PRAISE FOR *PLEASE DON'T LIE*

"Getting away from it all has never looked more sinister or ill-advised than in this deliciously dark version of the small-town idyll."

—Ruth Ware, *New York Times* bestselling author of *The Woman in Suite 11*

"Christina Baker Kline and Anne Burt take suspense to the next level with a creepy small-town setting, shady characters, and an unpredictable, twisted web of deceit. Lock the doors, grab a blanket, and settle in—you won't be able to put this one down anytime soon. *Please Don't Lie* is unsettling, atmospheric, and propulsive."

—Mary Kubica, *New York Times* bestselling author of *Local Woman Missing*

"Psychologically rich and bone chilling, Christina Baker Kline and Anne Burt's serpentine and timely thriller *Please Don't Lie* will make you question everything you think you know about those closest to you, and make you wonder how vulnerable we all are—in our weakest moments—to deceit, manipulation, and a surrender of control."

—Megan Abbott, *New York Times* bestselling author of *El Dorado Drive*

"This twisty-turny tale spins the riveting story of Hayley Stone, a newlywed who leaves New York to move to the idyllic Adirondacks with her husband Brandon. But what happens there plunges her into a mystery underlying her marriage, as well as her tragic past. It kept me breathless until its surprising ending. I loved it!"

—Lisa Scottoline, #1 bestselling author of *The Unraveling of Julia*

"*Please Don't Lie* ratchets up the tension, twist by twist, until the suspense is almost unbearable. It will make every woman ask herself: 'Do I know who I really married?'"

—Tess Gerritsen, *New York Times* bestselling author of *The Summer Guests*

"*Please Don't Lie* is a nail-biting, fast-paced thriller that had me on the edge of my seat from start to finish! Just when I thought I had it all figured out, another shocking twist caught me by surprise! I highly recommend."

—T.R. Ragan, *New York Times* bestselling author of *Best House on the Block*

PLEASE DON'T LIE

ALSO BY CHRISTINA BAKER KLINE

The Exiles

A Piece of the World

Orphan Train

Bird in Hand

The Way Life Should Be

Desire Lines

Sweet Water

ALSO BY ANNE BURT

The Dig

PLEASE DON'T LIE

A THRILLER

CHRISTINA BAKER KLINE
and ANNE BURT

THOMAS & MERCER

This is a work of fiction. Names, characters, organizations, places, events, and incidents are either products of the authors' imaginations or are used fictitiously. Otherwise, any resemblance to actual persons, living or dead, is purely coincidental.

Published by Thomas & Mercer, Seattle

www.apub.com

EU product safety contact:
Amazon Media EU S. à r.l.
38, avenue John F. Kennedy, L-1855 Luxembourg
amazonpublishing-gpsr@amazon.com

ISBN-13: 9781662524394 (hardcover)
ISBN-13: 9781662524400 (paperback)
ISBN-13: 9781662524417 (digital)

Cover design by Caroline Teagle Johnson
Cover image: © alvarez, © Angus Clyne, © Eric Stark / 500px, © John Rensten, © Sergey Ryumin, © Tony Anderson / Getty
Trees used throughout: © Baks, © Yulyu / iStock / Getty Images

Printed in the United States of America
First edition

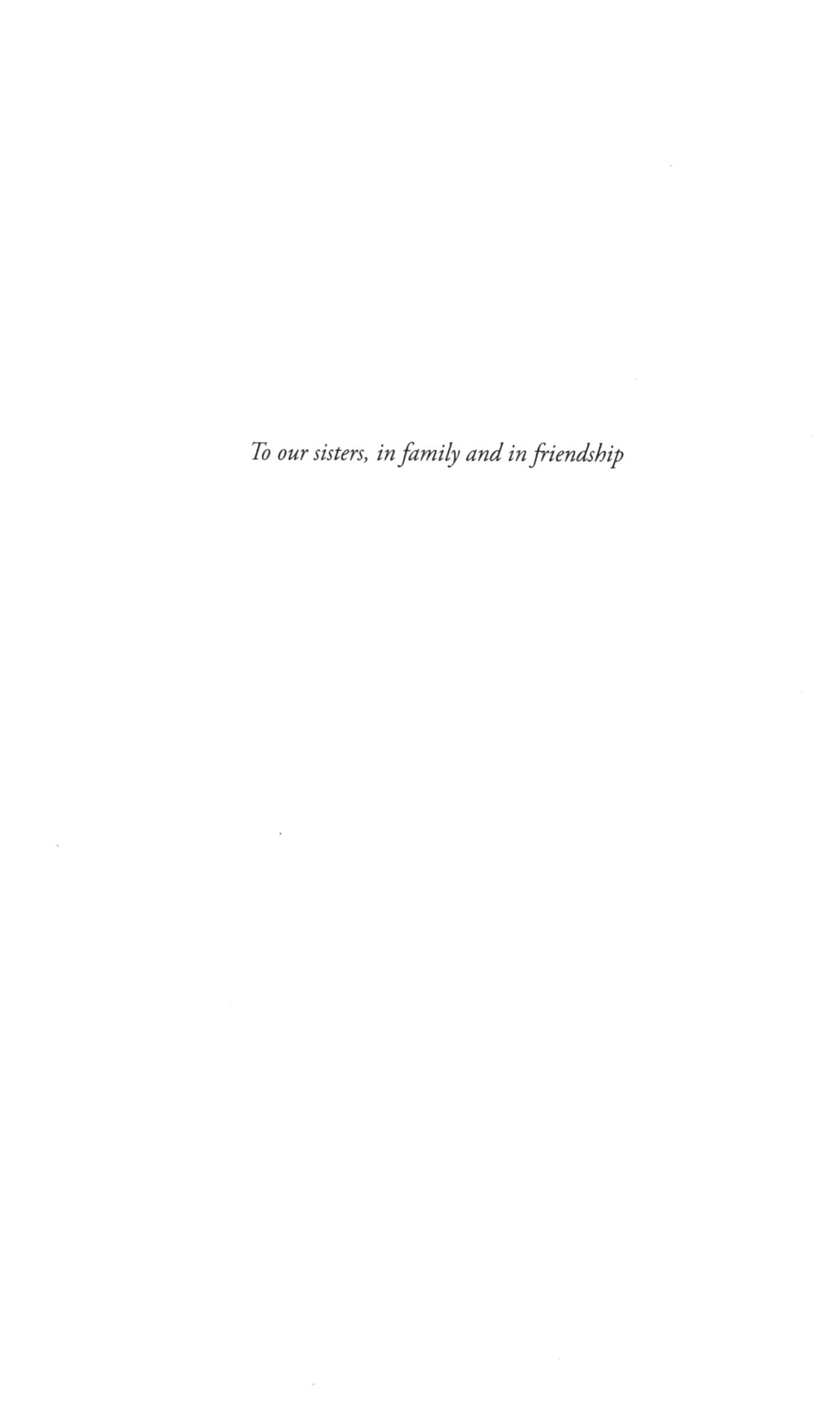

To our sisters, in family and in friendship

Above all, don't lie to yourself.
—FYODOR DOSTOEVSKY
(tr. Constance Garnett)

PROLOGUE

November 2023

The wind blows into Hayley's face as she stumbles forward in the darkness, half blinded by snow. Heart racing, panicked and terrified, she can't get her bearings. The familiar bluestone path between the main house and the guest cottage is completely obscured. Every direction looks the same: a swirling white chaos. Icy flakes sting her unprotected neck and shoulders.

A guttural shout, muffled by the wind, sends a wave of fear through her. Glancing over her shoulder, she sees a shape moving toward her through the shadowy gloom. She thought she was safe on this beautiful property, where she has lived for the past two months. Safe with the man who loved her.

The smokehouse comes into view, its outline barely visible. Hayley is determined to get there. As she runs faster, struggling to keep her balance, she slips and falls on a sheet of ice. A stab of pain shoots through her ankle. She scrambles to her feet, limps forward, falls to her knees. She pulls herself up and stumbles again. *Don't look back.* She hobbles as quickly as she can, despite the sharp jab each time her right foot hits the ground. Hayley senses, rather than hears, footsteps in the snow behind her. She lunges for the handle of the smokehouse door and pulls the iron ring, then scrambles inside. A ladder against the wall is all she can find for a barricade. Desperately, she grabs hold of it. Her arms strain as she tips it over with a grunt, wedging it against the doorway. Her breath comes in ragged gasps as she stands in the dark.

As her eyes adjust, Hayley looks around the shed her husband built so meticulously earlier in the fall, with its hand-planed two-by-fours and wrought iron hooks to hang the wild game he'd hunted and cured for the long winter ahead.

A weapon. I need a weapon. She scans the shelves stocked with tools and spies a metal spade.

Gripping the wooden handle with both hands, she waits for the pounding on the door.

SEPTEMBER

ONE

Two months earlier

“Could today be more perfect?” Hayley gazes out at the majestic peaks of the Adirondacks.

“Oh, this is nothing.” Brandon grins at Hayley from behind the wheel of their new cherry red Jeep. She loves his smile—it lights up his entire face. “Wait till a month from now, when it’s prime leaf season.”

With her hand over his, Hayley shifts her attention to the nearly empty upstate New York highway stretching ahead. The road twists and turns, flanked by towering pines, as they wind their way higher into the mountains. The sky is a brilliant blue, the air crisp and clear, with just a hint of chill. A hawk glides overhead on outstretched wings.

“Look at how this baby handles the road,” Brandon says as the Jeep hugs a curve. “Just what we’ll need up here in the snow.”

She nods. Autumn is one thing, but the thought of winter and the isolation it will bring worries her. They only started coming up here to Crystal River in June. For the past few months they’ve been renovating Brandon’s childhood home, commuting back and forth between his remote rural property and Hayley’s West Village apartment. Now that the renovation is nearly complete and her apartment has sold, they've pulled up stakes for good.

Hayley's window is down, and her auburn ponytail flutters behind her. She looks at the ravine far below, a blur of dusky green with a few pops of yellow and orange. The air is thick with the scent of pine and damp earth. As the Jeep darts in and out of dappled shadows, she pushes away her doubts.

This, right now, she reminds herself, is the new start she's been longing for.

She steals a glance at her new husband. Brandon is lean and muscular, with a tight dark beard and a glint of intensity in his blue eyes. His skin is burnished bronze in the afternoon light. She still can't quite believe this man is now her husband.

Hayley had been in the depths of grief when her sister, Jenna, died two years ago back in Florida, where they grew up. After the funeral, Hayley spent the afternoon hiding out in the clubhouse kitchen at Platinum Shores Estates with the caterers to avoid perfunctory condolences from their distant relatives and Jenna's so-called friends. Brandon Stone, who'd worked as a contractor for her parents, literally stumbled into her, spilling his IPA down the front of her black silk dress. His profuse apology, and his awkward attempt to pat her dress with a napkin without touching her inappropriately, made Hayley smile for the first time since Jenna's death.

Now, as the Jeep rounds a corner, the grade steepens dramatically. Hayley grips her leather seat. These mountain roads are a far cry from the Manhattan grid she knows so well.

Brandon looks over at her. "Been on these mountains my whole life," he says with a smile. "You're safe with me."

Hayley has been a thoroughly urban creature ever since she left Florida for NYU. With relief she'd traded away her parents' vast McMansion for the close quarters of her Washington Square Park dorm, three to a room. She loved the vibrant chaos of life in the city—the wail of sirens and honking horns in the wee hours, the constant hiss of steam through the radiators, even the garbage piled high on the corner of East Ninth Street after a long weekend. She swore then and there, as a first-year college student, that New York City would be home forever. Her roommate, Emily, a born-and-bred Manhattanite, claimed that an hour in Central Park was as much nature as anyone needed. Hayley, laughing, agreed.

—

But that was before.

Before the photo went viral online of her mother and father, framed in the picture window of their bedroom suite, clinging to each other as flames licked the damask curtains around them.

Before the rumors that twenty-year-old Jenna, fueled by spite and opioids, set the fire that killed them.

As Brandon navigates the increasingly steep road, Hayley is only half-present, plunged back into those dark days. The night of the fire, Jenna had thrown a rager at their parents' home to celebrate her engagement to an older guy she hardly knew. A loser, Brandon had told Hayley, like the rest of her sister's crowd. Her parents had come home unexpectedly and infuriated Jenna by announcing in front of her friends that they'd disown her if she went through with the wedding.

Hours later, Tad and Matilda Pierce were dead.

If Hayley had stayed longer in Florida after their parents' funeral, might things have been different? Could she have saved Jenna from spiraling deeper into addiction?

She turns her gaze back to the mountain view. The wind is picking up, rustling through the trees and sending dried leaves skittering across the rutted pavement. Only a moment ago, the scene appeared idyllic to her: lush green foliage dotted with gold and crimson. Now the whispering of the pines carries an air of menace. The hum of the car engine has shifted to a disconcerting whine.

The road they're on narrows, becoming even more pocked and rough. They round a hairpin turn. "Is this a different route to the house?" Her own voice is at a slightly higher pitch than usual.

"This is the back way. I wanted to try the Jeep on some real terrain."

The faint pulse of an emerging headache throbs behind her eyes. Her seat belt, tight against her rib cage, digs into her skin. Despite the open windows, the car now seems confining, claustrophobic. She leans forward and opens the vent in front of her on the dashboard.

Looking up, she spots a dark object straight ahead.

"Brandon, watch out. There's an animal in the road!"

"It's just a shadow, Hayl." He drives, unperturbed, right over the dip in the pavement.

Hayley digs her fingers into the leather seat. *Handshake your fear.*

"What's that?" Brandon asks.

Hayley didn't realize she'd spoken the words aloud. It's a quote from one of her self-help books, *The Road Unbound.* Over the past two years, Hayley has found herself surprisingly reassured by advice from therapists, spiritual leaders, and ordinary people who've gone through hell and come back to write about it. In her private moments, she visualizes the authors of the books as a nurturing community of friends. "Oh—it's just a mantra. Meaning . . . if you turn toward something you're afraid of, you strip away its power."

"Here we go," Brandon says playfully. "The gurus in your head."

"Yep." She laughs, glancing at the tote bag at her feet and its proliferation of books.

Reaching down, she rummages through them, looking for *The Road Unbound. The Miracle of Mindfulness, Whole Again, Healing the Soul of a Woman*—ah, here it is. And . . . wait, how did this one end up in her bag? *Savvy Women, Senseless Choices.* A less-than-subtle gift from Emily after Hayley told her she planned to marry Brandon. She'll donate it to the Crystal River Public Library next time she's in town.

Emily has been skeptical of Brandon from the start. She's peppered Hayley with her concerns: *Don't you think this is moving way too fast? You met him at your sister's funeral, for god's sake. Aren't you too vulnerable to be making big decisions?*

Reasonable questions, Hayley has to admit. A quote from another book, *Follow Your Wild Heartsong*, helped her frame an answer: *What you gain from life is shaped by your willingness to embrace what lies ahead.*

Maybe she wasn't too vulnerable to know what she wanted. Maybe she was finally vulnerable enough to let true love in.

Emily ended up apologizing and was a gracious witness to their wedding. And she's planning to visit for a few days next month. But Hayley knows her friend still has reservations. Some of it could be the inevitable change that comes with growth. Friendships evolve, after all. Hayley is married now, and Emily hasn't had a serious girlfriend for more than a year. They're in different places in their lives. With a pang, Hayley remembers all the good times she's shared with Emily—the late-night confidences, the dreams they've spun together. But those memories are tinged with the pain of her friend's recent judgment. Emily doesn't seem to understand that when you've experienced as much turmoil as Hayley has, you seek peace. You crave solace. Even if you have to move to the top of a mountain to find it.

Spontaneously, Hayley reaches over to touch the side of her husband's face. The warmth of his beard reassures her. "Love you, babe," she says.

He smiles. "Love you too."

Hayley settles back in her seat. The wind in her hair, the cloudless blue sky: this is the true beginning of their life together. Here in the Adirondacks, she'll spend quiet mornings watching the fog lift from the pond on their property, lazy afternoons reading in the sun-drenched living room, evenings sipping cocktails with Brandon, recounting the events of the day. They'll have to rely on each other. And it will be good for them—good for their relationship. Their courtship was a whirlwind, and the fallout from the tragedies in Hayley's life has been all-consuming. This will be a space where they can grow together. Where what they build will be from scratch.

TWO

As they pull up the long, steep drive, the Jeep kicks up a cloud of dust. Once it settles, the reveal—the main house, surrounded by tall trees and framed by dense greenery—is dramatic. The floor-to-ceiling steel-framed windows create the illusion that the house has grown organically from the hillside. The roof slopes sharply upward in a series of triangular planes, giving it a sleek, geometric look.

A stone walkway leads from the garage behind the house to a front porch flanked by two boulders. A path curves through the grass to a snug guest cottage with a shingled roof, about thirty yards away. In the distance, between the house and the mountain range beyond, a small pond reflects the sky.

After Brandon parks the Jeep, Hayley steps out and takes a deep breath. What a transformation the small grounds crew has achieved over the past three months! At the pond, the once-overgrown banks are neatly trimmed, the tall grasses and reeds cut back to reveal a tidy shoreline. The willows and alders that had encroached on the water's edge have been pruned, their branches no longer dipping into the pond's surface. A new wooden dock stretches out into the water, its planks smooth and sturdy beneath Hayley's sneakered feet. She sits down at the end, brushing her hand along the pond's cool surface. How restorative it will be to spend long days here next summer, swimming and lounging, having picnics on the dock.

The pond's surface glitters in the afternoon sunlight. The water is now so clear that Hayley sees straight to the sandy bottom. Gone are the murky, greenish hue and the lily pads and aquatic plants that once choked the shallows.

Was it really only the beginning of June when Brandon learned his estranged father had had a fatal stroke in California, where he lived with his second wife and children? His father, an architect, left all his money to his new family—but to Brandon's surprise, he bequeathed him this property in Crystal River.

Brandon hadn't even known his father kept the house.

At first, when he found out that the property would be his, Brandon was indifferent. He wanted to sell off the place, pocket some cash. "Too many bad memories," he told Hayley. "After my parents split, it was so ugly between them. No one wanted to stay in that house."

"I'm the queen of bad memories," Hayley reminded him gently. "We can face them together." She suggested they take a day trip before making any big decisions. "I want to go to Crystal River," she said. "I want to see the place where you grew up."

So they rented a car and headed upstate. The drive was gorgeous; the food at the quaint diner they stopped in was unexpectedly delicious. Hayley breathed in the clean air, the beautiful surroundings. She felt surprisingly . . . free.

And as they toured the property, Brandon grew more and more animated. Despite two decades of neglect, the house his father had designed and built was in pretty good shape. Brandon's eyes lit up as he guided her through the open, airy floor plan inside. With pride, he pointed out the white oak floors, the huge windows that flooded the interior with light, the dual-sided slate fireplace between the living and dining rooms. "My dad worked on this himself," Brandon said, his hand brushing the stone. "He said it should feel like the heart of the house."

Gesturing to the basement, he continued, "He always wanted to put a wine cellar down there. He never got around to it."

Upstairs, he led her through an office space and two bedrooms, each with a private bathroom. "Look at this pocket door," he said, sliding the panel open and shut between the primary bedroom and its en suite bath. "After all these years, it still tracks smoothly."

"Where's the lock, though?"

Brandon laughed. "Why would you need a lock?"

"Privacy!"

"From me?" He wrapped his arms around her and kissed her neck. "We have no secrets."

As they made their way down the stairs, Brandon said, "It feels good to see this place again. I thought it would dredge up all the bad times. But they're just"—he made a *poof* motion with his hand—"gone."

Hayley hadn't seen him this happy since he'd left Florida to follow her to New York.

The memory of their first day in Crystal River washes over her as she sits on the dock. She looks over to the grassy bank—it was right there, on that very spot, that Brandon had clasped her hand, his eyes alight with excitement. "I want to bring this property back to life," he'd said. "For us. Can't you see it?"

She couldn't. Not really, not yet. But Brandon was deep in his vision of the future here. And she didn't want to ruin the moment. She had to admit, there were practical elements to his plan. He had the skills as a contractor to renovate the property. And she, frankly, had the money. Her double inheritance had seemed excessive, embarrassing, when matched with Brandon's modest bank account. He'd hated asking her for money while he waited endlessly for his NYC licensing paperwork to come through. The bequest from Brandon's father brought a new parity to their relationship. Acres of property in the Adirondacks, all his.

"This is going to sound crazy," said Brandon, "but I feel like . . . I don't know . . . something, or someone, is calling me back."

"Your father?"

"Maybe. My dad started something here. There's a part of me that wants to finish it."

"For him?"

"Or for me. Truth is, it's the only place that ever felt like a real home. Things didn't end well here. But for a while, when I was a little kid, it was good."

Hayley gazed out at the trees beyond the pond. "We'd be so far away from anyone out here," she said. "How would we make friends?"

He pressed his shoulder against hers. "You're the only friend I need." The tenderness in his voice made her chest ache.

Brandon proposed to her later the same day, spontaneously, in a fairy ring by the edge of the cliff along the side of Route 8, the steep back road between Crystal River and his property. He presented a makeshift ring—a twist tie salvaged from a snack bag—and dropped to his knees under a copse of tall fir trees, just steps from a dramatic drop-off.

Hayley's "yes" was heartfelt. She had no doubts about marrying him. But the prospect of moving to Crystal River filled her with misgivings. It was remote, rural, and would be colder in the winter than anywhere she'd ever lived.

"Look," Brandon sighed. "I'm willing to make a go of it in the city for now if you're willing to keep an open mind about Crystal River in the future."

How could she say no to that?

Back in the city, Brandon had stayed true to his word. He didn't push. But having seen him in his element in the Adirondacks, Hayley knew that the man she lived with in the West Village was a shadow of his true self. He belonged on that property in the woods. He hungered for it.

For a moment now, as she gazes across the pond to the line of trees, Hayley feels a vague disquiet. In the late afternoon, with the sun glinting through the pines, the place seems desolate. Is that a coyote howling in the woods, or only the wind? Her heartbeat quickens.

"Look at those clouds catching the light," Brandon calls from the Jeep. "Going to be an incredible sunset."

Hayley puts her hand on her chest and pats it. *Stop,* she tells herself. This place is perfect. Exactly where she is meant to be.

It's funny, she thinks as her breathing slows back to normal, how quickly her view can shift. With just a small twist of perspective, anticipation can turn to dread.

After everything that happened to her family, the world looks different to her now, tinged with an unease that won't easily fade. Her notion of safety was pierced, her sense of peace disrupted. Tranquility—even on a beautiful day like today—is elusive. No matter how she tries to feel safe, she knows security is an illusion. A threat can come from anywhere, anytime.

THREE

Hayley is setting up cocktails on the porch while Brandon finishes unloading the final boxes in the garage. She places a bottle of gin and two cans of tonic on a small table. As she sets highball glasses beside them, the afternoon sun catches her sparkling diamond ring. Beyond its obvious symbolism, this ring serves an important purpose for her. One of her dog-eared self-help books, *The Healing Journey: A Path to Wholeness*, suggests creating a connection in your mind between a current object in your life and a significant object from your childhood. For Hayley, the object from her past is the ring her father wore, a distinctive gold-and-black band with beveled edges. She remembers sitting on his knee, playing with his ring while he took another of his endless work calls. He might've been ignoring her, but she felt protected. Secure.

On one level, Hayley knows edicts like this are a little formulaic. But it's been working for her since the moment Brandon slipped the ring on her finger, so there's that.

Brandon emerges from the garage, and Hayley smiles, holding up a glass.

"Thanks, babe." He takes the sweating glass and lowers himself into the red wooden chair next to hers. "Got to get my application in for a hunting permit." He takes a sip and gestures to a patch of land beside the stone-lined path toward the guest cottage. "Then it's time to build the smokehouse."

"When does hunting season start?" Hayley asks. She takes a sip of her drink, nudging the rosemary sprig she plucked from the garden out of the way. The sweet-bitter hit of sharp gin, fizzy tonic, and bracing lime feels like an extension of summer, even as the air is beginning to tell her otherwise.

"Already has. I'm behind. Winter comes fast up here. I've got to get this place airtight before the first frost."

Hayley never imagined she'd end up with a man like Brandon. The guys she'd dated in the past tended to be fast-talking New York finance types. Brandon, on the other hand, had led a pretty free-range life. He told her that after his mother died, when he was eighteen, he'd spent weeks at a time roughing it in the Florida swamplands, living off the grid with some buddies and a fishing pole. Eventually, he went into construction and worked his way up as a contractor.

Hayley met him just as he was rounding the corner into his midthirties—the perfect moment, he told her, just when he was ready to settle down. They flew back and forth on weekends for a few months until Brandon joined her in the city. But city life was never a good fit. Brandon wasn't at ease there; he was unsure of himself and his surroundings. The clamor overwhelmed him.

Now the city is in the past. Florida is too.

Hayley takes another sip. The fizz of the cocktail suits her mood. The first day of the rest of their lives together, and the prospect of their future, is exciting, filled with promise.

She reaches over, puts her hand on his thigh. "This place is amazing, Brandon. I know I'm going to love it here."

Brandon looks down, a faint smile on his face.

"What is it?" she asks.

He takes a sip of his cocktail. "I like you in the woods."

"What do you like about it?"

"There's no one for miles. I've got you all to myself."

Hayley takes his hand and slides it inside her shirt. His fingers, cold and wet from the condensation on his glass, brush her stiffened nipple. She moans, letting it all wash over her.

Brandon slides off the chair and tugs Hayley with him, on top of him, onto the rug that spans the floorboards of the porch.

The sun, low in the sky, blazes on their faces and turns their skin golden as they strip off their shirts. They separate briefly to wriggle out of their jeans before Hayley straddles Brandon again and pulls him inside her.

"Howl for me," he whispers.

And she does.

The moon, bright as a new dime in the dark sky, casts an otherworldly glow across the sheets. Brandon wanted to leave the bedroom blinds open. The moon's passage through the trees, he told her as they collapsed into bed after their marathon day of unpacking, is a fond memory from his early boyhood. It helps him drift off to sleep.

Hayley agreed not to close the blinds. But as she lies awake beside him, that same cold sweep of bluish light that soothes him fills her with dread. During the day, the oversized windows let in natural light and offer a panoramic vista of the pond, the field, and the trees beyond. Now those dark sheets of glass are unsettling. She feels exposed. Brandon has been asleep for hours, but she finds herself staring at the ceiling.

Wind in the trees, crackling branches, rustling squirrels burying acorns for the winter—Brandon can explain the noises that surround them a million ways. "These are the sounds of nature, Hayley. This is what people leave the city for," he says. "Most folks would kill for a chance to live like we do."

Rationally, Hayley knows this. But to her, every branch is the boot of an intruder. Squirrels morph into bears.

Her mind races. Did she lock the front door? Are the windows secure? And . . . is that smoke?

Ever since the fire that killed her parents, Hayley smells smoke wherever she goes: in her apartment, at work, rounding the corner on a busy street, on the subway. The therapist she saw briefly told her it was a response to their traumatic deaths—that the photo of them surrounded by flames had seared itself into her brain. Even so, the smell seems all too real. She often finds herself overheated, drenched in sweat, on the verge of tears.

Never was Hayley more grateful for Emily and her wicked sense of humor. When Hayley described the phantom threat of fire that often sent her into a panic, Emily programmed both of their phones to ring to the opening beats of "Ice Ice Baby"—a sonic bit of irony that never fails to make Hayley smile.

When Hayley told her therapist about how the ringtone helped her, the woman nodded. "That's a whole phenomenon. Sights and sounds and smells and tastes can help us avoid triggers."

Hayley is slowly healing. Fireplace fires no longer scare her, and she's overcome her anxiety about gas burners leaping to life. But even now, two years later, she sometimes smells smoke, and her pulse quickens.

FOUR

Three hours later, Hayley glances at the clock: 2:17 a.m.

The house is eerily quiet. Brandon's even breathing beside her is a small comfort, but it's not enough to banish her anxiety. She knows she could wake him, share her fears, but something holds her back.

Sleep seems impossible.

She sits up and gingerly peels back the covers from her side of the bed, so as not to disturb him. She steps onto the cool floor and grabs her robe, then pads down the stairs.

The front door is bolted. Check. The window above the sink is open a crack; Hayley slides it shut. Check.

Pale moonlight streams into the kitchen. Hayley flips on the light, wincing in the brightness, then dims it to create a softer ambience. On the kitchen island, along with a few other bags and boxes still waiting to be unpacked, she spies her canvas tote and pulls out a black three-ring binder. Inside, news clippings and web article printouts chronicle the tragic events surrounding her parents' and Jenna's deaths. The lawyer Hayley consulted after the fire instructed her to compile this record. "Documentation is crucial, Hayley," he said. "Every article, every report, every word."

Hayley sits at the island. With a heavy sigh, she opens the binder to look at the raft of articles she printed out and cataloged, all lined up in their orderly plastic sleeves. She knows she shouldn't—but she can't help herself. It's like an addiction, the way she's driven back into the darkest corners of her past at these moments when she's most vulnerable.

Not that she needs to look. She has memorized every headline, if not every word, of the coverage of the events that upended her life.

She turns to the first article.

NEWS ALERT: Platinum Shores Gazette (FL), January 25, 2021

Tragic Fire Claims Lives of Local Couple

Theodore (Tad) and Matilda Pierce, both 60, were killed in a fire at their home. The couple, a prominent bank executive and his wife, perished early Sunday. Emergency services responded to the blaze around 2 a.m. after neighbors noticed the fire. Their daughter, Jenna, 20, found outside the house, was transported to the hospital with minor injuries. The investigation into the origin of the fire is ongoing.

When Hayley returned to Florida for her parents' funeral, Jenna was a mess: bingeing vodka, hooked on fentanyl. To make matters worse, a local striver with an obscure podcast, *Sinister Sands: Digging into South Florida's Bloodstained Secrets*, saw the photo of Hayley's parents online and glommed on to the story. While the community was abuzz with gossip about the cause of the fire, the host of the podcast, Olivia Blackwood, turned her high beams on Jenna. The potent combination of wealth, a gated community, an attractive, damaged female, and the specter of arson proved irresistible. The podcast took off.

Sinister Sands presented a version of Jenna that broke Hayley's heart. Yes, on the surface Jenna was all of these things, but she was young. She was just beginning to find her way—and learning to make better choices. The day after the fire, she broke off her rash engagement, admitting to Hayley that their parents had been right about her fiancé. She also swore to get clean and, this time, stay that way. Jenna seemed to be turning her life around.

Though Hayley was repulsed by the garbage churned out by Olivia Blackwood, she couldn't deny its effect. The internet lit up for weeks after each episode of *Sinister Sands*. Hayley's phone is unlisted for this very reason. The flood of social media, texts, and emails, not to mention the gawkers who stood outside the church hoping for a glimpse of Jenna as she left their parents' funeral, threw Hayley into a state of agitation. All she wanted was to get Jenna through the ordeal in one piece and get herself back home to New York, where she could process and mourn in her own way.

Taking a deep breath, Hayley turns the page.

NEWS ALERT: Platinum Shores Gazette (FL), February 1, 2021

Fire That Killed Platinum Shores Couple Ruled Accidental; Daughter Cleared

The Broward County Fire and Arson Investigation Unit has concluded that a house fire on January 23 at Platinum Shores Estates was an accident. Jenna Pierce, 20, has been absolved of any wrongdoing. Authorities attributed the fire that killed her parents, Tad and Matilda Pierce, to a malfunction in the home's wiring. Jenna and her sister, Hayley Pierce, 28, expressed relief and requested privacy following the ruling.

After Jenna's name was officially cleared, Hayley thought they'd be able to move forward. She'd managed to keep Jenna's addiction out of the papers and hoped the ruling would be a catalyst for her sister to commit to positive change.

But then came the terrible night a few months later when Jenna sent Hayley a manic series of texts.

Hayley flips the page and skims the printout:

I ruined everything

It's my fault Mom and Dad are dead

I cut Sean out of my life and I'm miserable

Olivia Blackwood is still fucking with me

I'm overwhelmed

There's nothing left for me here

The distant hoot of an owl sends a shiver down Hayley's spine. She shudders and pulls her robe tighter around her. Though she knows exactly what comes next in the folder, the headline is a slap in the face every time.

NEWS ALERT: Platinum Shores Gazette (FL), April 28, 2021

Orphaned Heiress Dead at 21; Sister Inherits Estate

The Platinum Shores Estates community mourns the death of Jenna Pierce, the bank heiress who recently lost her parents in a fire.

Her sister, Hayley Pierce, a New York City–based marketing associate for the online home store Domicile, inherits the family's considerable estate. Ms. Pierce has opted not to make a public statement.

Olivia Blackwood turned Jenna's death into a cause célèbre. Her podcast gained hundreds of thousands of followers seemingly overnight. Each week she devoted an episode to a new question: Why did Jenna throw an engagement party at her parents' house when she knew they hated her fiancé? Why did Jenna's parents object to her fiancé so much that they threatened to disown her if she married him? Why did Jenna really dump him after her parents' death? Why did her sister, Hayley, run back to New York so soon after her parents' funeral, leaving Jenna to fend for herself? And the biggest questions of all: Was the investigation tainted? Was justice served?

As the serial gained traction, listeners lapped up every word. Week after week, Hayley's image and personal information were splashed across the internet. Even more painful, she couldn't help but feel that maybe Olivia Blackwood was right about her: she did abandon her sister when Jenna needed her most.

The guilt weighed heavily on Hayley's shoulders.

And then, an explosive new episode of *Sinister Sands* dropped, exposing Jenna's fentanyl addiction and insinuating that she had set fire to her parents' house in a drug-filled rage. Public opinion swayed abruptly from sympathy to condemnation. Hayley had been so careful to keep her sister's struggles private. Someone close to Jenna had to have been Olivia Blackwood's source. For weeks, Hayley cowered in self-exile in her West Village apartment, hiding from the gossipmongers who accosted her online—and sometimes in person. Only Emily and Melinda, Hayley's cubicle mate at Domicile and the one new friend she'd let into her life since the fire, could coax her out for the occasional coffee or cocktail.

Then came Brandon.

Hayley looks back down at her tote bag. The stark black title of Emily's gift—*Savvy Women, Senseless Choices*—accosts her like a finger-wagging scold.

She doesn't need a book to remind her that she jumped into a relationship with Brandon too quickly. As much as she tried to assuage Emily's doubts, Hayley knew it was fast. But the way Brandon looked at her when they bumped into each other in the clubhouse kitchen at Jenna's funeral made her feel alive. After everything she'd been through, what could be wrong with that?

Brandon brought levity into her world, and great sex—someone to hold on to in the dark. At first, Hayley thought that was all it was. Why not hook up with the hot guy she'd met after her sister's funeral? Didn't she, recently orphaned and now completely without family, deserve a modicum of joy? Did everything have to be so . . . solemn?

But the seeds of connection between her and Brandon flowered into something more. To her surprise, the support he offered felt deep. A bit blindly, with a lot of fumbling around, they crept toward each other from their very different backgrounds and met in the middle.

Now, standing at the island, Hayley is about to close the black binder when a more recent story catches her eye. It appeared on a trashy true crime gossip site the morning after their private wedding at City Hall. And it changed everything.

CrimeHive.com, June 21, 2023

Banking Heiress with Sketchy Past MARRIES Mystery Man in Hush-Hush Ceremony!

Hayley Pierce, the 30-year-old banking heiress with a shadier past than a palm tree at noon, has shocked the world by tying the knot with a small-time contractor from her hometown—and CrimeHive has all the juicy deets.

The super sus wedding went down at NYC's City Hall, and get this—hardly anyone was invited. What's the deal, Hayley? You got something to hide?

In case you live under a rock, Hayley's been dodging major heat ever since *Sinister Sands* spilled the tea on her family's shocking past. We're talking a suspicious fire that killed her parents, a dead sister who may or may not have been shady AF . . . and Hayley bouncing from Florida faster than you can say "guilty conscience."

Now she's wifed up to Brandon Stone, 35. The newlyweds are begging for privacy, but this whole thing reeks of a desperate attempt to bury Hayley's secrets. After all the bombs *Sinister Sands* dropped, the public wants answers.

CrimeHive was even less reputable than *Sinister Sands*—but it still got under Hayley's skin. She felt violated and miserable on the one day she was supposed to feel joy and hope. A slightly unflattering image of her at her desk appeared alongside an out-of-focus shot of her and Brandon on a bench at City Hall and a picture of their prewar West Village apartment building on Perry Street. Emily, who worked in tech, did some digging. Two days later, she called Hayley with the news that Melinda—the only other witness at the wedding—had sold the story and photos to the press.

Melinda's betrayal rocked Hayley to her core. The resurgence of gossip about her, and the revelation of her address, was the final push she needed to say yes to Crystal River. Hayley gave notice at her job. Put the apartment on the market. Brandon commuted back and forth between Manhattan and Crystal River, getting the place in shape for them to move in and fielding deliveries of furniture, rugs, linens, and kitchen supplies. He applied for a permit to hunt wild turkey and deer so he could stock the smokehouse he planned to build. "Winter can be brutal upstate," he told her. "We need to be ready."

Whiplash fast, but it all felt right. She spent hours buying furniture and decor for her new life in the mountains. Why not, after all, use some of the money that had landed in her lap to speed along their transition from city to country life?

It was a fun challenge for Hayley to use the design know-how she'd developed at work. And entertaining to figure out how to dress both of them for this new locale. After years in Florida, Brandon had a wardrobe of worn T-shirts and cargo shorts. And Hayley's smart-casual dresses and blazers would be of little use when she was making sourdough and pickling vegetables.

It is all too easy, and enjoyable, to shop for Barbour jackets, Vuori sweats, and Blundstone boots online when you have a Platinum Amex, a handsome husband to clothe, and an overwhelming desire to shed the skin you're in.

Or at least cover it in soft flannel and indigo denim until you don't recognize the woman in the mirror who lost so much, so fast.

Though she would always love New York, Hayley could no longer find peace there. Other than Emily, there wasn't a single person in that city she could trust.

Hayley closes the binder and turns to the window. The sun will rise soon, and everything will feel normal again. But now, in the predawn stillness, the dark expanse of the pond reflecting the moonlight is an inky abyss. Hearing a mournful howl in the distance, she hugs herself tightly. She's surprised to find her arms are shaking.

FIVE

A few days later, Hayley and Brandon head into Crystal River to stock up on supplies. The afternoon sky is bright and clear; the air is brisk. Bracing even. But Hayley finds herself drifting off in the passenger's seat, only to jerk awake with every turn.

Another sleepless night has left her drained, her mind haunted by thoughts she can't shake. Nothing seems to help—not sex, not melatonin, not shutting off her phone long before bedtime. She vowed not to, but last night she wound up poring over the black binder again until the first light of dawn appeared in the sky.

Brandon fiddles with the radio until Taylor Swift's voice drifts through the speakers, singing about red flags and reckless love. Hayley sighs, resting her head against the window. Outside, the colors seem too sharp, the sun harsh against the trees. She blinks, and the landscape blurs.

"I'm dying for a coffee," she says. "Can we stop at that little place on Main? What's it called, Sticks & Stones?"

"Bones & Leaves." He shakes his head. "Don't get your hopes up," he says, signaling left off Route 8. "It's not exactly a charming espresso bar in the West Village."

They turn onto Crystal River's only commercial street, a three-block stretch nestled between Anderson's Hardware on one end and an open field on the other, where the farmers' market sets up on Saturdays. They pass a row of vacant buildings, their facades faded and peeling, and North Country Sporting Goods, its window display dominated by guns and crossbows.

They park in front of the library next to a bar called the Frostbite Lounge, with its flashing neon signs for Miller High Life and Pabst Blue Ribbon. Even in the early afternoon, the parking lot at the Frostbite has more cars than the library's.

As Hayley emerges from the Jeep, two ponytailed women in black leggings approach, carrying babies in front-facing pouches. Two small boys cling to either hand of the mom on the left.

Hayley gives the women a smile, but they breeze past her as if she isn't there.

She sighs. It's not going to be easy to make new friends. If she's honest with herself, she hasn't made a real new friend since college. She'd thought she might get there with Melinda, but the CrimeHive article showed her how wrong she was.

"Guess I won't be hanging out with those two," Hayley says as she watches the women head up the library walk.

"We didn't come here to be with other people anyway," he says. "We came to get away from them."

"Yes, but at some point we'll want friends, won't we?"

"Aren't we still newlyweds?" He takes her hand. "Now, let's get that shitty cup of coffee you're dying for."

"So what's your poison?" A heavyset man in his thirties with a full beard and long ponytail leans toward her and Brandon from behind the counter. "Holy hell . . . could it be?" He squints dramatically. "Dude. I heard you were back, but I didn't believe it. *You?* No way."

A look crosses Brandon's face that Hayley can't quite read. "Anthony Pelham," he says. "So you never left."

"Nope. And they still call me Pellet, thanks to you."

"Ha." Brandon turns to Hayley. "Seventh grade. BB gun," he tells her. "You killed how many squirrels in your barn that day, dude?"

"Don't know why you had to make such a big deal of it. Farm life, y'know?" he says to Hayley.

How is she supposed to respond? "Um . . . sure?"

"I was young. Just messing around. You probably don't know that your husband had a nickname too."

Hayley raises her eyebrows at Brandon. "Oh?"

He gives a quick shake of his head.

"Yeah," Pellet continues. "We called him the Coyote Kid. He used to run around the playground at recess, howling his ass off. Stirring up trouble." Pellet's voice is rough, as if he's recounting something that happened yesterday, not decades ago. "He was a scary little dude."

Hayley and Brandon walk past a smattering of mismatched tables, their tops a mosaic of broken plates, and sit by the window to wait for their order, out of Pellet's earshot. She takes in the dust motes in the air and the half-moon brown stains on the tabletop. She has to admit Brandon is right—this place is a long way from charming.

"So what's up with the 'Coyote Kid' thing?" she asks in a low voice.

"Pellet's just trying to get a rise out of you." Brandon rubs the back of his head. "But I guess I was kind of a loner," he says. "I used to spend a lot of time in the woods. My mother said I was a wild animal, always running off on my own adventures. I could mimic coyote calls perfectly. Used to freak people out, hearing what they thought was a pack of coyotes, only to learn it was me."

Hayley isn't sure whether to be impressed or unnerved. "That's . . . quite a talent."

"It came in handy," he continues. "Made it easy to keep people away from my territory."

"Your 'territory'?"

"Everybody needs a place that's theirs, Hayley. Somewhere they can be themselves without anyone interfering."

"Like the school playground?"

"I couldn't stand being cooped up. At home too. I only wanted to be in the woods. I'd disappear for hours out there."

"Didn't your parents worry?"

"Sure. But I always came back eventually."

"That sounds dangerous, Brandon."

"Probably was," he admits. "One time I got lost. It was pretty scary. My dad found me right before dark. He said I should always howl when I'm in the woods, to keep the other animals away—and so he'd know how to find me. My dad was good at stuff like that." Brandon stares out the window at Main Street, a pensive expression on his face. "After he left my mom and we moved to Florida, I pushed him away. But now that I'm here, the memories of how he cared for me are coming back."

"Yo, Stone!" Pellet's voice breaks into their conversation. He beckons toward Brandon from the counter. "Order up."

Alone at the table, Hayley mulls over Brandon's nickname, trying to integrate the man she knows with the boy who ran around the playground howling like a coyote. Ugh—coyotes are so creepy. Those awful howls at night. During the day she spies evidence of their nocturnal wanderings: paw prints in the soft earth near the pond, tufts of fur caught in the shrubs. At dusk, when the light fades to a murky blue, she sees their lean, ghostlike figures slinking along the edge of the woods. Their eyes catch the last rays of sunlight, yellow green in the glow.

Brandon sleeps so soundly here. She, on the other hand, is deeply attuned to the disquieting stillness that surrounds them, punctuated by those howling coyotes. And the creaks and sighs of the house itself, settling on its foundation as the evening cools, only add to her unease.

Each night, lying in bed beside Brandon, she thinks, *Maybe tonight I'll finally sleep.*

Each night, the house whispers: *Not yet.*

—

Brandon returns, setting two mugs on the table between them. "Hey, Pellet invited me to go hunting with a group of guys in town once the season starts. Crossbows. They take overnight trips."

Hayley's eyes widen in surprise. "Hunting? With him?"

"Not just with him." Brandon's voice has an edge of defensiveness. "I'm planning to hunt anyway. And these guys know where all the good spots are." He takes a sip of coffee, grimaces, pushes the mug away.

Hayley takes a sip. Yep, swill. Still, she'll drink it. "He just seems kind of . . . off," she whispers.

"It's not like we're gonna be best friends."

She glances over at Pellet behind the counter and is startled to find that he's staring at her. She blinks hard. "You don't think he knows my story, do you?" she asks Brandon.

He scoffs. "I doubt he knows what the internet is, let alone your story."

"I just wonder—"

"He doesn't recognize you, Hayl."

She is not convinced.

"Muffin on the house," Pellet calls from the counter. He walks over and drops a plastic-wrapped corn muffin on the table between them. "Welcome back to town."

Brandon gives Hayley a half smile. *See?*

Just then, the wind chimes clang. A disturbance in the air announces a new visitor.

It's a woman in her midsixties, holding a large white cardboard box, dressed in denim overalls and a plaid shirt with a fraying collar. She has intense brown eyes and short, steely hair poking out from under a John Deere cap. Pellet leans in close to Brandon.

"Watch out, dude. Here comes Cheryl."

"Figured that old bird would be dead by now, one way or another," Brandon says under his breath.

"Still runs the orchard north of your folks' place," Pellet says. "We source our pies from her. Don't worry—we don't serve booze, so she doesn't stay long." He heads back to the counter.

What would Brandon have to worry about? Hayley gives him a questioning look.

He shakes his head. "Just—ignore her."

Before Hayley can ask anything more, Cheryl catches sight of Brandon. "Well, what do you know," she says in a loud, raspy voice, plonking her box on the countertop before coming over to their table. "Brandon Stone." She eyes him up and down. "Look at you, all grown up."

"Cheryl Snyder." Brandon's voice is curt. "What a surprise."

Cheryl has an upright, solid stance and a frank demeanor. Her brown leather work boots are flecked with paint and specks of mud. "Really? I never left. You're the surprise."

"I suppose I am." Brandon fidgets with his keys.

"Last I heard you'd hightailed it to Florida. Rumor has it your father couldn't move far enough in the other direction."

Whoa. Whoever this woman is, she's rude. Hayley starts to respond, but Brandon puts out his hand. *No.*

Abruptly, Cheryl turns to Hayley. "And who are you?"

"Um . . . I'm Hayley. Hayley Stone." Unnerved by this woman's brusque manner, she doesn't know what to do other than offer her hand.

Cheryl ignores it. "Brandon's wife, eh?" Giving Hayley an unabashed once-over, she says, "City girl. Guess he did all right for himself. Never would've predicted it, but hey, what do I know? Good for him."

Hayley feels like a prize pig at a county fair. Abruptly, Brandon stands. "Well, it's been fun catching up, Cheryl, but we've got stuff to do. Take care now."

Hayley pushes her chair back too.

"Oh, don't you fret, I'm leaving." Cheryl turns toward the door before either Brandon or Hayley has time to move. She pulls it behind her with a hard tug, setting off the wind chimes in a discordant clatter.

As soon as the door closes behind her, Brandon lets out an exasperated breath. "Jesus Christ."

Hayley meets his eyes. "She's—"

"A sad case," he finishes. "That woman was a piece of work back when I knew her. Looks like she's only gotten worse."

"Why was she so nasty about your dad? That was the rudest—"

"Doesn't matter." Fishing in his pocket, Brandon throws a couple of bills on the table. "Let's get out of here."

"It does matter," Hayley says. "Why would someone talk to you like that?"

"It's nothing," Brandon says sharply. "Leave it."

SIX

Stepping inside the cavernous space of Anderson's Hardware and Building Supplies, Hayley inhales fresh-cut wood and the earthy smell of mulch. Anderson's couldn't be further from the cramped single-aisle hardware store on Seventh Avenue where she occasionally ventured for a light bulb or a picture hook. This store is clean and brightly lit, its towering shelves packed with gadgets and equipment. Bins are filled with nails and screws, lumber is piled in stacks, neatly organized tools hang from hooks on the walls.

"I'll be in Outdoors," Brandon announces, grabbing a cart. "I'm looking for a crossbow. Meet you at the front in, what, fifteen minutes?"

"Sure." Hayley pulls a cart of her own from the line. She's still a bit off kilter after the scene in the café.

Slipping his free hand around her waist, he tugs her close. "Bet you never imagined you'd be shopping for weapons in an upstate hardware store, did you?"

Hayley knows that Brandon's flirting is his version of an apology for snapping at her. "Can't say I did."

"You like it, though. Kind of turns you on."

He's clearly trying. Okay. She's ready to let it go. Apology accepted. "The sooner you find your weapon, the sooner we can get home."

A grin spreads across his face. "Yeah? Any reason to rush?"

"Maybe."

"Meet you in ten, then."

She smiles as he steers his cart toward Outdoors, and she pivots toward Home.

—

As Hayley walks slowly past the endcaps, aisle by aisle, her fingers graze the merchandise: rough sandpaper, smooth gold door pulls, the sharp edge of an axe. She smells cleaning supplies, lemon and pine, and metal—and . . . is that smoke?

No.

Stop, Hayley. Use your senses.

At the paint kiosk, she runs her fingers along the rows of cans, feeling the cool metal against her fingertips. Her heartbeat slows. She takes a breath, then lets it out.

Better.

On a display wall, strips of paint swatches are arrayed in a rainbow-style plastic holder. She plucks two samples. Meditating on the blue-green-gray hues, Hayley envisions the study she's creating for herself on the second floor, a place where she'll work on designing tranquil living spaces for herself. And maybe someday for others.

The house Brandon's father built is undeniably beautiful, but truthfully, after a few days of living there, Hayley is finding the sleek lines and polished surfaces a little cold. It feels like living in a fishbowl. Not that there's anyone around to see them.

The guesthouse is closer to Hayley's style and personality. Built in the 1940s, with small rooms, a stone fireplace, and a butcher-block island, it is unpretentious and comfortable. Brandon told her it was the only dwelling on the property when his father purchased it in the early 1990s. He'd considered tearing it down but decided to keep it for household staff.

When she first toured the property with Brandon, she was tempted to suggest they live in the cottage instead of the main house. But she knew it would never happen. He was so proud of his father's work, so excited to make the place his own.

Still, over the past few months, in between stockpiling furniture from Design Within Reach and Arhaus for the main house, Hayley has been accumulating vintage dishes, floral curtains, and upholstered furniture, hoping to create the look and feel of a quaint cottage in the English countryside.

Holding up paint swatches now, she thinks about how she wants to make Brandon's father's office her own. She's drawn to two samples, Sea Salt and Tidewater. Both are calming. But is Tidewater a little . . . warmer? Hmm.

She slides the strips into her bag.

Announcements blare through the speaker above Hayley's head: "We're having a postseason sale on patio furniture and gas grills! And an early promotion on tire chains, with a bonus twenty-pound bag of ice melt for your driveway!"

"Ice melt? It's not even Halloween yet." A woman's voice floats toward Hayley. It's coming from the direction of plumbing supplies. She spies a couple, their hipster chic in marked contrast to the oversized sweatshirts and sturdy work boots of the local clientele.

Hayley's interest is piqued. The woman has olive skin and long dark hair that falls down her back in loose waves, and she's wearing a belted maxi skirt and a floral top. She moves with an effortless grace that isn't marred in the slightest by the fact that she's holding a plunger. The man has tousled, blond-tipped hair and a strong jawline. He's trim and fit, with a tattoo of . . . She squints. Some kind of bug? . . . on his bicep, just visible below his rolled-up sleeve.

Hayley pulls a glossy trifold from the paint kiosk and opens it so she can peer surreptitiously over the edge at the couple. They radiate a playful intimacy. The man places his hand on the woman's back and slides his fingers beneath the crisscrossing straps of her blouse, drawing her closer. He says something Hayley can't hear, and the woman murmurs a response.

The man leans in, brushing her ear with his mouth.

Clutching the trifold, Hayley meanders over to the wall of paint cans that abuts their aisle.

Their conversation is nothing like what she imagined.

"What kind of landlord refuses to snake the toilet in a tenant's apartment? He's such an asshole," the woman is saying.

"It's not a big deal," the man says, holding up a toilet auger. "See? $12.98."

The woman shakes her head. "That place is such a dump. The shower sucks, the ceiling leaks, it smells like mold. We've gotta get out of there."

"Well, maybe if you'd stop buying all those self-help books, we could afford to move."

"They're research. It's a business expense!"

"Right. And when's the 'business' part starting again?"

"As soon as I get the bookshelf painted, I can post photos online. Writers need a platform. As I've said a thousand times." The woman crosses her arms. "What about you? You don't exactly have clients banging down the door."

"I'm working on it."

"Playing pool and drinking beer at the Frostbite Lounge does not count as networking."

He drapes an arm over her shoulders. "That's exactly what it is, darlin'."

The woman shuts her eyes and holds out her hands performatively, fingertips touching. "Serenity now," she stage-whispers.

The woman's bold humor, her unfiltered honesty, stirs something in Hayley. She imagines speaking her mind so freely with Brandon, but the thought makes her stomach clench. Years of tiptoeing around her detached father and sidestepping her mother's barbs have left their mark. Her need to smooth things over with Brandon, she knows, is a reflex born of deep-seated insecurity. She wonders, not for the first time, what it would be like to shed that weight.

The man holds up a scrap of paper. "I'm gonna grab the rest of the stuff. Gotta get back to networking."

The woman gives him a bemused smile.

The couple parts ways, and the woman pushes her cart in Hayley's direction. Hayley busies herself with the trifold in her hand, as if she's studying the various shades of gray: Slate, Fog, Flint, Shadow, Iron . . .

"Excuse me."

Hayley looks up.

"I'm sorry to bother you." The woman's voice is warm, a little shy, even. "But you look like you know what you're doing."

"Oh . . . I do?"

The woman gestures at the paint strip in Hayley's hand. "I'm trying to decide on a color for the bookshelf in my yoga space, but I'm overwhelmed. So many options. Those shades have great energy."

This self-assured woman is asking her for help? Well . . . okay! Hayley smiles. "I get it. There's this book called *The Choice Conundrum—*"

"*—Why Limitless Options Are Limiting Our Potential!*" The woman jumps in before the words are out of Hayley's mouth. They stare at each other.

"'True happiness is found in simplicity.'" The woman quotes the exact sentence Hayley had taped over her desk in her cubicle at Domicile. "That book actually changed my life. 'Seek simplicity' has become my mantra."

"Mine too! I moved to Crystal River with my husband because . . ." Hayley pauses. The real reasons she moved here with Brandon crowd her mind, but she's not going into all that. "Partly because of what I learned from reading *The Choice Conundrum*."

"Wow. Same. With my boyfriend, last month." When the woman stretches her hand across her cart, Hayley catches the light scent of patchouli. "I'm Megan."

Hayley shakes her hand and introduces herself.

Megan holds Hayley's hand in hers for a long beat. "It's really great to meet you. You're the first interesting person I've talked to since we got here." She places her other hand over Hayley's as well. "Your aura is so . . . glowy."

Hayley feels the back of her neck flush. "Oh . . . um, thank you?"

Megan laughs. She lets go of Hayley's hand. "Sorry, I can come on kinda strong when I feel a connection."

"It's okay! Refreshing, actually." Hayley feels a familiarity too—the same kind of *us versus the world* vibe that she and Emily shared during their early days at NYU. She senses how much she wants Megan, this total stranger, to like her. She's already spinning scenarios in her head: Megan texting her to meet for hikes. The two of them practicing yoga together (note to self: buy a yoga mat).

Hold on. Hayley's already deep into this imaginary friendship, and she's only just met the woman. What if this is another Melinda—someone who appears to be genuine, only to turn on her when she least suspects it?

"Do you live in Crystal River?" Megan asks.

Hayley shakes herself back to the present. This is a perfectly nice person asking perfectly simple questions. "Brandon—my husband—and I just moved here. We live outside of town. It's beautiful, but pretty isolated."

"Oh, I'd kill to live in the countryside," Megan says. "Tyler and I are renting a shithole apartment in the middle of town. It's all we can afford. He's a skilled handyman, but he's just starting to build his customer base here. Speaking of which . . ." She rummages in her bag and pulls out a sheet of paper with her boyfriend's xeroxed photo and the tagline *No Job Too Small.* "I made up these lame flyers. Want one?"

"Sure." Hayley looks at Tyler's photo. He's flashing a dimpled smile at the camera. "Your boyfriend is really cute."

Megan grins. "I figure the photo won't hurt."

"Maybe Brandon could use his help on the property. There's a lot to do." She tucks the flyer into her bag. Hayley isn't ready to let Megan slip away just yet. "So you teach yoga?"

"Sometimes. But that's not my main hustle. I write about wellness."

"For a website?"

"I'm planning to launch a Substack. I have about four nonpaying followers, but hey, it's a start."

Hayley glances at Megan's cart. In addition to the plunger and the toilet auger, there's an off-brand set of dish towels. She eyes the price tag: $1.99.

Hayley has so much. Too much. The property and houses that Brandon inherited might have balanced their emotional scales, but in a funny way they make her sudden wealth—and the way she inherited it—even starker. Every time she pays a Design Within Reach bill for an Eames chair or a Nelson lamp, she thinks half of this money should've been Jenna's. And none of it should've been either of theirs for decades. Her spending follows a predictable cycle: a dopamine hit, followed by a guilt wallow, followed by a mantra recitation to ease the self-reproach.

Seeking simplicity means one thing when it's about buying fewer pricey objects and quite another when it's about being frugal because you can't make a living.

"Hey, Meg. I knocked out the list."

Hayley turns around. Tyler has come up behind them. He's a few inches taller than Brandon, and wirier. She glances at his bicep: the insect is a vibrant green, its front legs folded as if in prayer.

"Awesome. This is Hayley," Megan says.

Tyler gives Hayley a nod. He's undeniably charismatic, with a boyish charm and deep-brown eyes.

"Hayley is helping me find a paint color," Megan continues. "She's got spectacular taste."

"Well, I don't know about that, I just—"

Megan plucks the strip that peeks out of Hayley's bag. "I love these. Which one's better for my bookshelf? Tidewater?"

"That's the one I'm drawn to. It's soothing but also . . . generative."

"'Generative'?" Tyler laughs. "You speak her language. Good thing someone around here does."

Megan gives Hayley a little eye roll. "Ty is about as enlightened as that plunger."

He slips a finger through Megan's belt loop and tugs her toward him. "The snake, you mean."

She laughs, pushing him away.

Tyler catches Hayley's eye over Megan's shoulder. His smile deepens.

"Hayley?"

She turns. Brandon is standing behind a flatbed cart stacked with merchandise: a couple of saws, an electric heater, a box labeled SNIPER CROSSBOW, three axes in various sizes. There's an unsettling look in his eyes that Hayley doesn't recognize. How long has he been there?

"Hey!" She makes her voice bright. Hurrying to Brandon's side, she bangs her thigh against the sharp edge of the crossbow box. She puts her arm around his waist. He doesn't reciprocate. Did he see her make eye contact with Tyler? Did he think she was flirting? "I was just helping these guys pick a paint color!"

He stands there, statue-still.

"You must be Brandon," Megan says. "Your wife is a lifesaver."

"Hey, man. I'm Tyler." He leans forward, ready to shake hands. "Good to meet ya."

"Uh-huh." Brandon keeps his arms by his sides.

Hayley feels a flash of embarrassment. Now she knows he's jealous. But does he have to be so hostile?

Tyler lowers his hand, and he and Megan exchange a loaded glance. "Well, we're out," he says.

Hayley pulls away from Brandon and heads back to her own cart. She's heavy with disappointment and a little annoyed.

Just as she's about to resign herself to a missed connection, Megan turns back, surprising her. "If you ever want to do yoga—"

"I'd love to!" Hayley hears herself being overly effusive, but she can't help it. Megan taps on her phone, and Hayley feels her own vibrate. AirDrop. She accepts Megan's number.

Hayley watches the couple walk away. Megan's easy confidence seems to float around her like a magic blanket. What would it feel like for that blanket to settle gently over her own shoulders?

Despite Brandon's surliness, this intriguing woman wants to be her friend. And Hayley could really use a friend.

SEVEN

"They're a cute couple, her and Tyler. Don't you think?"

"Didn't like the guy."

Well, that was blunt.

Brandon stares straight ahead as he drives them home from Anderson's. Hayley pretends to scroll through design posts on Instagram as a tense silence settles between them.

"Megan seems nice," she finally ventures.

Nothing.

"I'm psyched to start yoga again. It's been a while."

"I thought you said yoga is boring."

"Well . . . up here, 'boring' is relative." She looks over at him, hoping he'll crack a smile. Nope. "Just kidding. But who knows, maybe it will help me sleep."

He nods, mouth tightly closed, as if wanting to say more but choosing not to.

Back home, as the two of them work together to unpack the car, Brandon is quiet and a bit removed. They bring the crossbow and axes and a handsaw to the garage and carry boxes of pickling supplies and mason jars down to the basement room that will become the larder.

"Let's plan to build shelves over here," she says as they stack the goods along the back wall.

He taps his chin, appraising the room. Now he's back in his element. "I think we can probably fit, what, four units in here?" He walks around the space, arms out. "We'll need two-by-fours for framing and one-by-twelves for the shelves themselves. It'll take four pieces for each shelf: two for the sides and two for the front and back." Gesturing toward a corner, he says, "And maybe a flat surface to work on over here?"

"Great," she says.

After everything is put away, they sit in the red porch chairs in the late-afternoon sunlight, drinking iced tea. Brandon turns and puts his hand on Hayley's knee. "I'm sorry about earlier."

"Oh—it's okay. You don't have to—"

"I can be an asshole sometimes. It's just . . . I don't know. Weird things trigger me. Strangers."

She tilts her head. "What do you mean?"

"I don't know," he says again. "Those two just seemed overly familiar. I don't want anybody in our business. You've been burned before. And my past here is . . . complicated."

She puts her hand over his. "Hey, I get it."

He kisses her cheek. "More than anyone."

It feels good for him to say that, and maybe it's true. But she doesn't *really* get it. She still only knows a bit of Brandon's history in this place. What actually happened here? Why did his parents break up? All she has been able to glean so far is that the divorce was so bitter that his father and mother put a whole country between them. And that his father's engagement, less than a year later, hit him hard. His dad had invited sixteen-year-old Brandon to the wedding but didn't even offer a plane ticket to San Francisco, so there was no way he could afford to go. That was the last contact the two of them ever had.

He'd been so angry, he told Hayley. For years. He felt responsible for his mother, who spiraled after the divorce. She drank herself into oblivion, couldn't hold down a job. After she died, only a few months after she was diagnosed with liver failure, he was entirely on his own.

Clearly, for Brandon, Crystal River is more than just a fresh start. It's a do-over. A way to reclaim the time and place before his parents' marriage ended, now with Hayley at his side. Other than hunting, he's shown no interest in connecting with people. As much as Hayley loves him, and as much as she shares his vision of a private paradise, she doesn't want to cut herself off completely. Her instant rapport with Megan brought these feelings to the fore.

Maybe that's what made Brandon jealous.

Or maybe it was just typical guy stuff. He felt threatened by Tyler.

Whatever the reason, Hayley senses it's best to let it go for now.

So much so that when, an hour later, while she's chopping bell peppers at the kitchen island and Brandon is a few feet away, unpacking boxes in the living room, and her phone buzzes with a text from Megan, she ducks into the pantry to read it.

Loved meeting you!

Hayley hesitates before responding. She starts typing apologies: Sorry my husband was so . . . Sorry my husband wasn't very . . .

She backspaces. It probably seemed like a bigger deal to her than it did to Megan. The look that passed between Megan and Tyler, though, when Brandon stood there, glowering . . .

Hayley sighs.

She looks down at her phone. Three bubbles. I'd invite you here for yoga, but this shithole is a biohazard. Hike?

Hike. Good. Perfect for this area, this new life. She has the boots, after all. She has never relished the idea of wandering into the woods alone, but if Megan is up for it . . .

Sure! she types.

You're out there in the wilderness somewhere, right?

Hayley smiles. Pretty much.

She's seen a trailhead marker in the state park land a few hundred feet from the back edge of their property. When she asked Brandon if hikers would be tromping through their backyard, he'd laughed. "The Adirondack Trail is about ten miles south of Crystal River. That's where the real hiking is. Up here it's more like a stroll through the trees."

Brandon lived off the map in the Florida swamps, she reminds herself. And he grew up hiking trails that few would attempt in this area. His idea of an easy amble is probably most people's idea of strenuous exercise.

I'll come to you, Megan texts. When's good?

Ugh. Brandon will be annoyed. She needs to figure out how to broach it.

I'll check, she texts back. Stay tuned.

But there never seems to be the right moment to raise the subject.

After two gin and tonics, a dinner of grilled fish and vegetables at the island, and a spontaneous dance to "Purple Rain" on their Sonos, she and Brandon stumble up to bed, laughing, pulling off each other's clothes as they climb the stairs. The sex is teasing and slow at first, then intensely passionate, ending in a tangle of limbs and sheets.

"Gotta love makeup sex," Brandon murmurs. "Worth the fight before, don't you think?"

"That wasn't fighting," she says, playfully pushing his shoulder. "That was . . . communicating."

"Okay, sure." He rolls toward her, his hand drifting down her stomach. "What do you say we communicate a little more?" She shivers with pleasure, closing her eyes as he stokes the heat between them.

Hayley traces Brandon's bicep lightly with her fingers, thinking about the day. Sure, he has a moody side. He shuts down quickly when he feels threatened. But she knows, from her own experience, that loss changes a person. No matter how old you are when tragedy strikes, it can bring out the saddest, loneliest, most bitter parts of you, and it's damn hard to tuck it all back in.

Even so . . . as wrenching as her loss was, it opened up a current of feeling she'll never regret having access to. The fact is, she probably wouldn't have been attracted to someone like Brandon before the fire. Her New York life was a whirlwind of sharp quips and knowing glances, chasing the next trendy bar or restaurant. If she'd met Brandon sooner, she would've dismissed him as an outsider—too volatile, too sincere for her carefully curated world. But grief reshaped her. It peeled away layers, leaving her exposed to new possibilities. The very qualities that might have pushed her away from Brandon before now draw her in, a testament to how profoundly loss has changed her perspective on others, on life.

She looks over at her husband, his sleeping face illuminated in the light. Leaning on her elbow, she slides closer, nestling against him. He stirs but doesn't wake, and he doesn't move away. Despite her own insomnia, she loves watching Brandon sleep in this house, where he rests more deeply than he ever did in New York. She sees glimmers of the boy he must've been, fully at home in this idyllic place before the events that tore his family apart.

Something haunts her, though, that she can't quite put her finger on. She's tried to push away this uneasy feeling, but it only grows more oppressive, a weight on her chest. It's as if the air in the house is charged. She imagines she can hear whispers from the past, the memories of a couple who built a life and a family here. Brandon's mother, young and hopeful, raising her son in a home custom-built for them by her talented husband.

Such an auspicious beginning. So much promise.

The ghosts of the past are strong in this house, their presence rooted in its very foundation. They had free rein of these empty rooms, left untouched for twenty years.

After it all collapsed. Right here.

The sadness Brandon won't speak about surrounds them. The walls pulse with it.

Hayley is afraid to push, but she wants to know.

Why?

EIGHT

Now she's really awake. The sleep experts Hayley has consulted online all say that tossing and turning is a sign you should get up and do something else. Pulling on her robe, she tiptoes into her study.

Hayley turns on a small desktop lamp, adjusting the shade to keep the room soft and dim. She lifts the top of the cardboard banker's box that sits on her desk, labeled in black Sharpie: *Florida Mementos.*

One by one, she removes objects from the box: a threadbare stuffed tiger. A set of nesting dolls, the largest one faded and peeling. Her diploma, unframed, from Platinum Shores High. It's a pitifully meager collection. Below these few objects lie her scrapbooks—an archive of how she made sense of her life when she was young.

She pulls out the top one. When she opens it, an index card flutters from its pages and lands on the desk. It's written in her own neat handwriting from when she was . . . how old, twelve? Thirteen?

The future is a blank canvas, waiting for me to paint it with my dreams.

Hayley picks it up and stares at it. Did she copy this line from somewhere? Make it up? She doesn't remember. Gazing out the window above the desk, studying the contours of the moonlit mountains, she ponders its meaning. The sentence feels like a message from her child self to her adult self: *You're in the future you dreamed of. It's up to you to make it your own, to fill this house with love and laughter. To banish the ghosts of the past.*

She tacks the card onto the bulletin board that leans against the wall by the window. Closing her eyes, she visualizes her children-to-be playing in the yard, their laughter ringing out across the grass, a labradoodle romping beside them. Vegetables in the garden and chickens in the coop, winter nights around the hearth, summer afternoons on the dock by the pond.

On the gray walls of the study, Hayley can see the trace outlines of frames where Brandon's father's architectural blueprints used to hang. Brandon took them down and is storing them in the basement until they finish painting the living room, where he wants to hang them in a place of honor. Tomorrow she will return to Anderson's and pick up a gallon of paint. Tidewater. She wants to erase these gray lines that frame nothing, yet make her think of windows, portals into an unhappy past. By the time Emily comes to visit next month on her way to a long-planned thirtieth birthday trip, Hayley wants her study to hum with purpose. She feels an irrational need to prove to Emily that she didn't just quit her job to follow a man on his own quest; she has a plan for her future too.

Hayley turns to a project she's in the middle of, stacked in two piles on the desk: a collection of frames and a heap of photographs. She plans to make a photo wall in this room and has already framed two pictures that now sit propped against the wall. One is a formal portrait, commissioned by her mother when Hayley was ten and Jenna two. Their parents on a cream velvet love seat, Jenna perched on their mother's lap, Hayley standing with a hand on their father's shoulder. The memory of posing for the photo isn't exactly pleasant; just looking at it conjures the scratchy fabric of her pink dress, the way her father's back stiffened when the photographer cupped Hayley's hand on his shoulder, her mother's mounting exasperation when Jenna wouldn't stop squirming. But at least it captures a moment in time when her family of origin was intact.

Hayley's mother was better suited to lunching at the country club, planning charity galas that yielded gauzy photos in the *Platinum Shores Gazette*, and golf-and-spa getaways with her girlfriends than mothering. After Jenna was born, when Hayley was a shy and awkward eight-year-old, things only got worse. Jenna was rambunctious, then rebellious—a tantrum thrower who hurled and broke objects if she didn't get her way (toys, phones, a valuable antique vase). Hayley's mother brought a parade of child-rearing experts in to stare at, analyze, and medicate her. Her father, already a distracted workaholic, withdrew even more.

Hayley's response had been to disappear into her bedroom. She found solace in her mother's collection of shelter magazines—*Southern Living, House Beautiful, Garden & Gun*—stacked in piles in the family room. For entire afternoons, lying on her bed, Hayley cut out photos and pasted them into scrapbooks. She envisioned herself in these rooms—cozy sunlit spaces warmly decorated with books and flowers and wallpaper, in stark contrast to the reality of her parents' sterile showpiece home.

When she joined Domicile just after graduating from college, her job was to post and share design influencers' photos—not unlike the pictures she used to paste into those scrapbooks in her childhood bedroom.

The next photo on her desk makes her smile. It's the only picture from her wedding that truly conveys the magic of that day. Emily snapped it outside City Hall, on their way down the steps after the ceremony. Hayley and Brandon are holding hands, both beaming.

Hayley likes the two images together, the candid wedding snapshot, relaxed and joyful, as opposed to the clipped formality of the childhood portrait. They remind her that as an adult, she has the ability to choose joy. She can paint her canvas however she wishes.

As she's dismantling a picture frame, a high-pitched, eerie sound cuts through the silence of the house. A coyote. Hayley cups her hands around the window and peers out at the dark woods, backlit by moonglow. She can see the faint outline of the animal, a shadowy figure moving through the trees. It stops, waits. Does it see the light from her window?

She knows it's irrational, but she feels as if the coyote is studying her.

Fingers trembling, she lowers the shade.

Is this a sign, a warning of some kind?

Don't be silly. Shake it off. She takes a breath.

Seeking distraction, she turns to the box she's been avoiding ever since the move. *Jenna Mementos.*

After her sister's death, Hayley went through Jenna's phone, searching for clues to help her understand what had happened. But Jenna had deleted almost everything. Any picture, or even mention, of her brief engagement was gone. All Hayley knew about Sean Wilder was what Jenna told her after she dumped him: he'd charmed her at first, but ultimately he was bad news. Anyone else from Jenna's life at that time was impossible to identify, stripped from photos and her address book.

Hayley had grilled Brandon for any details he might have to offer about her crowd. It was a rotating group of heavy partiers, he said; he couldn't tell one from the other.

Almost everything in the Platinum Shores house had been destroyed in the fire. But after Jenna's overdose, once the legal issues were resolved, Hayley received a package of her sister's effects from her parents' lawyer's office. She'd been too distraught to go through it then, so it went into this box.

Now, in the soft light of her study, she opens the top folder and pulls out an envelope. It's filled with photos. Polaroids, glossy squares with thick white edges. The retro craze for the nostalgia of low-res, no-filter images—staged ironically in well-lit clusters by the design influencers Hayley used to promote—clearly reached Jenna and her crowd too.

Hayley upends the envelope and spreads out the photos that fall across the desk. There aren't many, a dozen total. She picks one up and studies it. Jenna's platinum hair is shot through with streaks of blue, and she has raccoon rings around her eyes. This photo would've been snapped not long before the fire, Hayley realizes, probably within the same year.

Her sister is almost as old here as she would ever be.

In the photo, Jenna's holding a red Solo cup in one hand. Her other arm juts into the frame: black chipped fingernails, a small tattoo Hayley has never seen before on the pale white skin of her wrist. Squinting at the tattoo, Hayley makes out a hummingbird, green and magenta, beak raised, wings outstretched.

Oh—right. Their father used to compare Jenna to a hummingbird, though it wasn't necessarily a compliment. Her frenetic energy, her bright darting eyes—she flitted through life with an intensity as dangerous as it was beautiful. For all her buzzing speed there was a fragility to her, a sense that she could be damaged by a single touch.

The rest of the photos on the desk are all selfies, apparently from the same night. It's obvious that Jenna is drunk or high or both. Is this how Hayley wants to remember her? Yet how can she destroy what are probably the last remaining images of her sister?

Gathering up the photos and sliding them back into the envelope, Hayley sees the white edge of one more Polaroid, caught in the corner. She pulls it out. Another selfie. But this one has been sliced in half, the ragged edge created by a hasty scissor causing it to cling to the envelope. In the photo, Jenna looks to her left, toward the missing person. Whoever's been ripped out was holding the camera. Their other arm is draped across Jenna's shoulder. With a start, Hayley realizes that this must be her sister's former fiancé.

Hayley recognizes the look on Jenna's face: infatuation bordering on obsession. When she fell for someone, she fell hard and fast. There was never any half measure in her emotions—her passions tended to become addictions. Jenna must've cut the photo in half to eliminate his face. Just as she deleted him from her phone and her life and tried to delete him from her memory.

But she couldn't. Instead, she deleted herself.

This is one photo Hayley doesn't want to keep. The last thing she needs is a reminder that this asshole contributed to Jenna's vulnerable state after the fire. But wait . . . there's something odd . . .

She brings the cut Polaroid to her face. Inspects it closely.

The man's hand—Sean's hand—sports a black-and-gold ring with beveled edges.

Their father's ring.

Hayley glances back at the framed photograph of their family. Here it is, on her father's left hand. And here it is on Sean's.

What the actual fuck?

Tears of fury prick the corners of her eyes. The one talisman that mattered to her, the only object from her past that gave her any sense of security—and it's on the finger of some piece of shit who knew Jenna for all of five seconds.

She drops the Polaroid onto the desk and lowers her face into her hands. She'll never shake the guilt she feels about fleeing Platinum Shores after their parents' funeral instead of taking the time to make sure Jenna was okay. Sure, she reached out by text and email in the weeks that followed—but it was mostly to keep her sister informed of legal developments and other business matters to do with the family estate.

Lame. So lame. And selfish.

Predictably, Jenna sent cursory responses: Fine. Sure. Whatever you want. Whatever you say.

Until, out of the blue, that final heartbreaking barrage of texts . . .

"Hey, babe. What's wrong?"

Startled, Hayley turns to see her husband in the doorframe. "Oh, Brandon." She sighs. "I was such a bad sister. I can't believe I left Jenna alone after the fire."

He opens his arms. "Come here."

She lets him hold her close, kiss the top of her head. "I should've done more. I should've—"

"You can't keep dwelling on the past."

"But I abandoned her."

Brandon shakes his head. "Hey, I knew Jenna, remember? She was so . . . broken."

Hayley picks up the photo and shows it to him. "She gave Sean our father's ring. He probably sold it."

He glances at it briefly. "It's just a ring, Hayl. I'll buy you any ring you want."

"It's not the same."

"That ring is gone."

"But Jenna—"

"Some people are going to destroy themselves no matter what. And there's nothing anyone can do to stop them." He takes the photo from her hand and drops it into the trash.

"Brandon, wait—"

"That part of your life is over, Hayley," he says. "That's why we're here, remember? To create a new life together."

She glances back at the index card from her childhood, pinned to the bulletin board. *The future is a blank canvas.* He's probably right.

"Come back to bed," Brandon says. "It's almost morning."

"I will. Just give me a minute."

When he leaves the room, she retrieves the torn Polaroid from the trash. For a moment she stares at her sister's face, shining with anticipation. Maybe it's unfair to expect Brandon to understand the weight of what she carries.

She slips the photo into the junk drawer in her desk and shuts off the light.

NINE

Hayley scrutinizes the bag of coffee beans she's been feeding into the grinder. Could she have accidentally made decaf? Did she miss the fine print? Because the caffeine she desperately needs is not kicking in.

Nope. The label clearly reads *Pleasant Morning Buzz.*

Hardly. She sighs.

Even with Brandon holding her when she returned to bed last night, she couldn't drift off for more than a few scant minutes at a time.

"You gotta start getting more sleep," Brandon says as they stand at the island. He's just stopped her from absently spooning salt instead of sugar into his mug.

"I know," she says miserably.

He clasps her hand across the kitchen island. "If you were one of your own self-help gurus, what would you tell yourself to do to make yourself happier?"

Good question. She thinks for a moment. "Well . . . I'd probably say that your unconscious can be your teacher if you let it. Instead of running from your fear, try to embrace it."

He pats her arm. "Then do that."

—

In the warm light of midmorning, Hayley watches Brandon through the picture window as he stacks bricks from a wheelbarrow around the base of what will be the smokehouse. He moves swiftly, with assurance, as he angles the wheelbarrow so there will be no wasted motion.

Now he's laying the foundation. One brick, a swipe of mortar from the trowel. Another brick, repeat.

Brandon is imbued with purpose in this place. He's been making swift progress on everything from organizing the garage to building out the wine cellar. This is the guy she fell in love with—not that tin man who'd languished unhappily, stiff and rusting, in her West Village apartment.

She sips the last of her cooling coffee, rinses the mug, and puts it in the dishwasher. If Brandon can find his happiness here, so can she.

Impulsively, she pulls out her phone and opens the text conversation with Megan. Why does she think she needs Brandon's okay to invite a friend to her own home? He wants her to embrace this life, after all.

Morning! she types. Is today good for you? Perfect weather for a hike.

Within seconds, three bubbles.

You read my mind. Get me out of this apartment! Trees for the win.

Hayley smiles. She drops a pin in Google Maps and forwards the location.

Got it. I'll be there around 3, if that works.

Oh shit. She's actually coming. Brandon might want Hayley to be happy, but he doesn't love surprises.

Hayley taps out a text to her husband. Hey babe, good news! That woman from the hardware store reached out and asked me to go on a hike today.

Just a little white lie.

I'm embracing my fear of the woods.

As she hits Send, she hears the buzz of Brandon's phone on the kitchen counter. Damn, he didn't take it outside. So much for technology helping her get out of a face-to-face.

She scoops his phone off the counter to bring it to him, and the screen lights up with an incoming call.

Unknown number, 754 area code. South Florida.

An old friend? There'd be a contact name. A former client? Maybe she should answer.

But maybe it's spam . . .

The call goes to voicemail before she can decide.

Hmm. Brandon has five voicemails from this number, she notices, all from this morning. And it's only ten a.m. It must be one of those robocalls that mimics the area codes in your contacts and spams the hell out of you.

Hayley heads outside. The sun is beginning to warm the air. Soon the Fair Isle sweater she's wearing will feel oppressively thick. Maybe she should wear her fleece on the hike. Or should she avoid synthetic fabrics in case Megan opposes them? She does seem pretty earthy, what with her wellness Substack and all. She'll probably be wearing flannel.

Brandon looks up, surprised to see her.

"You left your phone on the counter," Hayley says, holding it out to him. "Hey, you got a bunch of calls this morning from a Florida number. Maybe you need to get on a 'do not call—'"

He swipes the phone from her hand, an odd look on his face. Alarm? Or is it . . . guilt?

"Brandon?"

He pockets the phone. "Hayley, I . . ."

Her brain might be foggy from lack of sleep, her nerves jangly from caffeine, but there's no mistaking his cues. This is how someone reacts when they have a secret to keep.

"Who called you?" Is it a former girlfriend? "And why don't you want me to know?"

He fixes her with an inscrutable stare.

Maybe not so former.

A gust of wind stirs up the fallen leaves around the ankles of their jeans, rustling them into a percussive dance.

Hayley's stomach tightens. She and Brandon have discussed their exes, of course. Her list is pretty lame: two guys during her entire four years at college, a few regrettable hookups when she was briefly on the dating apps, an ill-fated summer fling with a guy she met at a Hamptons house share. Brandon, on the other hand, has an extensive sexual history. One-night stands. Bar hookups. Bored housewives whose homes he renovated while their husbands were at work. But no serious relationships before Hayley, or so he'd told her.

Brandon fidgets with the bill of his baseball cap. "Well, you saw the number. So . . . uh . . . I guess I have no choice."

With trepidation, she crosses her arms. "No choice about what?"

He clears his throat. "I wanted to protect you from this. But . . . okay. That troll from Platinum Shores—the one with the voice you hate, who kept hounding you after Jenna . . . you know . . . died—"

"Olivia Blackwood," she breaks in.

"Yeah, that one. She found me somehow. She's trying to reach you for some *Where are they now?* feature."

Brandon isn't cheating. God, of course not.

Her relief is short lived, though.

Olivia Blackwood is back. Hayley feels a flare of rage. How dare that woman rise from the swamps and threaten her happiness again, after all the damage she's done?

And how dare she try to go through Brandon?

"Don't call her back," she tells him. "Don't even call to say no."

Holding up his phone, he flags all five messages, then hits Delete. Then, Delete Trash.

"Gone," he says. "When she sees she can't get to you through me, she'll give up. I'll keep deleting anything she sends, I promise."

She watches Brandon as he slowly pockets his phone and picks up the trowel, scraping a smear of hardened mortar from its tip with a dirt-streaked rag.

—

When Brandon comes inside for lunch, he says, "I saw your text about the hike."

Handing him a tuna sandwich, Hayley smiles. She's had a chance to think about how to finesse this. "Good timing, right?" she says. "I can really use the distraction from Olivia fucking Blackwood."

"Is the boyfriend coming?"

"Only her."

A sharp thud against the kitchen window makes them both turn.

"Damn birds." Brandon moves toward the glass. He stands there, frowning. "This one's hurt."

Hayley joins him at the window. A small chickadee lies stunned on the bluestone path, its wing bent at an odd angle.

Brandon is already heading for the door. She watches from the kitchen as he approaches the bird and scoops it up in one swift motion, cradling it in his palm.

"Get me that cardboard box from the recycling," he calls. "And one of my old T-shirts."

With precise, careful movements, he lines the box with his shirt, places the bird inside, then sets the makeshift nest in a sheltered corner of the porch.

Brandon comes back into the kitchen and washes his hands. "It'll either make it or it won't," he says matter-of-factly. "But at least the hawks won't get it."

Hayley studies his face. This pragmatic tenderness—it's so him. And so different from the guarded way he's been acting lately.

Brandon catches her watching him. "What?"

"Nothing," she says. "Just . . . that was so sweet."

He shrugs. "Circle of life and all that. But we can tip the scales sometimes."

"So . . . ," Hayley says, leaning closer. "You're okay that I'm hanging out with Megan, right? It would be nice to have a new friend."

After a moment, he nods. "I suppose. But take it slow. Your old friends haven't done you any favors."

—

At 2:45, Hayley is sitting at the kitchen island, sipping lemonade, her never-worn Blundstones laced up over brand-new merino wool socks. Despite this high-end gear, and less than fifteen minutes from Megan's likely appearance, she has metaphorical cold feet. What are they going to talk about in the woods for an hour? Yoga poses?

The truth is, Hayley has no idea how much to reveal about herself. Female bonding is built on mutual self-exposure, and even an innocuous question like "How did you and Brandon meet?" will inevitably lead back to the shit show of Hayley's past. And there's no quicker way to scare off a new person than drowning the conversation with sadness.

She takes a sip of lemonade. If Megan doesn't work out, how in the world will she meet someone else? Will she need to hang around the farmers' market and bribe little kids with candy apples so their moms will talk to her? Post a flyer in Anderson's on the bulletin board next to the beefcake photo of Megan's boyfriend: In the market for a yoga buddy?

But Brandon's words resonate. How can she trust anyone? She was so burned by Melinda, and here's Olivia Blackwood, back in her life again, dredging for dirt.

Hayley sighs. She flips open her iPad and types: "How can I make friends again after my trust has been broken?"

She scrolls past a stream of generic quotes about trust and friendship until an Emily Dickinson poem she had to memorize in high school stops her:

"Hope" is the thing with feathers—
That perches in the soul—
And sings the tune without the words—
And never stops—at all—

Hayley feels the familiar thrill of recognition that happens when she comes across the right words at the right time. The words resonate in a way that feels deeply personal and more complex than the advice she's been seeking from self-help books. The poem is not prescriptive. It cracks open something inside her that has felt too complex to articulate, giving her room to feel several things at once. She can be both wary and hopeful; the states don't have to be in opposition.

She stands up and puts her glass in the sink. Olivia Blackwood might be back, but that doesn't mean Hayley has to take the bait. She refuses to obsess over this woman who caused her so much grief.

Despite her fears, unless she makes a leap—takes a chance on someone new—she'll never move on.

TEN

Hayley pulls on one of Brandon's flannel shirts and heads outside to wait for Megan. One thing's for sure—she doesn't want to show Megan around the house today, in its current state of disarray. Unopened boxes dominate the space in teetering piles. Each day, she promises herself and Brandon that she'll tackle the clutter. But she finds herself unable to focus. She opens a box with good intentions, only to get lost holding a gray ceramic vase or staring at another midcentury modern lamp. Everything she ordered was carefully chosen, yet it all feels soulless.

Where is the soul? Where is her soul?

She knows.

The little cottage across the property came together so easily. Sometimes, when Brandon is running errands, Hayley slips down the path and sits in the living room on the English roll-arm sofa. She imagines Brandon fetching her a mug of tea from the sweet little kitchen while a snowstorm swirls outside the windows . . .

She can't confess this to her husband. Not when he's so invested in making his parents' house their home. She looks back at the soaring living room windows. The place is objectively beautiful, but it still feels cold despite her efforts to warm it up.

Hayley sighs. She knows in her heart that the cottage represents a part of her that is truly different from Brandon. When it comes to the main house, her husband is driven by an obsession she can't fully share.

It occurs to her that she hasn't seen her husband around since lunch. The trowel he was using on the smokehouse foundation sits abandoned in the wet, clayey mortar. Who knows? He's probably taking a break, wandering the woods, off-trail in the park land.

The grinding sound of an overtaxed muffler pops from the bottom of their steep driveway. Several moments later, a dilapidated black Hyundai inches around the curve. Megan, behind the wheel, gives Hayley a quick wave before turning toward the garage behind the house.

Hayley walks up the driveway to meet her. She reads a few of the peeling bumper stickers that adorn the back of the car—*I brake for wildflowers*; *Don't follow me, I'm lost too*; *My other car is a broom*—before Megan steps out.

Dressed in leggings, a well-worn flannel shirt, and beat-up hiking boots, with her long hair in a loose updo, Megan looks casually stylish. "This place is unbelievable!" She sweeps her arms wide as if embracing the entire property, earth to sky. "Even breathing feels cleaner up here. You're so lucky."

Hayley is about to mumble some excuse about stumbling into luck through Brandon's family when Megan laughs. "True confession," she says, "I almost turned the car around, like, three times. I was gonna text you some lame excuse. I had this sudden fear you're a psycho killer luring me into the mountains alone. I mean, who are you, really? We met once at a hardware store."

Hayley laughs too. "Yeah, that's me, all right. Psycho killer." And with that, her trepidation melts away. "I was worried you wouldn't like me, and you were worried I'd murder you. I feel better now that I know you're even more paranoid than I am."

With an arch look, Megan says, "If you're not paranoid, you're not paying attention. So—are you going to show me around this Eden of yours?"

Hayley rolls up her sleeves. The afternoon has grown warm. "Let's hike. The weather's so nice. We can save the house tour for another time."

Megan follows Hayley across the yard and through a winding trail into the woods. Sunlight filters through the canopy of tall pines, casting a dappled glow on the forest floor. A breeze carries the earthy scent of pine needles.

"So what are your plans for the property?" Megan asks.

"Well," Hayley begins slowly, "I'm starting with planters on the front porch. And in the spring, we'll expand the vegetable garden. Brandon's pretty obsessed with the smokehouse he's building to preserve what he brings back from his hunting expeditions, but I gotta admit, it's not really my thing."

Megan shudders. "I'm vegan. Killing animals is definitely not my thing either."

Hayley feels a little defensive on Brandon's behalf. She thinks about the chickadee he rescued, how gently he handled it. "Brandon has a philosophy that he'll only kill what we can eat. It's about survival, he says."

"Is it?" Megan's tone is light but insistent. "I mean, I'm surviving just fine with no meat at all."

"Oh, we eat a ton of vegetables too," Hayley says quickly.

Sounds of the forest rise up around them: leaves rustling softly, a woodpecker rat-a-tat-tatting against a treetop. Megan is quiet. Is she upset?

"Hunting is just part of Brandon's philosophy," Hayley says, looking over at Megan. "It's his dream to live off the land."

Megan smiles. "It's cool. I respect having a philosophy. Since mine is 'live and let live,' I won't judge other human animals for their choices. I'm just a little surprised you're on board with it. You seem so kind-hearted. You and Brandon, is it like 'opposites attract'?"

"In some ways, I guess. What about you and Tyler?"

Megan makes a face. "Tyler." She shakes her head. "Let's just say the two of us are . . . living in the moment. My wellness vibe is a little woo-woo for him. But I've gotten him into composting, and it's his new goal to be somewhere where we can build out a whole system for it. Raised beds, different types of waste. He's all over it now. He even got a tattoo of a praying mantis. Ty says mantises are nature's composters."

Hayley remembers the green ink peeking out from Tyler's sleeve at Anderson's. "I found an ink master a few towns over," Megan continues. "I got this." She pulls up her flannel and rolls down the waistband of her leggings to show Hayley a delicate mandala in three shades of blue just over her left hip bone.

"Nice."

"Want to come with me and get one next time? I'm saving up for something bigger. Maybe a tree."

Hayley's not into tattoos herself, though most of her friends have at least one. Brandon has a Florida crocodile on his ankle. Emily has a whole sleeve.

"Tyler might get another bug," Megan continues. "He actually surprised me with all his research on insect digestive systems. He didn't even finish high school."

She grimaces a little. "It's kind of a pain point between us. But I'm trying to practice radical acceptance."

Hayley nods. "That's what relationships are all about, isn't it?"

"Well, to be honest, 'relationship' is kind of a strong word for what Tyler and I have. We're together, but we're not really doing the whole ownership thing."

"You mean . . . ?"

Megan shrugs. "We're open."

Hayley nods again. Interesting. "So where did you move from?"

"Syracuse. What about you?"

Hayley has stumbled into a conversation she's not ready to have. "New York City. I mean . . . Florida originally."

"Do your parents live in Florida?"

Hayley just . . . cannot. "They died when I was little."

"I'm so sorry. What happened?"

Hayley rubs the back of her neck. "They had cancer. Different kinds. I know it's crazy, both at the same time. What are the odds, right?"

Megan shakes her head.

Hayley tenses—she knows what an awful liar she is.

"That's terrible, Hayley," Megan says.

Ah, it's just pity. "I'd rather not talk about it, if that's okay."

"Of course. I understand. Just know I'm here for you if you ever do."

"Thanks." Hayley doesn't like making up stories about herself, especially not to someone she hopes to call a friend. But it's too soon. She can't bear to expose the salacious details of her family tragedy. Not yet.

For a moment both of them are silent. Leaves crunch beneath their boots as they walk.

"Tell me more about you and Brandon," Megan says. "What's your love story?"

"We're pretty traditional, I guess. We got married a few months ago."

"How did you meet?"

Another land mine. She tries to keep it vague. "Oh . . . mutual friends. The typical story."

"There is no typical story. So what's yours?"

Hayley doesn't want to lie again. "We met at an event. I ran into him in the kitchen, and he spilled his beer on me."

"That's cute. In New York?"

"No, Florida. He lived there; I was visiting from the city."

"How long were you dating before you tied the knot?"

"About a year."

"That's fast," Megan remarks. "So—Florida . . . New York City . . . how'd you end up here?"

Whoa. So many questions. Hayley is trying to be open, but this is too much for her. She sighs. "Brandon liked Florida, but I didn't want to live there. He came to Manhattan, but it was never a fit. He inherited this house. I guess it was a compromise." Hayley hears the slight note of exasperation that's crept into her voice despite her attempts to stay light.

Megan shakes her head. "Sorry, I don't mean to pry."

"It's okay." Hayley reminds herself that Megan has no idea what she's been through. These are ordinary questions any new friend might ask.

A rustling noise from above makes both women look up. In the clearing above their heads, three enormous birds are winging through the sky in a slow, mesmerizing pattern. Then, all at once, there are a dozen—no, more. Hayley shades her eyes to see them clearly.

"Broad-winged hawks!" Megan marvels. "They're migrating. I've never seen so many at once." The two of them stand side by side, watching the birds of prey glide on the wind. They circle higher, dark shadows in the sky.

"Gorgeous," Megan says.

Hayley's eyes dart from bird to bird as she tracks their movements. She swallows hard, forcing a smile. "To be honest, hawks have always creeped me out. They're so menacing."

"You really are a city girl, aren't you?"

"I guess I am. People everywhere, lots of activity—it reassures me. There are too many trees out here for my liking. What if a giant oak falls on the house?"

Megan laughs. "An oak would have to uproot itself and literally grow feet to walk over and fall on your house."

Envisioning this makes Hayley laugh too.

"You just need to learn more about this environment," Megan continues. "I gave myself a crash course on Adirondack trees and trails before Ty and I relocated. Content prep for my Substack. 'Woods and Wellness'!"

"I'd love to read your posts."

"Oh, nothing is up yet. Still getting my shit together. But yeah, subscribe. You'll be one of the first."

Hayley watches Megan as she continues to move through the forest. She isn't glancing around anxiously, worrying about hawks, or coyotes, or whatever invisible menace may lurk around the corner. Hayley wishes she had half her confidence. What would it be like to be in

Megan's skin, to see the world through her eyes? To trust her gut the way she seems to?

"Can you show me?" she asks.

Megan looks at her. "Show you what?"

Hayley gestures around them. "How to be in this place. To really . . . I don't know, inhabit it."

Megan shrugs. "Just look around," she says. "All of this is yours. This land, those houses. It's perfection. What could you possibly need from me?"

"I don't know how to feel safe here."

Megan looks at her intently. "You are safe, Hayley."

Hayley feels, irrationally, on the brink of tears. "I can't explain it; there's a feeling from the past that lingers here. Brandon's family . . ."

"What about them?" Megan's curiosity is clearly piqued.

Hayley stops. It's too much. What would she even say? "I don't know."

A silence falls between them as they continue their walk.

After a long moment, Megan asks, "Do you meditate?"

Hayley shrugs. "I've tried, but—"

"I could teach you a few techniques if you want. It doesn't have to be anything formal."

"That'd be great." Hayley remembers the cheap housewares in Megan's cart at Anderson's. The beater car, the nasty apartment. "And I can pay you! I don't expect you to give your time away for free."

A cloud passes over Megan's face.

Hayley feels herself flush. "Oh, I didn't mean to suggest . . . I just meant—"

"That you feel sorry for me?"

"God, no. I didn't want to take advantage of your expertise."

Megan is shaking her head. "I was nervous about the obvious financial difference between us, but I told myself I was being silly. This makes me feel like you think our relationship is, I don't know . . . transactional."

Hayley, slightly panicked, blurts out, "Look, can we start over? I put my foot in it, and I'm sorry. Money doesn't matter to me."

"Money always matters, Hayley. Especially when you don't have it."

The words pierce Hayley with a sting. "You're right."

A howl rises from the woods, closer than feels comfortable to Hayley. She stops cold. A coyote. Hawks are one thing, but . . . "Megan, let's—"

Megan raises a finger to her lips. "Shh."

"Should we get out of here?" Hayley whispers.

"No." Megan smiles. "It's probably a female calling to her pups to let them know she's found food. I'm trying to hear what direction she's calling from. The sound bounces around in the forest, and you can't always tell."

"'Food' meaning . . . us?"

Megan laughs. "You'd be pretty tasty. I'm too gristly."

Owooo . . .

This time both of them flinch. But now Hayley realizes what they're hearing. It's not a coyote—it's a person. The Coyote Kid. "Ugh, Brandon! He must be on the mountain. He told me he uses that call to establish animal dominance."

"You weren't kidding about 'back to the land.'"

Now that she knows the source of the howl, Megan is back to rubbing leaves between her fingers and placing her hands on tree trunks. "Look." She points at a patch of fungus growing near an old oak. "That's nature's artwork, if you ask me."

Hayley follows her gaze. A bright-orange mushroom stands out against the backdrop of the lush forest.

"And over there. That one," Megan says, pointing. "Look at those colors! Like all of autumn."

Hayley steps closer. Brilliantly hued fungus clings to the trunk of a dying tree. She touches the fronds of the mushroom cap. It's velvety.

Megan points to another blooming patch of mushrooms. "Do you mind if I forage from your extended backyard?"

"Sure."

Megan gets to work. "Have you seen what those posers at the Crystal River Farmers' Market charge for 'locally sourced morels'? Please."

Hayley has. She paid $25 last weekend at the farmers' market for locally sourced morels.

Megan grins. "I'll cook up something special with these. And bring you a sample."

"Could they be poisonous?"

"I guess you'll have to trust me."

Hayley watches her gather a bundle of mushrooms in a bandana she fished out of her bag and then knot the red cloth. "You're welcome to come back for more anytime."

"Deal. As long as my car can make it up and back. I was praying her brakes wouldn't give out the whole way up the mountain. Ursula can't survive another winter on Tyler's duct-tape repair jobs."

Owooo.

Brandon's howl floats toward them, even farther away now. Megan and Hayley look at each other.

"He forgets that it might be scary to humans," Hayley says.

Megan lifts an eyebrow. "Maybe he wants to be scary to humans."

ELEVEN

Hayley has slept soundly for the first time since moving to Crystal River. And what a difference it makes. She's filled with energy. In the kitchen, she grinds beans, pulls a glass bottle of milk from the fridge, and, when the coffee is ready, sets two steaming mugs on the island. The aroma of French roast wafts through the light-filled room. As Brandon comes down the stairs to the kitchen, she butters his toast and slides a pile of scrambled eggs onto his plate.

"Good morning, sunshine." She gives him a deep kiss, handing him one of the mugs.

"Good morning. And wow."

Hayley perches on a stool next to his at the island, sipping her own coffee. "I'm finally ready to tackle the living room," she says. "I'm getting a vision for how to make it work."

"Excellent," he says, munching a piece of toast. "Well, I'm heading into town to deal with the bank. Paperwork. And I'll go to the Verizon store. New phone, new number. When you changed yours, I should've done it too. I don't want those Florida trolls to find us ever again."

Hayley squeezes his arm, feeling a surge of love toward her husband. When Brandon leaves, Hayley stands in the center of the great room. The sun, streaming through the windows, washes the pale floors in cold white light. Pushing up the sleeves of her sweatshirt, she steadies herself for the daunting task ahead. She appraises the angular built-ins, the swooping ceiling, the stone fireplace big enough to roast an ox.

What did Brandon's mother think about this place? Hayley wonders. Did she share her husband's minimalist eye, or did she, like Hayley, prefer the comforts of the homey cottage?

Hayley has been hoping to come across a dusty box of Brandon's childhood photos in the basement, a forgotten album stashed in some corner. So far, she's turned up nothing. Brandon has expressed little interest. When she asked him directly about his parents, he provided scant descriptions of how they looked back then. "She was pretty," was all he said about his mother, "before the drinking." And his father? Did Brandon look like him? A shrug. "I guess. Maybe. The dark hair."

And what was it like for Brandon to grow up here? No secret nooks, no cozy hiding places, no tree house, despite the acres of trees as far as the eye can see. Other than the forest, where did he hang out when he was a kid? When she asks him about his past life in this house, he brushes her off. "Let's make some new memories, Hayley," he says. And when she asks for his input on making the place theirs, he says, "Do whatever you want."

But Hayley doesn't know what she wants. Her design sense, usually so reliable, has abandoned her.

Hayley flips open her iPad and returns to the saved home design tabs on her screen. She clicks through to DWR, where her shopping cart is already full. With one more scan of the great room, she decides: Enough perseverating. It's time. She's ready to purchase what she selected.

The total is huge. For a moment, she's taken aback. Is it too much? Too extravagant?

No. This is furniture. The house is big and empty. They need it.

After a quick scroll of the items, editing out a few, she hits Purchase. A window pops up on her screen: Card denied. Limit exceeded.

Huh?

Hayley hasn't exactly been paying attention to the bottom line. Between her inheritance and the return on her New York apartment, there's plenty of money in her various accounts. But this particular credit card is just for new house purchases.

She texts Brandon to see if he knows anything.

Sorry babe, he texts back. Huge week for me with lumber and the tractor and other stuff.

Equipment is that expensive?

She really wouldn't know.

Heads up please next time, she answers.

My bad comes back in return. Didn't know you'd bought so much too.

She pulls out a different card. Brandon is right. Her spending—between furniture and clothes and kitchen supplies—is probably equal to, if not greater than, his. It has been all too easy, and enjoyable, to shop online for high-tech down coats, ultra-cozy sweats, and fleece-lined boots with her Platinum Amex for the winter ahead.

Maybe she needs to increase the limit on their shared account. And she should keep better track of where the money is going. She has to stop being passive about the balances in her accounts. There's so much loss associated with how the money came to her. Maybe the pain she feels has left her an indifferent steward of her own wealth.

The thought sends Hayley into a spiral. Is she unconsciously trying to spend away the portion of the inheritance that should have been Jenna's? She considers this possibility. As chaotic as the last years of Jenna's life became, and as determined as Hayley has been to leave the past behind, she misses her sister. Hayley feels the sting of tears. It's unbearable to acknowledge that she's even richer because Jenna is dead.

As Olivia Blackwood never failed to mention on her podcast.

When it first aired, Hayley couldn't help herself; she skimmed a few reader responses on the website. But after reading what OBStan23 wrote—How curious that the sister ended up with everything. And then there were none.—Hayley swore she'd never look at the site again.

But now, despite her better judgment, she clicks out of DWR and pulls up the *Sinister Sands* website on her iPad.

As she scrolls through the comments, the words blur before her eyes, a cacophony of judgment and speculation:

> Fentanyl + family fortune = motive. Just saying.
>
> "Accident" is code for "we can't prove it was the daughter."
>
> Addicts will do ANYTHING for their next fix. Even burn down the family mansion.

Hayley's fury flares as she scrolls.

She clicks through to the landing page for the episode that featured her and scrolls to the bottom.

> Olivia's right. How could anyone abandon their sister like that?
>
> Jenna's behavior was obviously a cry for help. Hayley is a selfish narcissist who only cares about herself.

And the occasional reasonable voice: Maybe there's more to the story? Seems harsh to judge without knowing everything.

Hayley's hands tremble as she continues to scroll, each comment a fresh wound. She pauses on a particularly vicious one: Hayley is a coward. Partying in New York while her sister fell apart. Disgusting.

And then she reads one that makes her stomach drop: I was friends with the sister! She ghosted me. What a headcase. Melinda1995.

Melinda. Adding insult to injury.

Hayley's finger hovers over the "Leave a Comment" button. Part of her still longs to defend herself, to make a case for her behavior even two years later, to persuade people she's not a villain. But no. Engaging with the trolls will only feed the frenzy that Olivia Blackwood clearly still thrives on.

Hayley doesn't want to keep running away. She may not be able to erase the past, but she can fight to protect her future—and Jenna's memory—from those who would exploit it. She remembers her Florida lawyer's advice: *Documentation is crucial.*

With a determined breath, she opens her email and begins to craft a letter.

> To: legal@truecrimeproductions.com
>
> Subject: Cease and Desist–Response Required
>
> I am writing to formally request that Olivia Blackwood and the Sinister Sands podcast immediately cease all attempts to contact me or my family. If I do not receive written confirmation within 45 days that all such activities have been halted, I will have no choice but to initiate formal legal action . . .

TWELVE

Hayley is making quick work of unpacking boxes and finding places for each kitchen implement, each place mat, each throw pillow. After cutting through yards of padded plastic wrap, Hayley uncovers a glass vase and sets it in the middle of the kitchen table.

Morning sun filters through the haze. After the fierce rainstorm that swept through the region, the mountains surrounding their home are vibrant with color. It's close to the height of fall now. She pulls on her puffer vest and steps outside into the chilly air. She walks down the steps from the porch, and her boots sink into the mud below the leaves that litter the ground. She picks her way carefully across the yard to gather cattails to display in the new vase. In the distance, the pond is shrouded in a mist that rises like steam, blending the line between water and sky. The velvety cattail heads at the water's edge sway and rustle, their green stems tinged with shades of yellow and brown. The distant call of a loon echoes.

Back indoors, Hayley arranges the cattails in the vase, then stands back to admire their effect against the mountain view. The dramatic arrangement can't fix everything that's wrong with the room, but it helps.

A knock on the front door startles her.

When Hayley opens it, she's surprised to find that awful woman they met at the café in town standing on the threshold. She's holding a foil-topped pie. What was her name again? Oh yes—Cheryl Snyder.

Cheryl thrusts the pie at Hayley. Her hands are calloused, with dirt under her short nails.

"Housewarming gift."

"Oh, wow."

"Honeycrisps. People love my pies. I sell 'em at the farmers' market."

"That's so nice. Thank you."

Cheryl peers over her shoulder, squinting into the house. Then she refocuses on Hayley. "My husband was the one who built this place, you know."

"Really?" Hayley is thrown. Weird that Brandon didn't tell her.

"Back in the nineties, when Brandon's father designed it. That man had some wacky concepts. Without Rick's help, this place would be a flying saucer."

"I had no idea."

Cheryl shakes her head. "I'm not surprised."

There's nothing neighborly about this visit, the pie notwithstanding. The tone of Cheryl's voice, the intensity of her stare—Hayley is growing more uneasy by the moment. "Well, the craftsmanship is gorgeous," she says, hoping a compliment might soften the exchange. "Your husband is obviously a master of his trade."

Cheryl just stands there, expressionless. Expectant.

As the uncomfortable silence between them grows, Hayley feels she has no option but to invite her inside. She gestures. "Would you like to—?"

Cheryl brushes right past her and walks in.

Hayley, sighing, follows.

"This house was empty for so many years," Cheryl says. "And now look at it. All shiny and new again." She runs her hand along the kitchen island countertop. "Marble?"

"Uh—Silestone."

"Fancy. I prefer good old laminate myself."

Sensing that her visitor doesn't plan on leaving anytime soon, Hayley resigns herself to playing hostess. "Can I get you a coffee. Or tea?"

"Tea. Black. None of that herbal nonsense." Cheryl waves dismissively at Hayley's newly arranged tea station, alphabetized from Anise to Zinger.

Now Hayley has no choice but to make small talk. Glancing with longing at the great room, where yet more unopened boxes await, she forces a polite smile while she fills the teakettle. "Brandon has told me a bit about growing up here," she says. "Were you neighbors?"

"I've lived in this county for forty years," Cheryl says. "Knew Brandon as a boy. We all figured the family forgot about this place after they left. Who would've thought we'd see him back in Crystal River."

Hayley is irked at Cheryl's barbed tone. But as she places the pie on a ceramic serving plate, inhaling the scent of baked apples and cinnamon, she decides there's nothing to be gained by meeting rudeness with more rudeness. She'll try neighborly warmth instead.

"Brandon wants to make new memories here," she offers. "We're excited to fix up the place and make it our home."

Cheryl gives a derisive snort. She casts her gaze around the great room, making it clear that she disapproves of the expensive new furnishings and accessories.

When the kettle boils, Hayley prepares two cups and brings them to the island.

"So where's the telephone?" Cheryl asks, looking around the kitchen.

"Oh, we took it out. We both have cell phones. Nobody really uses landlines anymore."

"I do."

"We've got pretty good coverage."

Cheryl clicks her tongue. "Not a great idea to go without one up here. Cell phones and snowstorms aren't exactly kissing cousins."

To Hayley's surprise, Cheryl pulls a flask from the pocket of her overalls and pours a generous splash of amber liquid into her tea. She offers the same to Hayley.

Cheryl gives a little laugh. "It's five o'clock somewhere, amirite?" She tops off her tea with another dribble and offers the flask to Hayley.

"No, thank you." Jesus, it's only 10 a.m.

Hayley cuts two slices of warm apple pie, pushes one across the table to Cheryl, and digs in. She has to admit: The woman makes a great pie. Flaky crust, a perfect combination of sweet and tart. "This is incredible. Thank you so much."

"Well, I figured it would be a novelty. Young people don't make pies from scratch anymore, do you? Despite your fancy ovens." She lifts her chin toward the gleaming Bosch induction range.

"Yeah. It has great features, but I'm still learning my way around it."

"Mine's easy. I light it with a match."

As they eat, Cheryl eyes the baseboards around the room. "My husband did all the woodwork in here, you know. Custom." She waves her fork vaguely in the direction of the wall. "Those joints are his signature. Sturdy as the day they went in."

An idea occurs to Hayley—maybe the way to ease the tension with Cheryl is to show some appreciation for her husband's craftsmanship. "You know, I'm renovating the second-floor office space. Do you think your husband might be available to make some built-ins?"

"Well, that'd be difficult. Considering he's dead," Cheryl says. She blows on her tea, then takes an audible slurp.

"Oh. I'm—I'm so sorry for your loss."

"He died twenty years ago. The time for sorry is long past."

Hayley nods. She's out of ideas now. Maybe if she just stays quiet and amenable, Cheryl will leave.

Just then, she hears the crunch of tires on the gravel drive. Oh, thank god—Brandon is back from town.

As he comes into the kitchen, his eyes alight on Cheryl, seated at the island. Hayley notices his jaw clench before he plasters on a smile. "Cheryl. What are you doing here?"

"Getting to know your lovely new wife."

"I see that." Brandon's eyes flick toward Hayley. She gives a helpless shrug, palms turned upward, behind Cheryl's back.

Cheryl gestures around the open space. "Big changes."

"Not as many as you'd think," Brandon says. "It's solid. My dad did good work."

"Right," she says. "It's your dad's good work that holds this glass shoebox together. Nothing to do with the builder. But of course he's the last person you want to think about."

Brandon's face goes carefully blank.

"Takes a lot of work to maintain a property like this," Cheryl continues, undaunted. "Those giant windows your father designed—it's been twenty years, you planning to recaulk 'em? Once storm season starts, I'll bet the ice feels like it's forming on the inside." She gives Brandon a scrutinizing look. "So what is it you're doing for a living these days, anyhow?"

Hayley sees his free hand tighten into a fist at his side. "Right now, getting the house and property in order is my main focus," he says. "As you point out, it's a lot of work."

Cheryl's eyes narrow. "And expensive. The heat alone . . ."

Brandon rattles his keys in his pocket.

Hayley bites her lip. She desperately wants this visit to end.

As if on cue, Cheryl claps her hands together. "Well, I best get going. Plenty more to do today." She drains the last of her spiked tea.

Hayley exhales.

"You two come visit my stall at the farmers' market Saturday. I'll have more pies."

"Sure thing," Brandon says quickly, ushering her to the door. "Take care now."

The second Cheryl is out the door, Hayley sinks onto the couch.

Brandon sits next to her, his jaw still tight. "I'm sorry you had to deal with her alone."

"It's okay. Almost worth it for the pie." Hayley rubs her temples. "She's intense."

He shrugs. "She never liked me or my folks."

"I'm surprised you didn't mention that her husband was the builder when we saw her in town. You must've known him if he was in the house all the time."

"Hayley, drop it." Brandon's voice is suddenly flat.

"I'm just curious whether—"

"Jesus Christ. I said drop it." He stands abruptly and heads back outside, slamming the door behind him.

What the hell?

Hayley moves to one of the enormous windows and watches Brandon retreat to the smokehouse. He picks up the axe he left there and starts hacking away at a log. Her chest tightens. Why is he acting like this toward her? What set him off?

She wanders the too-quiet rooms, trailing her fingers over the boxes. It's starting to feel like she and Brandon have hit a rough patch. He's spending more and more time outdoors—hunting, prepping, disappearing into the woods. When he does come home, he's uncommunicative when she craves conversation, closed off when she longs for vulnerability. Hayley finds herself tiptoeing around his moods, trying to placate him with small gestures (back rubs, fresh-baked brownies) that used to work. But these days, nothing lands as it once did. Except when they're in bed, he seems perpetually short tempered.

A creeping sense of abandonment has started to take root.

THIRTEEN

Hayley texts Emily from her half-finished study: FaceTime? Let's plan your visit. What are your exact dates?

Emily to Hayley: Busy today. Catch up next week?

Sitting back in her chair, Hayley feels a prickle of annoyance. Ever since she moved to Crystal River, she has been alternately irked and saddened by her friend's lack of attention. To be fair, Emily has always sucked at long-distance friendship. It's all quick takes and heart emojis with her, then days of silence. She gets caught up in her life and forgets that her friend on the other end of an ongoing text stream is waiting.

Emily tends to operate under the assumption that she can freeze time, disappear into her own world, and emerge when she feels like it, and everyone else will be exactly where they were when she left. Hayley has been exasperated by this for years. But Emily more than makes up for it by dropping everything when there's a real emergency, as she did when Jenna died. Hayley will never stop loving her for that, no matter how different their lives have become.

Mostly, these days, Hayley sends only quick missives, random updates and photos, carefully curated glimpses: A cup of steaming tea on the arm of a red porch chair. Cattails in a large glass vase with a view of the pond behind. A sherbet-colored sunrise from the kitchen window.

Emily's response, a few hours later, will be something minimal—a face with heart eyes or an exclamation point, both of which strike Hayley as perfunctory.

Hayley sets her phone on the desk. She and Emily have been on different wavelengths in the past, and they've managed to come through it. The first few months of Hayley's romance with Brandon, for example. And further back, a year after graduation, when Emily was dating a woman twice her age, then toyed briefly with becoming a nun after a heartrending breakup. And there was that time she went on a ten-day silent retreat without letting Hayley know.

Emily's lack of communication now probably means that she's thrown herself into her latest obsession—an adventure organization called Trailblazers, started by a woman who wrote a memoir about her life-changing solo hike through the Canadian Rockies. Emily is focused on planning her own thirtieth birthday solo trek in the Adirondacks. Hayley was shocked when Emily announced the news of her trip. "What happened to 'an hour in Central Park is enough nature for anyone'?" Hayley asked. Emily smiled. "Maybe you've had more of an influence on me than you know."

Hayley doesn't want to play mind games with herself about Emily. She is still her best friend. Their relationship is too important to Hayley, too deep. For now, she'll just give Emily lots of room.

—

Megan, on the other hand, is proving to be a delightful text buddy. After only a few days, Hayley finds herself texting her, not Emily, when a pretty bird with a yellow breast lands on her windowsill and she captures a photo before it flits away. Megan responds immediately: omg you're a phone camera genius! Without an old-school shutter lens I'm useless. Bird shots on my phone are all blur, no bird—and sends four hilarious examples of unrecognizable wavy lines she claims are birds, seriously!—making Hayley laugh out loud.

Then she feels guilty and texts the image to Emily as well.

Four hours later, Emily sends a lazy thumbs-up.

Over the next week, Hayley's trickle of texts with Megan becomes a steady stream—not to mention phone chats and one panicked FaceTime, with Megan patiently coaching her through removing a prehistoric-looking beetle from the powder room and releasing it into the wild instead of crushing it with her boot. Through Megan's eyes, Hayley sees how idyllic her life in Crystal River appears from the outside. The beautiful expanse of land, with all its potential. Not one, but two houses to make her own. And on top of it all, the money to transform the property into anything she desires.

Everything Megan wishes for, Hayley has.

And yet, there's a lot about Megan that Hayley envies. For one thing, she has purposeful life and work goals. She's naturally funny and clever, with a shrewd self-awareness. Most of all, Megan exudes confidence.

Hey, good morning! There's a bonfire at sunset tonight in the park in town. Wanna go? Sponsored by Little League, I think—no doubt it'll be embarrassingly wholesome, but I have gummies . . .

Hayley stares at Megan's text for a long moment. Bonfire. That's one she hasn't conquered yet. She feels that old familiar panic as the viral image of her parents in the picture window, engulfed by flames, flashes to mind . . .

I can't. Sorry.

A second later, her phone rings. "Are you uncomfortable that I brought up edibles?" Megan asks. "I shouldn't have assumed."

Hayley and Brandon don't indulge—weed makes her anxious, and Brandon prefers alcohol. But she's not opposed on principle. "It's nothing to do with that."

"Then . . . what is it?"

The lie she told Megan last week about her parents dying when she was young weighs heavily on her. She can't exactly undo that now. But she and Megan have already come this far. She wants to be seen for who she is. "It's the bonfire." Hayley sighs. "I know this makes me sound like I'm five. But I'm terrified of an open flame. Phobic, actually."

"Oh, Hayley. Why?" Megan's voice is gentle. Kind. Not a hint of ridicule.

"Someone I loved died in a fire." Her voice catches a bit. "It's irrational, but sometimes I even imagine I smell smoke when nothing is there."

The phone line is silent for a moment.

Finally, Megan says, "Gosh, that is so hard. You know . . . if you want, I have a practice for quelling fear that's pretty effective."

They meet at Bones & Leaves. Dolly Parton's clear soprano drifts from the boom box in the back of the café. Two mothers watch as their toddlers crawl on the floor beside their table by the window. Hayley spots Megan waiting at a far table, beside a bookshelf crammed with fraying hardcovers and tattered paperbacks. She gives her a wave.

"Yo, Mrs. Coyote." From behind the counter, Pellet calls to her. "You're still here."

"Of course. Why wouldn't I be?"

He shrugs. "Thought you might've hightailed it back to the big city by now. This place isn't for everyone."

"It's great. I love Crystal River." The words sound a little hollow, even to her own ears.

"Enjoying all that . . . privacy out there? Brandon keeping you happy?"

She forces a smile. "Always."

"Your man is living up to his name out there in the woods," Pellet says, ignoring her clear unease. "He's getting pretty good with that crossbow."

"Is he?" Hayley's voice is flat, her attempt at enthusiasm falling short. She searches for something more to say but comes up empty. "Oh—I see my friend," she says, gesturing toward Megan.

"'Mrs. Coyote'?" Megan asks when Hayley slides into the chair opposite her.

"Oh—long story. He and Brandon went to school together." Hayley breathes in the scent of chamomile from the mug waiting for her on the table. Much better than Pellet's shitty coffee.

A look of recognition dawns on Megan's face. "The howling."

"Yep. They used to call Brandon the 'Coyote Kid.'"

"That's funny." Megan takes a sip of her tea. "So he still has friends in town?"

"I wouldn't say they're friends, exactly." Hayley's not about to get into Brandon's involvement with Pellet's group of bowhunters. Or the disturbing visit from Cheryl Snyder. "But . . . yeah. He knows some folks."

"Hmm. Was his family a big deal around here?"

Were they? Hayley has no idea. She shrugs. "Brandon doesn't talk much about his parents. I got the sense that they kept pretty much to themselves."

Megan nods slowly. What is she thinking? Is it strange that Hayley doesn't know more about her own husband's past? Hayley is tempted to ask, but just then, Megan sets down her mug and tents her fingers on the table. "Well," she says, her voice suddenly businesslike. "Shall we begin?"

"Oh. Uh—sure." Hayley sets down her mug too.

"Okay. Plant your feet firmly on the floor."

Hayley glances around. She feels a little silly. "Shouldn't I be cross-legged on a pillow or something?"

Megan gives her a slight frown. "Hayley—we're doing this. You have to concentrate."

"Okay. Sorry."

"Now," Megan continues. "Close your eyes. Imagine a fire."

Bright-yellow flames flash before Hayley's closed eyes. Her pulse races. She sees her parents leaping from the window, smoke billowing around them.

"The key is to focus on a calming phrase," Megan says. "You need to send yourself a message of strength."

Hayley's mind is blank. "It's not working."

Megan sighs. "Try this. When you feel yourself going into a spin, slowly and quietly repeat: 'I am safe. This fear does not control me.' Keep breathing. Continue the mantra till you regain a sense of tranquility."

Hayley opens her eyes. "It's easy enough now. There's no fire anywhere."

"There's no fire when you imagine it either. Don't forget that. It's in your mind."

"But when there's an actual fire—"

"Almost all fires—like the bonfire I invited you to—are controlled."

"That's true," Hayley concedes.

"This mantra will help you manage the anxiety. It'll work whether it's banishing fires in your imagination or controlling your panic when you actually smell smoke."

Will it?

"Practice it now so when you do have an issue, it'll come to you in a snap."

"Well, thanks. I'll try that."

A look flits across Megan's face, something fleeting that Hayley can't quite place. "No, say it out loud. 'I am safe. This fear does not control me.'"

Oh god, really? Dutifully, Hayley repeats, "I am safe. This fear does not control me."

"Good. I think you'll find it helps." Megan's phone buzzes, and she picks it up. "Hey, sorry—I've got to reply to this text. My fucking landlord. You don't mind picking up the check, do you?"

"Uh—of course." Hayley stands, a little awkwardly. She starts to say more, but Megan is already tapping away on her screen.

FOURTEEN

Over the next few days, Hayley finds herself replaying the conversation in the café. Megan's high beam attention caught her off guard; it felt so extreme. But as she reflects on it, she begins to see it in a different light. Megan's approach was fierce and intense, yes, but also . . . fun. She wasn't just listening to Hayley; she was immersing herself in her world. Her engagement felt like a stark contrast to Emily's distraction and Brandon's recent short fuse. It was refreshing for someone to be so fully present. Maybe, Hayley thinks, this is what true empathy feels like.

This new friendship with Megan is unlike anything she's experienced before. And perhaps it's exactly what she needs.

—

Hayley's phone pings. She puts down the ream of paper she's stacking in her printer and picks up the phone.

Tyler and I have to move ASAP. Can you talk?

Hayley taps the Call button, and Megan picks up after one ring. "What happened?"

"It's a nightmare," Megan says. "We asked for some basic mitigations. Our apartment is practically condemned. There's black mold in the kitchen and a whole thing with the toilet I won't even talk about. Our landlord finally said he's sending someone over. But he's using it as an excuse to double the rent."

"Is that legal?"

"We're on a month-to-month. This was never going to be permanent, but now we're scrambling. We only have a few days. We have to find somewhere cheaper. Like—I don't know." She sighs. "Vermont."

Ugh. Not now, when Hayley is just starting to feel a real connection. Vermont is hours away. The thought of Megan leaving sends a pang of disappointment through her. "What can I do to help?"

"If you hear of anyone looking to rent something we can actually afford, let me know. Otherwise, just keep your fingers crossed."

Hayley doesn't have to cross her fingers. A solution is already forming in her mind.

It feels like a big leap at first, but the more she thinks about it, the more logical it seems. Megan has so little. Hayley has so much. The guest cottage is just sitting there, empty, on their enormous property. It could be a temporary fix, just until Megan and Tyler find their footing.

Once the idea takes hold, it makes perfect sense. Now all she has to do is convince Brandon.

—

The rain comes down in heavy sheets as Brandon navigates the Jeep along the winding roads, on their way back from running errands in Crystal River. Droplets pelt the windshield, blurring the view of craggy cliffs and colorful foliage glimpsed between wiper blades.

Hayley studies his expression. He hasn't spoken a word since they left the hardware store.

"Are you okay?" she asks. As she hears the words come out of her mouth, she winces. This is Brandon's least-favorite question. (Well, second-least. "What are you thinking?" shuts him down completely.)

"I'm fine." Outside, the wind bends and rattles sturdy pine boughs. "I mean, this drive is a little stressful. And I have a lot on my mind."

"Like what?"

"I have a shit ton to do before the first frost."

"It's so much work. Trying to winterize the property by yourself."

"I'm racing against the clock. I've got to get the smokehouse finished."

Brandon's hunting permit is plastered to the windshield. She glances quickly at the dates, then turns back to him. "Is hunting season really only through November?"

"Yep."

"Well . . . maybe I could help you."

He shakes his head, rejecting her offer, as she knew he would.

Here's her opening. "Hey, so—I have a thought. Megan mentioned that she and her boyfriend have to leave their apartment. What if we offer to let them stay in the guest cottage for a few months in exchange for helping out around the property? Tyler's a handyman. And the cottage is just sitting there empty, after all."

They drive in silence for a few minutes, listening to the swish of the wipers and the sizzle of tires on wet pavement. Hayley stares out the rain-streaked windshield.

"I don't know," he says finally. "We're newlyweds, Hayley. I don't want anyone horning in on our privacy."

She pokes him lightly, attempting to be playful. "They'd be in their own house, on the other side of the property. We'll hardly see them unless we want to."

Brandon frowns.

"And think how great it would be to have a handyman around to help you prep for winter."

"I've got it under control."

"I know you do. But . . . Tyler could help with the mundane stuff. Stack firewood, shingle the smokehouse roof." She speaks quickly, trying to convince him. "Leave you more time for the big jobs no one else can do. And time to go hunting."

She brushes his hand with hers, then quickly withdraws it as they bump through a pothole, water splashing across the windshield.

"Then we'll be stuck with them all winter," Brandon says. "Complaining about the shitty internet and getting their crappy car stuck in the snow. Trudging up to the main house all the time for every little thing."

"They'll probably be gone by then. It would just be a stopgap." She looks out at the passing trees, bent and swaying in the storm. Thunder rumbles in the distance. "At least let's invite them to take a look at the cottage. We can make it clear they have to respect our privacy."

Brandon is silent again.

Lightning cracks the sky, illuminating the mountains. Hayley flinches. She's not used to the violent power of storms up here. The shift in the air feels perilous.

Her panic begins to mount. If Megan leaves Crystal River, Hayley will have to start over, try to find another friend. "Brandon, I think . . . I need this." She surprises them both with the intensity in her voice.

"I know you like hanging out with her," he says. "But all the time?"

She swallows hard and forges ahead. "If Megan is on the property over the winter, the isolation won't feel so overwhelming to me. It would start to feel like a—a neighborhood." She looks down at her hands in her lap. "We have so much. And the way the money came to me . . . Shouldn't we try to help people in need when we can?"

It's a risky gambit, she knows, calling attention to her inheritance. A finger on the scale that might irritate him further.

"Sounds like you've already made a plan."

"I didn't mention the idea to her, I promise," she says. "I came to you first."

The tires slip and slide through the mud. Hayley grips the door handle, anxiety rising again as they fishtail around each bend. "Take it slow, it's slick here," she says, her voice shaky.

"I've got it," Brandon says. But he eases slightly off the gas.

He is, she reminds herself, an experienced driver. But as the Jeep thuds through another deep rut, Brandon pumps the brakes, and they hydroplane for a terrifying moment before the tires grab hold.

Neither of them speaks, the air between them thick with fear.

Slowly, slowly, the road levels out. As they clear the worst of the muck, Hayley releases her grip on the door handle. She gazes out at the valley unfolding below them, a sea of gold and crimson trees blanketed in mist, both treacherous and beautiful.

After ten more minutes of cautious driving, they reach the steep incline to their property. Brandon turns the Jeep up the deeply rutted, muddy drive, and it inches slowly forward. At last he pulls to a stop in front of the house. Hayley shuts her eyes and lets out a long breath she hadn't realized she was holding. For a few moments they sit in the car, recovering, as rain peppers the roof and the driveway around them.

Feeling Brandon's warm hand on her cold one, she opens her eyes.

He glances over at her, his eyes softening a bit. "If it means that much to you, I guess it can't hurt to let them check out the cottage."

"Really?"

He shrugs. "No promises. But I'm . . . open, I suppose."

Hayley smiles with relief. "That's all I ask."

FIFTEEN

That night Hayley has a dream so vivid that when she rises out of it into the blue-gray early dawn, she's truly unsure whether it was real or imagined.

She stands at the edge of the property, her heart fluttering with excitement when Tyler and Megan pull up the drive in a gold Cadillac convertible. The main house shimmers—its windows, tall as the trees, mirror the landscape back to itself. The cottage has shrunk, Alice in Wonderland–style, to the size of a dollhouse.

Megan and Tyler float out of the car and wrap her in a warm hug.

"Welcome to our little slice of heaven," Hayley says, beaming.

Brandon, brooding, stands off to the side.

All at once the sun plummets to the horizon line, casting eerie shadows across the landscape: green, purple, black. The house now resembles a giant bruise. Hayley glances at the cottage, but it isn't there. It's disappeared, as if swallowed whole by the encroaching night.

Hayley opens her mouth to scream—

And that's when she wakes up, heart pounding.

Brandon snores lightly beside her, oblivious, his arm flung over her hip. She glances at him as she tries to slow her breathing. Yes, she knows it was a dream. But she can't help feeling unsettled.

With a little jolt, she has a realization. The car in the dream is her father's. His vintage Cadillac convertible, stored under a custom fabric cover in their garage for use only on Sunday afternoons. After lunch he'd unwrap the car, pull it out into the driveway, and wipe every inch with a chamois until it gleamed brighter than the Florida sun. Hayley and Jenna, freshly bathed, would slide onto the cream leather back seat behind their parents, wearing white gloves to protect the upholstery. (Her father actually kept sets of gloves in his glove compartment—a detail that later became a running joke between Hayley and Emily every time they were in a car together.)

Even Jenna—once she stopped squirming and trying to yank the gloves off with her teeth—loved the breeze on her face, the whoosh of the air as they drove.

Sitting beside her little sister, staring at her father's neat haircut and inhaling the scent of her mother's lilac perfume, Hayley could believe, for a moment, that this was the family she'd always dreamed of. Her mother's irritated scowl transformed into a genuine smile. Her father's distraction gave way to laugh lines and dad jokes. Jenna no longer screamed with fury but giggled with delight.

For an hour on Sundays, young Hayley could daydream it all into being.

Quietly, carefully, she extracts herself from under Brandon's arm. She grabs a cashmere throw off the slipper chair in the corner of the bedroom and tiptoes into her study. Closing the door behind her, she rummages through the papers in her desk drawer and unearths the photo of Jenna she'd hidden there.

Under those raccoon rings of makeup, despite the dilation of substances and flashbulbs, her sister's eyes are the same hazel as her own.

"Oh my god, Hayley, I love it." Megan gazes around the great room.

"You do?" Really? Despite her attempts to get the arrangement of the furniture right, the vibe of the room still feels off.

"Are you kidding?" Megan says. "This is my dream house."

"I prefer the cottage, honestly," Hayley says. "But don't tell Brandon; he's crazy about this place. He thinks he can re-create the childhood he had here before his parents' marriage imploded."

Megan nods slowly. "So you don't like it here. But you're willing to live in this house to help him repair his past?"

"I mean, I . . ."

Megan shrugs. "I'm not judging. Just saying. If it's really what you want, then great."

"It's really what I want," Hayley says. She's aware that her voice sounds a little hollow, as if she's not only trying to convince Megan but herself.

She thinks about Emily's quizzical face when Hayley told her she'd be quitting her job to move to Crystal River. The echo disturbs her.

"Great." Megan smiles.

Running her hand along the slate mantelpiece, she says, "I love this. It's so freaking grand." She touches the cashmere throw on the back of the chaise. "Every lousy thing Tyler and I own is from Goodwill."

"Even your mattress?"

"God help us. It's a miracle we don't have bedbugs."

Hayley laughs, relieved that the strain between them seems to have dissipated. "Do you want to see the cottage now, or shall we wait for Tyler?"

"He'll be here any minute. But he'd be fine living in a hollowed-out log. I'm the one who makes the decisions."

As they cross the path from house to cottage, Megan takes Hayley's arm. "Hey, I didn't mean to overstep earlier. It's just that you never talk about yourself or your past. It's cool, you don't have to. I'm just curious about where *you* are in all of this."

A pit in Hayley's stomach reminds her that she lied to Megan about her parents' deaths. She knows she's going to have to give her a little something more. Walk back the lie. Megan is too perceptive. "So, my family . . ." Hayley sighs. "You know how I told you my parents died when I was young? Actually . . . it wasn't that long ago. Only about two years."

"Oh! I'm so sorry."

"Yeah. It's still pretty fresh. That's why I don't like to talk about it. I'm sorry I lied to you."

"I get it. That's a lot to drop into a casual conversation with someone you just met."

Hayley feels a rush of gratitude. "Yeah."

The sound of tires rumbling up the drive interrupts the moment. Hayley turns to see Tyler, in a rusty flatbed Ford, come around the bend and up the final crest of the hill. He turns into the driveway by the cottage and parks the truck. "Hey," he says, nodding to them as he climbs out.

Hayley hasn't seen Tyler since meeting him in the hardware store. She's struck again by his wiry physicality. He has the kind of presence some actors and athletes possess without even trying. She feels a little shy. "Hey," she says.

"Perfect timing," Megan says. "We haven't crossed the threshold yet."

Hayley beckons them to follow her onto the porch. Her heart is pounding a bit with nervous anticipation. She's proud of how she's decorated this cottage. She pushes the latch on the farmhouse door and leads them inside.

Megan stands with her hands on her hips, surveying the living space. "Well," she says. "This is . . . cute."

"It's fully furnished." Hayley tries to ignore the disappointment in Megan's voice. "There's a bedroom upstairs with a study to the side. Maybe that could be your yoga space."

"Maybe."

Hayley can't help seeking a little affirmation. "So . . . how do you like it?"

Megan shrugs. "It's . . . way better than what we've got now! Hey, I'll be right back. I'm going to grab my tape measure from Ursula."

"Okay. And really, feel free to move anything around in here." Hayley feels a little deflated by Megan's lack of enthusiasm. But she reminds herself that it's human connection she wants, in all its messiness, not ego gratification.

When Megan goes out to her car, Tyler stands in front of the bluestone fireplace, looking out the window.

"What do you think?" Hayley asks him.

He turns and looks at her. "What?"

"Do you hate it?"

"Are you kidding?" He smiles, flashing a dimple. "I love this place."

"I . . . I didn't take you for a cozy cottage kind of guy."

"What kind of guy do you think I am?"

"Um, well . . . more surf shack, I guess."

Tyler laughs. "I guess I should be offended that you're stereotyping me. But you're not the first. I'm more in touch with my feminine side than I look."

"In what ways?"

"I'm kind of a nester. And I really like to cook." He wanders into the kitchen, and Hayley follows. Patting the butcher-block island, he says, "This kitchen is perfect. I can see myself making a big Bolognese in here."

"Lucky Megan."

"Ha. She won't touch it. I cook for her sometimes, but I can't deny my own basic instincts. I'm a carnivore through and through."

Megan steps into the kitchen, carrying a box overflowing with stuff: the tape measure, a yoga mat, several candles of various sizes. "I want to get a visual of how it's all gonna work."

"Okay!" Hayley says. "Make the place your own."

While Megan dumps the contents of her box on the island, Tyler goes over to the window. Following his gaze, Hayley sees that Brandon is out there with a spade, digging into the muddy ground next to a pile of bricks and metal pipes. "I should say hey to your husband," Tyler says. "Brandon, right? What's he working on?"

"I'm not sure what he's doing," Hayley says. "He's juggling a lot of projects."

Megan nods toward Tyler. "Well, he can help. What do you need? Ty's got that vision for composting beds I told you about. Nothing turns him on more than saving banana peels and green pepper cores. Right, Ty?"

"Sure," he says flatly, still staring out the window.

Holding up the tape measure, Megan addresses Tyler's back. "I'm going upstairs. Why don't you see if you can give Brandon a hand?"

Tyler shifts his weight, tilting his head slightly as if considering her words. Then, with a barely perceptible shrug, he says. "Sure."

He pushes the door open with more force than necessary, and the screen slams shut behind him.

Megan purses her lips.

Hoping to shift the dynamic, Hayley says, "Megan—if you don't like the decor in here, I won't be offended if you change it. I want you and Tyler to be happy."

Megan pauses. Then sighs. "I'm having some . . . feelings. I can't deny it. That stunning house you and Brandon have—I'll probably never come close to affording anything like it. But seriously, this cottage is a gift. It's so sweet and homey."

Megan is obviously talking herself into it. How funny that Megan and Brandon both love the glass house, Hayley thinks, and she and Tyler prefer the cottage. Opposites really do attract.

Glancing out the window from the small upstairs study where she's helping Megan measure the room, Hayley sees Brandon and Tyler in the yard below. Immediately, though she hears nothing, she sees that something is wrong.

Brandon's face is tense. He gestures with his metal spade. Tyler steps back and crosses his arms.

"Hey." She waves Megan over to take a look. "Any idea what's up?"

Megan grimaces. "Jesus. Ty's kind of a hothead. Maybe we need to soothe the angry beasts."

By the time the women are out on the porch, Tyler and Brandon have moved apart. They're standing across the pit from each other.

Megan smiles at Brandon. "Hi. We love your place."

He gives a forced smile in return. "Thanks." Turning to Tyler, he says, "So you were saying: you're handy?"

Tyler meets Brandon's eyes. "I get the job done."

—

"What were you and Tyler talking about out there?" Hayley asks Brandon that evening as they stand at the island, fixing dinner.

Brandon, chopping carrots with the Japanese chef's knife he gave her as a birthday present, shakes his head. She tries to catch his eye, but he's intent on dicing. "No idea what you mean."

Brandon's jaw is set. She knows that expression all too well. A knot forms in her stomach. "You were arguing about something," she ventures. "I saw you from the window."

He scoops up the carrots and scrapes them into a simmering pot on the stove. "What would we have to argue about? I just met the guy."

"It seemed intense. You both looked kinda angry."

"I was just challenging him a bit about his work ethic." Brandon rinses his hands and dries them on a towel. "If we're letting them live here rent free, I don't want to feel like they're dead weight."

His words hang in the air, carrying an unsettling charge that Hayley can't quite shake.

She searches his face. "Megan said he's really good with repairs and stuff. And he told me he likes to cook." She offers this information tentatively.

"Oh, I have to socialize with these people now?"

"Only if you want to. We don't have to be couple friends."

Will Brandon ever warm to the idea of Megan and Tyler in the guest cottage? She hopes their friendship will evolve organically, but maybe she's being unrealistic.

Hayley moves to hug him. "You and me. That's what matters."

He gives her a quick kiss on the lips.

Hayley draws him into a deeper kiss. Pulling out of his embrace, she turns off the stove. "Dinner can wait." She takes the knife from his hand, places it on the counter, and leads him up the stairs. From the landing, her gaze drifts toward the cottage. Despite Brandon's misgivings and her own lingering doubts after today's tense start, she finds comfort in the thought of neighbors just a short walk away.

As twilight settles over the property, Hayley imagines the cottage coming alive. Tyler in the kitchen, preparing something vegan, something aromatic, for Megan. The soft clink of dishes and murmured conversation drifting across the leaf-strewn yard, through the whispering pines, over the moonlit pond. Later they'll ascend the stairs and sink into the bamboo sheets she so carefully chose.

On the bed, straddling Brandon, she almost senses, looking out into the dusk, that she can see the flicker of candles in the cottage windows.

OCTOBER

SIXTEEN

Hayley pulls her cardigan tightly around herself as she heads down the path to the cottage. It's the first gray, gloomy day they've had since Megan and Tyler moved in, and Hayley feels a portent of the cold winter days ahead.

It's midafternoon. A chill permeates the air. Walking across the property, she flashes back to her life in New York. There, October meant crowded sidewalks, bustling cafés, leaves dusting the tops of cars parked along the street. It was a month of pumpkin spice lattes and final rooftop parties before the cold really set in—a far cry from the quiet solitude here in the Adirondacks.

Though now, happily, Hayley has actual neighbors instead of just wailing coyotes.

She knocks on the door.

"C'mon in!" Megan calls.

Hayley finds her sitting cross-legged on the floor in the living room, surrounded by paper bags and cardboard boxes. Weak light filtering through the clouds outside the window casts the room in shadow.

"Hey!" Megan says with a big smile when she sees Hayley. "Thanks for coming over. I'm so overwhelmed!"

Hayley takes in the haphazard piles of belongings. "I'm happy to help you get settled." All in all, she's surprised at how few possessions Megan and Tyler have. "Once we dive in, it won't feel so daunting."

As the two of them hang jackets and stack boots in the front hall closet, Megan says, "You know, I was thinking. What if we move the sofa under the window? Wouldn't it make the space look bigger?"

"I tried it in a few places, but . . ." Hayley stops herself. "Sure."

"Want to move it now?"

"Uh—okay." Hayley takes one sofa arm, and Megan comes around to take the other.

Once they have it in place, the sofa is crammed in an awkward position against the wall, covering the vintage floral wallpaper that Hayley loves so much.

"I like it," Megan says. "More modern."

After they move the rocking chair closer to the hearth and experiment with three different arrangements of armchair, side table, and reading lamp, Hayley realizes what Megan is doing. She's attempting to mimic the open layout of the main house. The house she wishes was hers.

Finally satisfied, Megan crosses her arms and surveys the room. "Yup. Much better."

It's not better. Anyone with an eye for design would agree. But Hayley musters a smile. "You should have it the way you like it."

They move to the kitchen.

Megan puts her hands on her hips. "This is so . . . quirky. But Tyler loves it, and he does most of the cooking. I'm not touching a thing."

Back in the living room, Megan starts unpacking books and shelving them on a small bookcase. Hayley opens a grocery bag piled with dog-eared paperbacks. So many familiar titles—most of the same self-help and spiritual growth guides that fill her own shelves. Ah—here's *The Choice Conundrum*, the book that brought her and Megan together that day at Anderson's. She picks up another: *The Universe Is Your Ally*. "I love this one," she says. "Such a comfort when I'm feeling anxious."

"Me too! I've read it, like, five times."

"'Embrace the magic within,'" Hayley says.

"Yes!" Megan lifts another book from a box—*The Tenacity Code*—and sets it on the coffee table. "I never thought I'd be into self-help books, but some of them really speak to me. This one especially. I want to read it again."

"'Bend with grace' is a great mantra," Hayley says. "I use it a lot."

Like right now, rearranging this living room.

Megan nods in agreement. "I had it posted on my fridge at the apartment. It reminds me to stay flexible. Adaptable."

"Open to change."

"Isn't it wild how alike our reading tastes are?" Megan shelves the final book and looks around. "I don't like the phrase 'self-help,' though. I call them guidebooks."

"Guidebooks. I like that."

Hayley feels suddenly grateful—for this moment, for the cool autumn air, for a new friend who seems to understand her.

"Hey. Check this out." Megan digs in her canvas tote and pulls out a candy bar. She hands it to Hayley, who reads the hand-lettered label: "Magic Bar. Organic Cookies 'n' Cream."

She looks up. "What is this?"

"Psilocybin. Mushrooms."

"Wait. Are these the mushrooms you picked with me?"

"They are!" Megan starts to laugh. "I wasn't sure at first; I'm not that much of an expert. But I sent a picture of them to this incredible woman I found through Substack who does Reiki and energy healing. She said, 'Hell yeah, those are liberty caps. Totally organic and therapeutic.' She told me about this other guy who's licensed in Colorado, where it's all legal—"

"But . . . homemade?" Hayley shakes her head. "How can you regulate dosage?"

"Oh, I didn't make the candy bars. The Colorado guy got me in touch with a small-batch manufacturer living off the grid about an hour north of here. She barters with foragers. I brought her enough shrooms for a whole batch, and she gave me a couple bars in return."

Hayley gives her a hesitant smile, both wary and fascinated. "I thought when you said you were going to make something with those mushrooms, you meant a stir-fry."

"I thought so too. But when I found out how special they are, how could I resist?"

"If you say so." Hayley hands the candy bar back.

"So . . . have you ever tried shrooms?"

"Nope."

"Do you want to?"

Hayley's not sure. But she must admit she's curious. It's something that's never come up with Brandon. She is a little worried about how she might react to psilocybin—this dodgy homemade form of it in particular. "Maybe."

"How about right now?"

"Ah . . . I don't know."

"Don't worry, I'll guide you through it," Megan assures her. "Shrooms aren't even counterculture anymore. And they're therapeutic. All kinds of celebrities and influencers use them. Harry Styles!"

"And Prince Harry, right? I read somewhere that psilocybin helped him cope with his mother's death."

"Exactly. They help people process trauma. They take the edge off."

Hayley is tantalized now. But she hesitates, caught between curiosity and caution. She bites her lower lip, still undecided. "I told Brandon I'd get started on setting up the storeroom in the basement."

Megan waves her hand dismissively. "That can wait till tomorrow. Stay and do this with me instead. It's research for my Substack. Plus, c'mon, fun! I mean, no doubt setting up a storeroom is fun, but . . ."

Hayley smiles. Trying mushrooms with Megan does sound a lot better than organizing the basement. It's not like the basement is going anywhere. "Well . . . okay. If you say it's safe. Just a little piece."

Megan's face lights up. She breaks off three small squares and hands them to Hayley. "This is going to be amazing. Just embrace the magic within," she says.

—

They stretch out together on the sofa.

Before long, Hayley becomes aware that she feels floaty and tranquil. The world shimmers around the edges. She gazes at the play of light across the ceiling while Megan traces swirly patterns on her upturned palm. Folk music plays softly over the portable speaker Megan found in one of the cardboard boxes.

"I've only known you for a few weeks," Megan says. "But I feel like you've been in my life forever. Like . . . I mean, this is going to sound ridiculous, but . . . like our souls are connected. Is it wrong to say that?"

Hayley rolls over to face her, eyes wide. "No, not at all! I feel exactly the same way."

"Like lifelong friends."

Hayley feels a rush of—is it love?! "I'm so glad you're here."

"I am too." Megan is shining. Glowing. Is her face made of glitter and moonbeams? It might be.

Megan moves over, letting her head rest on Hayley's shoulder. "Do you know how important you've become to me?" she asks. "I mean, Tyler is fine, but it's different having a woman my age to confide in."

Hayley pulls back and looks at her. "Making friends seems to come so easily to you, Megan."

"Nothing comes easily to me. I have to work hard at everything I do. But living here has given me room to breathe. You've changed my life."

Hayley shakes her head. "You're the one who changed—well, everything for me. I thought I'd have no friends in this—"

"—odd, dumpy town."

Hayley feels so protected, so secure inside the cocoon of their friendship. Why hasn't she ever tried mushrooms before? Never, not even in the most intimate moments with Brandon, has she felt so safe. She can actually see a protective membrane surrounding her and Megan on the sofa, a yellow-orange ring vibrating around them, warming them like their own personal sun.

If this was the feeling Jenna craved, Hayley can understand it a little more. The glow of this moment . . . her sister's desire to escape . . . Maybe the psilocybin is helping. She's thinking about Jenna without sorrow or anger for the first time since she died.

"Do you have a sister?" Hayley asks.

"No," Megan says. "I'm an only child. I was adopted when I was a baby."

"Did you have a happy childhood?"

Megan shrugs. "I mean, define 'happiness.'"

"Were your parents kind to you?"

"They were . . . adequate. I always felt kind of lonely, like I didn't fit." Megan smiles a little, looking Hayley directly in the eyes. "I get the sense you might've felt the same way."

Hayley nods slowly. "I did."

"It seems like you're carrying a lot of sadness," Megan says.

Megan's words settle into her, precise and undeniable. Hayley takes a breath. "I haven't been totally honest with you about my past," she says, relieved that the words are finally coming out of her mouth. "About how my parents died. And what brought me to Crystal River."

Megan looks at her keenly. Then she reaches for Hayley's hand. "Tell me."

Hayley speaks slowly at first, afraid of spooking her with the sordid details. But Megan doesn't flinch. She's fully engaged, listening deeply, her facial expressions adjusting slightly with each revelation. Once Hayley relaxes into the story and really gets going, it's hard to stop. She shares everything about the fire, her parents, and Jenna. About Olivia Blackwood, the devastation her podcast has caused, how she won't leave the story alone, even now. Hayley finds herself reflecting in a way she's never done before on the impact of her family's tragedies. How they've changed her.

Megan shakes her head. "You've been through so much, Hayley. It's a miracle you're in one piece. Do you ever just . . . cry? I mean, really cry. Scream. Throw things. Let snot come out of your nose, you know?"

"Um . . . to be honest, no." Hayley muffles what little crying she does in her pillow in the middle of the night. "It kind of freaks Brandon out when I'm sad."

"Why?"

"He doesn't like it when I dwell on the past."

Megan makes a face. "What's that about? You need room to grieve. I have to ask, Hayley. Is Brandon really there for you the way you are for him?"

The directness of the question gives Hayley pause. "He wants me to be happy," she responds slowly. "He says it all the time."

"Exactly. He wants you to be happy. But unless you feel your grief, you'll never be able to fully feel your joy. And that's for you to figure out. Not Brandon."

Hayley feels a pang of recognition. Megan is tapping into an undercurrent of emotion that's been lapping at the edge of Hayley's consciousness.

"You know," Megan continues, "I wasn't going to say anything, but . . . remember that day we were at the café, when that guy behind the counter called you 'Mrs. Coyote'?"

Hayley nods.

"Well, after you left, he came over to clear the table, and we got talking about Brandon's family," Megan continues. "He said that when they left Crystal River, there were all these rumors going around. He wouldn't give me details, but the way he was talking . . . it was strange. He hinted at something dark, you know?" Megan regards her steadily. "Have you ever asked Brandon what really happened? Why his family left so suddenly?"

Hayley's stomach tightens. She has always skirted this topic, giving Brandon a wide berth whenever his parents' divorce and its aftermath comes up. His discomfort talking about this time in his life is palpable. But now, Megan's directness casts a harsh light on Hayley's reticence: Has she been avoiding difficult conversations in order to keep the peace?

She imagines actually confronting Brandon, pushing past his usual deflections. The thought fills her with both dread and anticipation. What might surface if she did? Is this Pandora's box of secrets about her husband's family too perilous to open?

SEVENTEEN

Dusk has deepened. Hayley makes her way up the path from the cottage, still feeling unsettled. The cold evening air clears her head somewhat, though she knows she'll have to pull it together even more before she sees her husband. As she left, Megan pressed the remaining half of the candy bar into the pocket of her cardigan. "Your place next time," she said.

Stepping inside, Hayley finds Brandon has finished his work for the day and is building a fire in the great room's hearth. She pauses for a moment, watching the light dance over his features.

"There you are," Brandon says, his voice tinged with irritation. "What were you doing at the cottage all this time?"

Hayley feels like a naughty teenager being scolded for coming home late from a party. "Megan and I were bonding. Girl time."

His brow furrows. "You said you were going to work on the storeroom."

"Well, I was helping Megan unpack, and we ended up chatting and hanging out."

"For the entire day?"

Hayley shrugs. "We had a lot to talk about."

He thrusts at the logs with a poker. "Was Tyler there?"

"Nope. Just us." Hayley moves to the couch. The room is warm. She slips off her sweater and settles back into the cushions.

Brandon remains in front of the hearth, focused on the fire. "I don't like you spending so much time over there," he says. "Didn't you say they wouldn't interfere with our lives?"

Hayley feels a flash of annoyance. "Come on, Brandon. You're out in the back, building things all day, or off on supply runs, I don't know, and I'm alone. How does spending time with Megan when you're working interfere with anything?"

Shaking his head, he says, "I just think you should be careful. We barely know them."

The mushrooms have heightened her emotions, making her acutely attuned to the hostility in his voice. "Sometimes I think I barely know you," she snaps.

Brandon is silent. He gives the logs a hard poke. Sparks fly and land on the edge of the stone hearth. For a moment, they grow kaleidoscopic in Hayley's vision, flaring up into a full-blown fire. Is the room filling with smoke? Her pulse pounds.

The mantra Megan gave her at Bones & Leaves appears in her mind.

"I'm not afraid. This fear does not control me," she says.

He turns to look at her. "What?"

"It's what Megan said. And she's right."

He snorts. "Jesus."

Hayley stands up. "Whatever, Brandon. I'm going to take a shower. I can't with this right now."

As she climbs the stairs, Brandon calls after her, "I just don't think you should trust her blindly."

She turns and faces him. "Why are you so down on Megan?"

"C'mon, Hayley. Remember what happened with Melinda? Don't be naive."

Standing under the rainforest showerhead, Hayley activates the steam setting. A warm mist fills the air. She tips her head back, reveling in the soothing caress of the hot water. She tries to recapture the floating sensation from earlier, but Brandon's attitude has made her edgy.

Bringing up Melinda is like pressing on a bruise.

Embrace the magic within. She narrows her focus to the water droplets glistening on her skin: the way they form, slide down her arms, and disappear. The simple joys of soap and a washcloth. As water and warmth and steam billow around her, she feels herself dissolving into a porous world of sensual experience, her stress evaporating in the softest rain. She closes her eyes, runs her hand down her thigh, and brings the cloth between her legs. The sensation inside her builds . . .

The glass door flies open.

Hayley screams and drops the washcloth.

Brandon, fully dressed, stands before her, clutching the magic candy bar. "What the fuck?"

"God, Brandon," she says, backing away from him, covering herself with her hands. "You scared the shit out of me!"

"Are you tripping right now?"

She reaches for the shower controls and turns off the water.

"Answer my question," he insists.

Her initial shock gives way to vexation. "Hand me a towel." He does, and she wraps it around her body, trying to ground herself in the sensation of fabric against skin. "Why are you acting so uptight?" The words pour out of her.

Brandon fixes his eyes on the candy bar in his hand. "Did Tyler give you this?"

"No."

"If that guy's high on shrooms all the time, he's going to be fucking useless."

The judgment in Brandon's tone grates on her. "I told you. Tyler wasn't even with us." Why is he being this way? "And Megan and I were just"—she repeats Megan's phrase, feeling a strange pride in it—"taking the edge off."

Her words hang in the air between them. Brandon scowls.

The mushrooms seem to have stripped away Hayley's usual filter, her tendency to smooth things over. Instead of apologizing or explaining further, she hears herself say, "You should try it. It might even help your back."

Silently, Brandon leaves the steamy bathroom, sliding the pocket door shut behind him.

After a moment, Hayley hears the front door slam. She slips on her robe and slides open the door. Through the bedroom windows, she watches her husband's shadowy figure disappear into the woods.

—

An entire day passes. Brandon is avoiding her. She tries to find ways to start a conversation, but he keeps ducking out, ducking away. As twilight settles over the mountains, she slices limes and pulls out tiny cans of tonic for their usual end-of-day cocktail, but Brandon just blows into the kitchen, fixes himself a PB&J, and says he's "gotta work on stuff in the basement" before brushing past her and down the stairs.

It's the first time in their relationship that a full night and day have passed without them making up from a quarrel. Hayley is both frustrated by Brandon's silence and a little wary of his simmering anger, which doesn't seem to have dissipated at all, just gone underground.

Her phone pings with a text. It's Megan.

Come over?

Can't, she answers. Brandon's pissed.

Why? Did you confront him?

Hayley thinks for a minute. She does want to broach the conversation with Brandon about the rumors, but she knows she needs to wait until they're on better footing.

Nah. He's just jealous I got high with you.

Tell him we're not exclusive. He's welcome to join anytime.

Ugh. Fuck it, she should just march over to Megan and Tyler's and salvage her evening. Let her brooding husband stew in his own juices till he gets over himself.

But she doesn't. Instead, she grabs a throw from the back of the couch and steps out onto the front porch to clear her head. A cool wind carries the scent of approaching rain. The porch light casts a glow around her, creating a small oasis. As her eyes adjust, she can make out the glistening surface of the pond and the silhouettes of the pines and maples that stand along its edge.

Hayley tries to put herself in Brandon's shoes. How would she feel if he'd disappeared all day with Tyler and come home in an altered state? She might be a little resentful. But surely she wouldn't hold a grudge for this long.

Her gaze drifts to the porch. The cardboard box still sits in the far corner where Brandon placed the injured chickadee weeks ago. It's empty—the bird either recovered and flew away, or . . .

She shakes her head. She doesn't want to know.

A snap of a twig pulls her attention back to the yard. She leans forward, squinting into the gloom. There—a flicker of movement. Is that a pair of eyes, reflecting the porch light from the periphery of the yard?

When she blinks, she sees nothing but shadows.

She's turned, ready to head back inside, when a sound freezes her in her tracks.

A low howl, closer than she's ever heard before.

Hayley fumbles for the door handle. Slipping inside, she shuts the door and turns the lock. Cupping her hands against the transom window, she peers outside. In the fog-shrouded grass, a coyote stands motionless, illuminated by the moon, staring directly at the house. It turns and lopes along the grass at the edge of the property, its sleek body moving with predatory grace.

—

Brandon comes to bed calculatedly late. Hayley pretends to be asleep, though she's sure he knows she isn't. His movements are deliberate, almost too quiet, as he lifts the covers and slides in. The bed dips slightly with his weight.

She listens to Brandon's steady breathing, waiting for the moment it softens into sleep. The moment doesn't come. Both of them lie there, eyes open, staring into the same darkness.

EIGHTEEN

When Brandon brings Hayley coffee in bed the next morning, it's a peace offering. "I was being an asshole," he says, sitting beside her and putting his hand on her leg over the covers.

Hayley sits up and takes the mug, studying his face. His apology seems sincere. "I'm sorry too."

He shakes his head. "I don't know what came over me."

Taking a sip of coffee, Hayley wonders if this might be an opportunity to confront Brandon about his past, to push against the soft resistance of his deflections. She feels torn between sympathy and frustration. Everyone has demons—god knows she does. But his instinct to shut down rather than share worries her.

She weighs her words carefully. "Coming home like that, expecting you to meet my mood when you clearly have a lot on your mind—"

"Nothing's on my mind. I just overreacted."

Hayley realizes he's still too defensive. She chickens out. "Okay."

"Having those two on the property, it just feels like . . . I don't know. An extra burden."

She leans back against the headboard. "Look, I know you're concerned. But Megan is becoming a real friend to me. And Tyler is here to help you."

"I guess." He sighs. "Of course you can do whatever you want. I think I was just tired. I took it out on you, and I shouldn't have." He leans forward and kisses her. "Seeing you in the shower, man—what a wasted opportunity. I'm so mad at myself for being mad."

"We should do shrooms together one of these days. There's half a bar left, you know."

He grins. "I'd like that."

She sets down her mug. "And in the meantime . . ." She cups his face in her hands and kisses him back. Makeup sex first. The difficult conversation can wait.

Hayley looks outside, later in the morning, to see Brandon and Tyler standing together at the smokehouse. Even through the closed window, she can hear Tyler's deep laugh. What a relief. Maybe this is all going to work itself out. With her second cup of coffee in hand, she wanders down the path to the cottage and knocks on the door.

"I know, I see them, I can't believe it," Megan says when she opens it. "What the hell happened?"

"Sex happened."

Megan grins. "Works every time."

Throughout the morning, the sounds of hammering and sawing fill the air. For Hayley, baking muffins with Megan in the little kitchen in the cottage, it feels like . . . a détente?

"I knew they'd get along once they stopped sniffing each other's butts," Megan says. "Typical male behavior, right?"

"Right." Hayley holds up a batter-caked spoon. "But enough about them. How is your Substack coming? Are you ready to post something yet?"

"Yeah. Oh. Um . . ." Megan gives a dismissive shake of her head. "Everything's just in draft."

"If you need another pair of eyes . . ."

"Not yet. I want my prose to be perfect before anyone reads it."

Hayley nods. "I get it."

"But . . ." Megan pauses. "I could use your marketing savvy. Would you help me with some headlines?"

Hayley feels a spark of pleasure. "Yes! How fun."

Megan reaches for her notebook. "How about a title for a post about . . . the idea that nature holds some kind of secret wisdom?"

Kind of vague, but . . . okay, she'll go with it. Hayley taps her chin. "Let's see . . ." She grins. "'Is Your Life Flow Stagnant? How to Follow Your Own Current.'"

"Oh, that's hilarious!" Megan says. "Okay, my turn. 'What a Hibernating Bear Taught Me About Getting Enough Sleep.'" Laughter fills the kitchen as they come up with increasingly ridiculous headlines.

"Let's get some photos so I'm ready to go when the posts are done." Megan grabs her camera, and she and Hayley head into the woods. The sun through the trees illuminates the forest in a surreal light. It's the perfect backdrop, Megan says, for the post they named once they got down to business: "From Chaos to Calm: What Nature Can Teach Us About Letting Go and Moving Forward."

"I haven't seen an actual camera in I don't know how long," Hayley says.

"I found it in a thrift store. It's great for photographing nature on a day like today. No blurry birds."

Hayley trails Megan as she moves purposefully through the trees. "I want to make a statement about finding peace and reflection in the natural world," Megan says. "I'm planning some posts that weave these themes together. These photos are gonna be great inspo when I start writing."

"Didn't you tell me you drafted a bunch of posts already?"

Almost imperceptibly, Megan hesitates. "Oh, yeah. Well, I have them in my head, almost ready to go. It's my process."

Huh. Hayley could've sworn Megan said she had some pieces drafted. Maybe she misheard.

As the weeks progress, the détente between the two men seems to be holding. Brandon has been making lists of projects around the property; he and Tyler are knocking off the items one by one. They fell trees to provide firewood for the winter months ahead, make supply runs into town, prep the vegetable beds for next spring, pour a concrete floor in the woodshed. Tyler starts building out the composting beds.

Maybe it's the increased urgency of winter coming. Maybe it's the grudging respect Brandon is gaining for Tyler's hard work. Whatever the cause, Hayley's grateful. She doesn't call any extra attention to it, afraid to disturb the fragile ecosystem of their alliance while it's still forming. And she's put off asking Brandon about his family, not wanting to raise his ire when everything is going so well. Also, Emily has nailed down her plans and is visiting next week—Hayley doesn't want to fuel her friend's narrative about rushed weddings and poor choices.

As soon as the smokehouse is complete, Brandon turns his attention to hunting. Several nights a week, he sets his alarm to rise in the predawn dark and heads into the woods with his crossbow. Sometimes with Pellet and his gang, sometimes alone. Hayley often wakes to the sound of the bedroom door closing softly behind him. He returns midmorning, usually with a wild turkey or two.

Hayley is intrigued by the ritual he describes: Hours of silent vigil, walking stealthily through the trees, then shooting swiftly when a turkey appears. He uses a four-inch hunting knife to make precise incisions, then field-dresses the kill, rinsing the cavity with water from his thermos. Back at the smokehouse, he skins the bird before applying a rub and hanging it on an iron hook.

In the evenings, Brandon scrolls through articles and Reddit threads, sometimes reading bits aloud to Hayley about biodiversity and ecofriendly hunting practices. "You know," he says, "eating wild game is way better for the environment than eating farmed animals. Livestock farming uses a ton of land and resources. Hunting is more in tune with nature."

Brandon buys a deep-chest freezer to store the overflow of smoked meat. Hayley and Megan, standing at the window in the main house, watch Brandon and Tyler unload the freezer from the truck. "Meat eating actually is a cult," Megan says. "Look at Tyler—he's thoroughly brainwashed."

—

Brandon is subsisting on a few hours of sleep a night, but—oddly to Hayley—he seems more energetic than ever. The urgency of shorter days and colder weather, he tells her, is what's driving him. Hayley misses their time in bed together in the early mornings, but she knows that hunting season is short. When winter comes, they'll have all the time in the world.

One morning, when Brandon is off on a solo hunt, Hayley is sipping coffee and gazing out the kitchen window when she spies a strange shape in the yard.

What the hell is that?

She grabs her puffer and steps outside, the cold air hitting her skin as she makes her way across the brittle grass, her breath visible. The crunch of dead leaves under her boots is unnaturally loud in the morning stillness.

As she approaches, the shape begins to come into focus. Comprehension dawns: It's a coyote, lying on its side. As she inches forward, the smell of wet fur mingled with the metallic scent of blood stings her nostrils. Her stomach lurches.

The coyote's coat is stained a deep red, its limbs grotesquely splayed, eyes glassy and fixed on the sky. The animal has been eviscerated, its insides exposed in a brutal display: a gaping wound fringed with ragged flesh. The grass around it is dark with congealed blood. Steam still rises from the body, curling into the frigid air.

This was recent. Too recent.

The coyote has been gutted so cleanly. It looks to Hayley like the work of a person, not another animal.

The fact that whoever did this has been so close to the house sends a shiver down her spine.

She turns and hurries back inside. This was no random act of cruelty. The carcass has been deliberately placed in their yard, in clear view of the house. And whoever left it wanted to be sure that she and Brandon would find it.

Is it a sick prank? A message? But . . . why?

When Brandon arrives home an hour later, Hayley leads him to the inert form. He circles the gruesome scene.

"Who would do this?" Hayley asks, her voice tight. "It's so . . . deliberate."

He squats to examine the carcass more closely. "Could be another predator. A bear, maybe."

She gestures at the coyote's wounds. "Look how clean the cuts are."

"Nature can be brutal, Hayl."

She shakes her head. "Someone put this here for us to find."

He sighs. "It's unsettling, sure. But you're overreacting."

"To a gutted coyote in our yard?" Hayley's voice rises.

"I'll get rid of it," Brandon says. "Try not to worry."

Hayley feels a surge of frustration. "How can I not?"

"Believe me, this isn't that unusual. I trip over dead animals in the woods every day." Running a hand through his hair, he says, "And don't say anything to Megan and Tyler. No need to get everybody all worked up."

She isn't convinced. But she doesn't want to freak Megan out. "Okay."

"Nothing's going to happen. I promise." Though Brandon's voice is firm, something in his eyes doesn't quite match his reassuring words.

Later that night, Hayley puts on her Spotify "Embrace the Magic" playlist and lights a cinnamon-scented candle as she gets ready for bed, but her sense of foreboding lingers. No matter how much Brandon downplays it, she can't shake the feeling that someone left the coyote, now buried in the woods, for them to find. The thought gnaws at her. But she's got to push it away. Emily arrives tomorrow; she's certainly not going to tell her what happened. There's no point in sullying the short time they have together.

She can hear Brandon downstairs cleaning up, along with snippets of the classic rock he listens to when he's alone. *We're just echoes in the shadow, lost in the flow of time. Wandering through the hollow, in search of the divine . . .*

Hayley wants her husband's arms around her tonight. She sheds the utilitarian sweats she's bundled herself in and slips on one of Brandon's whisper-soft T-shirts—a look she knows he loves. She walks halfway down the stairs and leans over the railing. "Hey there, you."

He looks up. "Hey."

"Coming to bed?"

His smile seems a little forced. "I've got a few things to take care of down here. Sharpening my hunting knife, stuff like that."

"You really have to do that now?"

"I'm meeting Pellet and the guys tomorrow night."

"Oh." She's not sure what's going on behind his eyes. "You didn't tell me you were going out again tomorrow. Emily's coming. I thought we'd all have dinner."

He shakes his head. "I have to go out every night I can before the end of the season. You know that."

Echoes fade to silence; shadows start to blend. In life's eternal cycle, beginnings meet their end . . .

"This is just how it has to be," Brandon says, turning back to the dishes in the sink.

Hayley knows the conversation is over. The exchange has left her feeling lost and frustrated. Why is he so elusive, so distant from her? She yearns for the warmth she relied on to carry her through so many dark moments. She sighs. There's a part of Brandon that remains as mysterious to her now as the first day they met.

NINETEEN

The morning of Emily's visit dawns bright and clear, the first Saturday without rain they've seen in weeks. Hayley takes it as a positive omen. She bustles around the house, tidying things that are already tidy, fluffing throw pillows, refreshing the cattails in the vase by the window.

"The place looks great. Don't worry so much," Brandon assures her. They hear the honk of a horn. Tyler's truck. "I gotta go," he says, kissing her as he heads out the door. "I'll be back too late to see Emily tonight. Pellet's dropping me off. Tell her I say hi."

"I will," Hayley says, though she knows Emily isn't his favorite person, not by a long shot.

"And I'll tell Pellet you said hi."

"Sure," she says, though Pellet isn't her favorite person either. "Hey, you'll be back in time to take her to the trailhead tomorrow, right? Remember, I have that furniture delivery coming. Last time I missed it, and it was a nightmare to reschedule."

"Yep. I can take her."

Hayley watches Brandon go, wishing he weren't heading straight from errands in town to an all-night hunt. She'd hoped he and Emily would find common ground in this new environment. Maybe when he drives her to the trailhead they'll have a chance to connect. Hayley checks her reflection one last time before grabbing her keys. She actually made an effort this morning, not wanting Emily to think she's let herself go completely out here in the country. Her auburn hair falls in soft, blow-dried waves, for a change, over the black cashmere scoop-neck sweater that's languished in the back of her closet ever since she left the city. Her usual uniform of flannel and leggings can wait until tomorrow.

—

At Crystal River's tiny bus station, Hayley waits in the foyer. She peers down the street. Only one express bus arrives from New York City a day, ferrying leaf peepers and extreme hikers headed to the High Peaks. When the bus finally pulls up, Hayley scans the faces behind the windows—and there's Emily! Waving at her with a huge smile.

Hayley gives her an enthusiastic wave back.

Emily has cropped her brown hair short and is wearing new glasses with thick, dark frames. She somehow looks both like an urban hipster and the kind of intrepid adventurer who'd hike for a week by herself.

Emily steps off the bus, and Hayley pulls her into a warm hug, navigating around her friend's gigantic backpack. Registering the familiar lemony scent of Emily's shampoo, Hayley feels unexpectedly emotional. Here's her old life, colliding with her new one.

—

Hayley is taking Emily to the Crystal River Farmers' Market to stock up for dinner tonight. She also wants to show her some of the charm of her new town. In the Jeep, she rolls down her window, cool mountain air rushing in as she follows the road along the crystalline river. She grins when Emily opens the glove compartment to look for actual gloves, playing out their longtime game. The familiar rhythm of Emily's voice and the warmth of her laugh stir a bittersweet ache for home that Hayley hadn't allowed herself to fully acknowledge until now.

As they drive, Emily chatters on about her plans for the solo hike that she booked months ago. "All these badass women are going on epic journeys, you know?" Emily says. "My clients were, like, yes, go for it! We can't wait to hear everything."

"That's fantastic," Hayley says.

"Right? I was freaking out about leaving in the fall, my busiest season. But they urged me to do it, to take a mental health break."

"Amazing."

Emily gazes out the window. "This consulting thing is working out so well for me, it's scary."

"So great."

"Being on my own is a revelation. I'm off the dating apps completely. Why would I want a girlfriend now? I feel so free without anything, or anyone, holding me back."

"Umm," Hayley murmurs in assent. *Fantastic . . . amazing . . . great.* She feels slow of brain and tongue in her friend's high-octane presence.

And she can't quite tell: Is Emily just being self-reflective about her freedom? Or is she implying that Brandon is holding Hayley back?

"It was only when I decided to go solo that I found my tribe," Emily continues. "Ironic, right?"

Hayley pastes a smile on her face, but she feels a little stung as Emily talks about a "tribe" that doesn't include her. Of course it's inevitable that friendships evolve over time. But is this disconnect she's feeling new, or was it always there?

". . . so then my friend Casey forwarded me this podcast episode about radical self-discovery," Emily is saying. "That was the sign I needed. I booked the next day!"

"That's really cool, Em." Hayley hopes her voice sounds brighter than she feels. A flicker of envy sparks inside her—for the thrill of solo travel, for Emily's comfortable place in the New York scene. Not that Hayley regrets her choices, but part of her misses that fast-paced life.

"Turning thirty is a milestone. I had to do something over the top." Emily looks over at her. "I guess you did too, huh?"

"I guess I did."

"You went all in."

The words hang in the air, sharp and ambiguous. For a moment, the only sound is the hum of tires on asphalt. Hayley fights the urge to defend herself, to explain. Instead, she keeps her eyes on the road and lets the moment pass.

Hayley tries to keep to lighter topics, like the recent day she spent with Megan making pear butter and dilled green beans. "Megan's indifferent in the kitchen," Hayley says, "but she's up for pretty much any kind of experiment."

"Sounds like she's a lot more than a tenant," Emily says.

"It's nice to have a friend up here."

Emily nods.

"She's really excited to meet you."

"Same," Emily says, but her tone is noncommittal.

Hayley and Emily arrive at the farmers' market. It's a gorgeous day. Leaves of orange, red, and yellow rustle in the breeze, and the blue sky is dotted with puffy white clouds. Sunlight bathes the surrounding mountains.

Hayley finds herself hoping Emily will be charmed by the wholesomeness of it all. The scent of fresh bread, kettle corn, and dried eucalyptus; the pre-Halloween excitement in the air, with vendors dressed in costumes unpacking their trucks and setting up stalls and tents along the edges of the field. Here's a witch, arranging bushels of multicolored corn and spiky gourds. There's a vampire, filling baskets with orange and yellow mums. At a craft stand, a scarecrow adjusts a sign advertising goat's milk soaps and candles.

She notices a cardboard sign propped on a table in red block letters: PIE ALERT SYSTEM. Order now! Thanksgiving will be here before you know it. Sign up now for the Crystal River Herald's breaking news updates.

Hayley adds the number to her phone.

Emily, amused, says, "I can't believe you live in a place where a pie shortage constitutes breaking news."

Hayley laughs.

As Hayley and Emily wander through the market, more people begin to trickle in. Parents search for the perfect pumpkin while their kids play tag. An elderly couple walks hand in hand, stopping to sample maple syrups and homemade jams. Teenagers take selfies with their friends, dressed for Halloween parties later in the day.

"I want to buy you a pot of mums." Emily pivots toward the vampire's booth. Hayley follows, absently scanning the sea of unfamiliar faces around them. And then one comes into focus. Oh shit. It's Cheryl Snyder, waving vigorously at her from behind a stall. Hayley hasn't seen her since her surprise visit to the house.

"Hayley! Over here!" Cheryl calls.

"Who's that?" Emily asks under her breath.

"She owns an orchard near us," Hayley says. "She's a character. She knew Brandon's family back in the day."

There's no polite way to avoid Cheryl now. Hayley and Emily make their way over to her stall as she's handing a customer a white box tied with string.

"Well, hello." Cheryl's green poncho flutters in the breeze. "Glad I spotted you. I made my famous bourbon apple pies this week! And fresh-pressed cider."

"Oh!" Hayley says. "I'll have to—"

"Who might this be?" Cheryl interrupts, turning to Emily. She gives her a once-over. "Those glasses are a bold choice. Bet people can't help commenting on them."

Emily smiles faintly, adjusting the frames. "They save me a lot of time actually," she says, her tone light but pointed. "If someone makes them into a big deal, we probably don't have much in common."

Cheryl pauses for a moment, then lets out a surprised laugh. "Touché," she says, a hint of respect in her voice. "Here's to ya." As she pours herself a cup of cider from a steaming thermos, Hayley gets a whiff of whiskey.

"So where are you visiting from?" Cheryl asks.

"New York City," Emily says. "I'm doing a solo hike here in the Adirondacks, and I'm stopping over first to see Hayley's new home."

"It's quite a home." Cheryl takes a sip.

"So I hear. She just picked me up from the bus."

"My husband Rick was the builder."

"Cool!" Emily gives Hayley a *Can we get out of here?* look.

"In fact . . ." Cheryl pauses, her fingers tightening around the cup. "It was the last job he ever worked on." A shadow passes across her face. "A tragedy."

Hayley, unsure how to respond, glances at Emily.

"Um . . . I'm so very sorry," Emily offers.

Cheryl turns to Hayley. "Y'know, I've always wondered. Was your husband 'so very sorry'?"

Hayley's anxiety is spiking. What in the world—? She shifts her weight, her mouth dry. "I don't know anything about this," she manages weakly. "Brandon never—"

"He wouldn't, would he?" Cheryl takes another sip. "The less you know, the better you'll sleep at night."

Hayley and Emily exchange a look. What is she talking about? Neither of them wants to ask.

Hayley gives an audible sigh. "Well," she says, "jeez. That's . . . gosh. You know, we have to get going. We'll take one of your famous pies."

Cheryl makes a show of choosing the perfect one, putting it into a box, and tying it with red and white string. Hayley mumbles her thanks and hands her a twenty-dollar bill.

Her lungs don't fully reinflate until she and Emily have put some distance between themselves and the apple stall.

"What a fucking weird encounter." Emily matches Hayley's brisk stride toward the parking lot.

"She told me her husband died. It was twenty years ago. But that's all I know."

"And what was that about Brandon being sorry?"

Hayley chews her lip. "I have no idea. He's never mentioned a thing about it."

They walk in silence to the Jeep. Hayley sets the pie and the vegetables they bought in the footwell behind the driver's seat, then gets in and starts the ignition. Part of her wants to leave well enough alone. But she can't brush aside Cheryl's anger at Brandon.

"I'm going to poke around a bit online tonight," she tells Emily. "See what I can find."

Emily buckles her seat belt. "Hey. Finding shit on the internet is what I do for a living. I can sleuth around for you."

Hayley angles the heating vents toward her muddy boots. "I don't know."

"If you'd rather I didn't . . ."

Hayley thinks back to the terrible days after *Sinister Sands* first dropped. Never had she been more grateful that Emily worked in tech and knew hacks that enabled her to screen Hayley's texts, emails, and social media to make sure nothing traumatic got through. Emily had been her buffer, her safety net.

"No, I think you should," she says.

Emily pulls out her phone. "What was the guy's name again?"

"Rick Snyder."

Emily taps away. "Twenty years ago . . . obituaries . . . ah. Got it," she says. She starts to read out loud from her screen. "*Crystal River Herald*, December fourth, 2003. Hmm . . . it gives only minimal details—age forty-two, presumed cardiac event, survived by widow Cheryl. No children. No further information."

Hayley sighs. It's truly sad that Cheryl lost her husband so young. But if Rick Snyder had a heart attack while he happened to be working on the Stone family property, how could it possibly be Brandon's fault?

Enough catastrophizing. Cheryl is clearly a little unstable. If there's anything to learn from this, it's that Hayley should ignore her tendency to assume the worst.

TWENTY

After grabbing Emily's pack from the back seat, Hayley leads the way inside the house. Seeing the place through Emily's eyes, she feels a self-conscious twinge, suddenly acutely aware of the quiet luxury of it all, from the gleaming countertops to the exposed wood beams. Beautiful, but a little too . . . curated?

If Emily has the same critical thought, it doesn't show on her face. She masks whatever she's feeling behind a wondering smile. "Wow, Hayley, this is . . . wow!" she says as she wanders through the vast living space. She makes all the right noises as Hayley shows her the larder filled with home-canned goods.

They head outside for a tour of the property. Emily makes a show of marveling at the eggplant and zucchini still growing so late in the season.

"Hey there!" Tyler calls to them from the composting beds. He's wearing rubber boots, a metal spade in his hand.

As they get closer, Emily wrinkles her nose. "I've been with you so far on your back-to-the-land journey, but this is . . . yuck."

Hayley laughs. "Luckily, compost is not my domain."

After she introduces them, Tyler tells Emily more than she ever wanted to know about the coffee grounds and eggshells below his feet.

The spot he chose needed to have the perfect balance of sunlight and shade, not to mention good drainage. "The compost pile has to be just wet enough," Tyler says. "If it's too dry, you gotta add moisture. Too wet, more leaves or wood chips."

Emily grins. "Reminds me of my last girlfriend."

Tyler laughs. "You're funny," he says. Turning to Hayley with a playful grin, he adds, "I like her."

As they continue toward the cottage, Emily leans in close to Hayley. "He's kind of hot."

"Oh?"

"And I think he was flirting with you."

Hayley shakes her head, amused. "If you say so."

"If I were Brandon, I might be jealous."

Just then, Hayley spots Megan through the window and waves, gesturing for her to come out. Megan emerges wearing wide-legged jeans and a cream-colored sweater. It's obvious to Hayley that she's not the only one who's put some effort into her wardrobe today.

Holding her hand out to Emily, Megan says, "Hello." Her tone is oddly formal.

"Hey." Emily shakes it firmly. "I've heard a lot about you."

Has she, though? Whenever Hayley brings up Megan in conversation, Emily has shown little interest.

"Good things, I hope," Megan says. "Hayley and I are spending a lot of time together these days."

"Making pear butter, I hear." Is that sarcasm in Emily's voice?

Megan gives her a slow nod. "Yes," she says stiffly. "Our way of living out here is the opposite of life in New York. We're trying to be more connected to the earth. Less . . . frenetic."

Tiny alarm bells go off in Hayley's head. This is escalating in a way that she hadn't anticipated. "Megan is about to launch a Substack," she says.

Emily nods, glancing at her smartwatch. "Cool."

"And you're off on a big hiking adventure," Megan says.

"Sure am. In search of my version of inner bliss."

Megan doesn't react.

They all stand there awkwardly for a moment.

"Well. I should head back inside," Megan says. "I need to finish writing while it's quiet in the cottage. Nice to meet you, Emily." She gives a perfunctory smile.

"You too." Emily waves vaguely at her departing back.

Hayley feels surprisingly deflated. She'd had such high hopes for bringing her two closest friends—really, now, her only friends—together. Why did she assume they would click? The fact is, Emily is both protective of Hayley and suspicious by nature. And Megan, quick to pick up on social cues, clearly—and correctly—read Emily's attitude as dismissive.

Making small talk as they walk back to the house, Hayley is aware that she's straining for glimpses of her world through Emily's eyes. The rapid succession of changes she's undergone in the past few months still feels a bit surreal to her. In the brief silences that punctuate their conversation, she senses that Emily is searching too—maybe looking for traces of the ambitious friend who left New York behind.

When they reach the porch, a low howl echoes from the mountain, followed by a series of short, sharp yips.

"I know what that is," Emily says. "Trailblazers made us listen to recordings of wild animals and learn to identify them before they certified us to go solo. They sound creepy. But they're actually afraid of us." She smiles. "Fun fact: the Humane Society says you're more likely to be killed by a champagne cork than bitten by a coyote."

"Ha." But Hayley isn't laughing. Even though the gutted coyote is buried and gone, she still feels its presence—a prickle at the back of her neck, a shadow in her peripheral vision. She finds herself glancing over her shoulder, seeking its eyes as it slips through the trees, skirts the pond, blends seamlessly with the landscape, its bloodstained fur reflecting the colors of the changing leaves.

A few hours later, at the kitchen island, Hayley fills two shallow bowls for her and Emily with mushroom ragout—a signature dish at their favorite West Village bistro, Maison Champignon. The two of them ate there once a week, at least, often splitting an order of the ragout and a bottle of wine.

"So nice!" Emily exclaims, looking down at her bowl of mushrooms, triple-cream Brie, and aged Gouda. "Hayley, I'm touched."

"Aw, thanks, Em."

"I loved our old routine."

"I did too. I miss you, Em," Hayley says, and means it.

"I miss you too."

Hayley pours two glasses of rosé, and they clink them together. "To us."

"To us." Emily takes a sip. "Speaking of us, and you, and togetherness, where is that spouse of yours? I haven't wanted to ask."

"Oh! Yeah." Hayley knows she's been avoiding this topic. "Brandon wanted to be here, but he's on an overnight bowhunt with a group from town."

"Like . . . archery?"

"Not exactly. He has a ridiculously high-tech crossbow."

"So what do they hunt? Deer?"

"And wild turkey. Rabbits too."

"For god's sake, can't you just order from FreshDirect?"

Hayley laughs. "Well . . . their whole thing is that eating wild game is better for the planet than eating farmed meat."

Emily gives her a skeptical look. "C'mon—you really think that men prowling the woods with crossbows will save the planet?"

Actually, no—Hayley doesn't think that. But Brandon does. She wants to at least try to explain his worldview. "It seems weird and primal, I know. But these guys only kill what they can eat."

Emily scrapes sage butter across a piece of flatbread. "Huh. Well . . . sounds very 'end of days' to me."

Hayley takes a sip of rosé and sets her wineglass back on the table. "Yeah, I tease him about that," she says. "This place is a prepper's paradise."

Emily gives a pretend shiver. "You're making me wish I'd stayed in the city, where it's safe."

"Honestly? Sometimes I feel that way myself." Hayley smiles.

Emily reciprocates, holding her smile a beat longer than necessary. "But all's well in paradise, right?"

"All's well." Hayley takes a bite. The mushroom ragout, a strong sensory reminder of her life in the city, melts on her tongue.

After loading their plates into the dishwasher, Hayley refills their wine-glasses and leads Emily to the couch in the great room. She lights a few votive candles on the coffee table and puts soft jazz on the Sonos, and the two of them settle in, tucking their legs underneath them.

Hayley sips her wine, buying time before asking the question that's been lurking in her mind ever since she picked Emily up at the bus station this morning. She meets her friend's eyes. "Okay, Em . . . so, I'm dying to know. What do you think?"

Emily blinks at her from behind her oversized frames, as if not comprehending the question.

"I mean," Hayley says, "can you see it now—why I came here? What I love about this place?"

Emily looks away. She sets her wineglass on the coffee table and hugs her knees to her chest. When she speaks, her words come out in an apologetic tumble. "I don't know, I mean, you've got this massive house, and this big old plot of land, but . . . I gotta say, this is not what I imagined for you." Looking back at Hayley, she says, "You were killing it in New York—you kind of had it all, or at least it seemed that way to me. And now"—she waves a hand to encompass everything within view—"now you're canning your own food and decorating a lair for your bowhunting husband."

Hayley's hackles rise at Emily's words. She strains to keep her voice light. "This isn't a 'lair,' Emily. It's Brandon's home. He grew up here."

"I know," Emily continues slowly. "And I get that living up here is a big, beautiful dream come true."

Hayley stiffens.

"But, I mean, I look around and . . ." She actually looks around. "I don't see *you*. The . . . the compost heap, your husband killing what you eat—this is trad-wife shit, Hayley. You're living someone else's fantasy."

Hayley looks at Emily intently. "It's not just Brandon's fantasy. I choose to be here."

Emily's mouth tightens into a thin line. "You choose to be here with a guy who isn't being honest with you," she says. "Don't you think there's a problem when you have to search online for twenty-year-old articles to learn anything about your own husband's past?"

Hayley sits back, Emily's words punching the air from her lungs. "That's . . . harsh," she says finally, her eyes overbright. She takes another sip of wine.

Emily at least has the grace to act contrite. "Oh god, Hayley. I didn't mean to hurt your feelings." She scoots closer and puts a hand over Hayley's. "I just think the change has been really rapid, you know? One minute we're drinking Aperol spritzes in your apartment, the next you're moving to the middle of nowhere with a guy you met at your sister's funeral."

"It's not exactly the middle of—"

"Wait till the first winter storm," Emily breaks in. "I hope you have a monster generator, because you're going to be totally cut off from civilization." She hesitates, then adds gently, "In all the years I've known you, Hayley, you never once talked about wanting anything like this. So it just feels . . . strange."

Hayley shakes her head, bristling even as she fights back tears. "Things change. People change." She takes a shaky breath, grasping for the words to make Emily understand. "This is my life now, Em. I'm committed to making it work."

Just then, Emily's phone lights up. The opening bars of "Ice Ice Baby" shatter the moment.

Despite her agitation, Hayley can't help but smile. "I can't believe that's still your ringtone. I changed mine back a year ago!"

Emily smiles too. "I know. I love it, though." She holds up her phone in its custom case—blue hands cradling an orange flame, with *Trailblazers* in a jaunty font beneath—and turns it around to show Hayley the caller: Mom. "I gotta take this. It's the last time I can talk to her till I'm back from my hike."

She steps away to take the call.

Hayley is glad for the interruption, the intensity of their conversation put on pause.

"Hey!" Emily greets her mother cheerfully. "I'm at Hayley's." She turns to Hayley. "Mom says hi."

Hayley waves from the couch.

Emily's mother's voice buzzes faintly through the phone.

Emily sighs. "I know, I know. But you can text me."

More protestations from the other end.

"Mom, relax. You and Hayley have the emergency override code. My phone will ring if you use it, but"—she pauses for emphasis—"only for real emergencies. I'm trying to commune with nature here." A beat of silence, then Emily laughs. "No, the Thanksgiving menu is not a real emergency."

Hayley lets the back-and-forth between Emily and her mother fade into the background as she gathers the wineglasses and brings them to the sink. Emily's assessment of her relationship with Brandon has rattled her. A small part of her has to acknowledge that there's a grain of truth in what Emily said, despite her blunt delivery.

Only a grain, she tells herself. Not the whole truth.

They head upstairs. While Emily repacks her gear for tomorrow's hike, Hayley retreats to her study to work on her latest photo collage, but her mind keeps wandering back to their earlier conversation. She mechanically arranges frames and ribbons on her desk. Emily's blunt questions have stirred something unsettling within her. Not just about her own dreams, but about Brandon. His past in this house. The shadows of his family's history here. The frames in her hands suddenly feel like puzzle pieces that don't quite fit.

Hayley picks up a photo of her and Brandon, taken last summer. She studies his smile, familiar yet enigmatic. The way his gaze holds something just out of reach has always intrigued her. Now, that same quality gives her pause. What is he hiding behind that smile?

Hayley tries to shake off the doubt. This is the man she loves. This is the life she's chosen. Blue skies instead of skyscrapers, trees instead of cubicles. A life that challenges her to grow in new ways every day. But now, another question nags at her: Is she truly growing, or just adapting to fit the negative spaces of Brandon's secrets?

There's a light rap on the door. Hayley looks up.

"Can I come in?" Emily's voice is conciliatory. She's clearly ready to turn the page on the confrontation from earlier. Hayley is too.

"What are you doing?"

"Working on a collage."

Emily wanders to the desk, absently looking at the photos spread out there. Something in the open junk drawer catches her eye. Beneath scissors and paper clips and Scotch tape, the top half of a Polaroid is visible. "Ah—Jenna," she says softly. Lifting the torn photo from the drawer, she holds it close, inspecting it. "Whose arm is this?"

"That loser she was engaged to for about five minutes."

"Ugh." Emily shakes her head. "I don't blame you for cutting him out of the picture."

"I didn't cut him out. Jenna must've. I found it this way." Hayley feels a flare of anger. "That's my dad's ring. She gave it to him. Now that's gone too."

Emily contemplates the photo. "It's interesting that she kept this picture. Maybe she cut Sean out because she wanted to turn over a new leaf but kept the Polaroid because she couldn't quite let go."

Hayley considers this. "I hadn't thought of it like that. Maybe you're right."

Emily puts a hand on her shoulder. "Jenna had an illness." Her voice is deep with feeling. "It got the better of her. But I think if she'd lived, you would've had the chance to be the big sister you always wanted to be."

Hayley turns slightly misty eyed as a wave of affection crests inside her. Of course Emily understands her feelings for her sister, and why the loss of her father's ring cuts so deep. "This means the world to me, Em. You're the only one who really knows my past." She grasps Emily's hand.

Emily squeezes back, her usually guarded brown eyes softening behind her glasses. "You'll come stay with me in New York for a weekend when I'm home, yeah?"

"I'd love that. Just promise you'll be safe out there by yourself." Hayley stands and pulls Emily into a hug.

"You and my mom are on speed dial, and I'll be in and out of service areas," Emily says, hugging her back. "There are plenty of shelters along the way."

They separate. "Okay. Fine," Hayley says. "Don't let any bears steal your freeze-dried mac and cheese."

Emily laughs. "'If it's brown, lie down. If it's black, fight back. If it's white, good night'—isn't that how the saying goes?"

"You're in the Adirondacks. The bears are black here. Fight back."

—

It's close to midnight. After steeping a cup of chamomile tea to bring to Emily's bedside, Hayley wipes the kitchen counters, starts the dishwasher, and turns off all the lights except one that she leaves glowing for Brandon beside the door.

In her bedroom, Hayley crawls under the heavy down comforter. Curled on her side, watching the shadowy tree branches sway outside her window, Hayley falls into a dreamless sleep, rousing slightly when Brandon finally slides into bed beside her.

He smells vaguely feral, as if the hunting trip has seeped under his skin.

TWENTY-ONE

The next morning, while Emily is showering, Hayley steps onto the porch with her mug to find Tyler kneeling in the grass beside the steps, tinkering with the sprinkler system.

He looks up as she approaches, squinting into the autumn sunlight. "Hey."

"Hey. What are you doing?"

"Shutting off the pipes for the season."

She leans against the porch railing, staring out at the pond. Ripples break its glassy surface. "Beautiful morning, huh?"

Tyler rakes a hand through his hair. When he smiles, his dimple deepens. "It was cloudy till you showed up. You brought the sunshine." He holds her gaze a moment too long.

Her cheeks grow warm. Was Emily right? Is Tyler flirting with her?

There's a clang from the garage. They both turn sharply. It's Brandon.

Tyler's expression shutters, and he sits back on his heels. "Did you need something?"

"Oh, no. I'm just here for the view." Realizing that might sound suggestive, she adds, quickly, "I can't believe how soon the trees will be bare."

"Yep." He turns back to the sprinklers. "Winter's right around the corner."

Hayley retreats inside, slightly flustered by her own behavior. Why does she feel so . . . breathless?

—

"Em, Brandon's almost ready," Hayley calls up the stairs.

Emily comes down to the great room. She has an odd expression on her face, and she's clutching her phone.

"You okay?" Hayley asks.

Emily glances over Hayley's shoulder to the door. Hayley, sensing Emily's concern, closes it behind her and walks closer. "What's going on?"

Emily shakes her head. "It's Rick Snyder," she says in a low voice. "Something about his obituary kept nagging at me. It was so . . . anodyne. Small-town obits are usually pretty chatty, but that one seemed like it was written by a robot."

Hayley nods, a knot forming in her stomach. "And?"

"I did some digging last night," Emily continues, her words careful. "I found a police report." She types briefly on her phone, then turns the screen toward Hayley. The PDF is small and poorly reproduced; Hayley has to lean in, squinting, to read the blurry text. As the words come into focus, her breath catches. It's a summary of Rick Snyder's death in 2003. A car skidded on ice, crashed into a tree on the Stones' property. Snyder pulled an inebriated teen from behind the wheel, but the car rolled back, crushing him.

The teen was Brandon.

Hayley stares at the document, her mind reeling.

"Someone covered up Brandon's involvement and the true cause of death," Emily says. "But here it is, in black and white. Cheryl's husband died saving Brandon's life."

The words settle like a palpable presence in the room.

When Hayley and Emily come outside, Brandon and Tyler are hooking bungee cords over a load of black trash bags in the back of Tyler's truck. Hayley is surprised. "You're not taking the Jeep?"

"Too much going on," Brandon says. "It's bulky waste day at the dump, a two-man job. Then I've got errands to do in town while Tyler picks up slate at the quarry."

"What about Emily? You promised her a ride."

"There's room for three in front."

Hayley frowns. This was not her plan. But . . . maybe it's just as well that Emily won't be alone with Brandon right now.

She glances at Emily, standing in the doorway with her enormous backpack. "Is this okay with you?"

Emily hitches her pack higher on her shoulders. "Does Uber come here? I don't want to trouble anyone."

"Uber's iffy. And it's no trouble," Tyler says genially. "You can tell us about your trip. I hiked the High Sierra Trail once, in my twenties."

"Really?" Emily says.

"Six days. Hope your hiking boots are better than mine."

"Merrell," she says, holding up a foot.

He gives the boot an approving nod. "Nice. I had some off-brand shit that fell apart after four days."

Hayley helps Emily load her gear into the truck bed. Emily gives her a fierce hug. "Love you. No matter what," she whispers. "You know that, right?"

"No matter what," Hayley says into her hair.

Emily pulls back, hands on Hayley's shoulders. "You'll talk to him about this, right?" she whispers.

"Absolutely. But please don't say anything to him about it, Em. I need to do this my way."

"I know."

Hayley feels a rush of gratitude toward her friend—for being tactful, and generous, when her feelings are clearly mixed. "Text me sometimes when you have service, okay?"

"I will."

Tyler slides behind the wheel, and Emily climbs in next to Brandon. She gives Hayley a little wave as the truck rumbles down the drive.

An hour later, Hayley's phone pings with a text from Emily. I'm proud of you. Honestly. You're a trailblazer too.

Hayley shoots back a string of red heart emojis. Then she taps out another message, this time to Megan: Yoga this afternoon? I need it.

After the delivery truck arrives, Hayley spends a few hours unpacking and arranging two leather club chairs, a bookcase, and several lamps in the den. When she crosses the yard to the cottage with her yoga mat tucked under her arm in the early afternoon, the sunlight streaming through the whispering pines feels surreal—too bright, almost accusatory.

She takes a breath, trying to center herself.

Megan meets Hayley at the door. "I'm so glad you texted," she says in a rush. "I've been feeling awful about yesterday. The way I acted with your friend . . ." She shakes her head. "I was giving off weird vibes. I don't know what came over me."

"It's okay, really. Em can be a bit . . ." Hayley pauses, searching for the right word. "Territorial, maybe. We've been friends for so long."

"It's totally understandable."

In the living room, they unfurl their mats across the smooth wooden floor. As Hayley attempts to mirror Megan's movements, her mind keeps drifting.

"Inhale, reach up," Megan instructs. "Exhale, fold forward."

Hayley tries to focus, to lose herself in the movement. But the weight of what she knows presses down on her, making it impossible to find peace in the familiar stretches.

"Is everything all right?" Megan asks, noticing her distraction.

Hayley forces a nod. "Just a lot on my mind."

She's tempted to confide in Megan, but this is not the time.

She has to talk to Brandon. She won't feel right until she does.

By the time Brandon returns from Crystal River, rain is pelting the windows. Over dinner at the kitchen island, Hayley steels herself for the conversation she needs to have.

As he scoops the last bits of white bean chili from his bowl, she begins. "I've learned something that we need to talk about. Cheryl Snyder's husband was fatally injured right here, on the property."

Brandon is silent for a moment. Then he says, "Maybe. I don't remember."

Hayley's stomach tightens at his evasiveness. "Brandon, I know you were involved."

His face clouds. "I'm not sure what you—"

"Please don't lie."

Brandon swallows hard, staring at his empty bowl. When he looks up, his eyes are guarded. "What else do you know?"

"That you were driving the car that ran him over. And you were drunk."

The rain drums on the roof, filling the silence between them. Brandon puts his head in his hands.

When he finally raises it again, Hayley presses ahead. "Why did you keep this from me?"

"I wanted to forget the whole thing. It ruined our lives. My parents' marriage fell apart, we had to leave . . ."

Hayley tries to absorb what he's saying. "I understand it was terrible for you. But surely you knew I'd find out eventually."

"I didn't think you would. I was fifteen, a minor. My parents kept it out of the news."

She sets down her fork. "I've always been honest with you. I thought you were being honest with me."

"I know, I am. I mean . . ." He shakes his head. "I was afraid you wouldn't want to live here if you knew."

That's true. She probably wouldn't.

"Look, I'm—I'm really sorry," he says. "I should've told you."

She nods, her feelings a tangled mess.

Brandon's expression shifts. "So how'd you find out?"

Before Hayley can respond, realization dawns on his face. "Emily," he says with a disparaging shrug. "Of course. The tech whiz. She's always hated me."

Abruptly, he stands. "I need to clear my head. Go for a walk."

"It's pouring," Hayley protests.

"I don't care. I'm not going to melt."

After the door slams behind him, Hayley sits alone at the island, listening to the rain. There's more to this story, she's sure of it. And Brandon's reaction has only deepened her doubts. She's left with the creeping sense that she's just scratched the surface.

NOVEMBER

TWENTY-TWO

The wooden stairs groan as Hayley descends to the basement, a cardboard box filled with mason jars, lids, bands, and other canning supplies heavy in her arms. Squinting in the dim light, she makes her way to the still-unfinished room that will serve as their larder.

After setting the box down with a thud, she flips on the light and stands, hands on hips, surveying the space. Wooden framing lines the opposite wall, with rough lumber sheets propped against it, waiting to be transformed into shelves and storage nooks. In the absence of shelves, she's been stacking her homemade preserves on overturned boxes. The floor is cluttered with jars, and there are still potatoes and carrots and late-season squash to process.

She's been waiting for Brandon to frame out the larder shelves, but he never seems to have the time.

An uneasy truce has settled between them over the last several days. Brandon is out of the house most of the time, hunting and getting the property ready for winter. She has thrown herself into her own projects, preserving the last vegetables from the garden, cooking and freezing as much as they can store. Brandon's past and all she doesn't know weigh heavily on her. But the urgency of the tasks at hand now provides a welcome distraction from the intensity of her thoughts. There's time, she tells herself. The past isn't going anywhere.

Now, in the basement, she unpacks several mason jars and stacks them against the opposite wall. As she opens another box, she hears footsteps overhead, followed by the creak of floorboards at the top of the basement stairs.

She pauses. "Hello? Someone there?"

Peering out the door of the storeroom, she sees work boots, then legs in faded jeans—ah, it's just Tyler coming down the stairs.

He lifts his chin when he spots her. "Hey."

"Hey! You surprised me."

"Oh, sorry." He steps into the room. "Brandon asked me to double-check the insulation throughout the house. Figured I'd poke around and see if there's anything down here that needs repair. I'll stay out of your way."

But instead of leaving, he approaches the wall and studies the wooden framework across the long expanse. "Want me to finish up these shelves? I have time."

"Oh! Sure. That would be great."

He drags a pair of sawhorses to the middle of the room and lifts a sheet of plywood across them, creating an improvised worktable.

Over the course of the afternoon, the two of them fall into an easy rhythm. As soon as Tyler hangs a shelf, Hayley lines up the jars in neat rows and stacks supplies. He's got the next shelf ready just in time for her to empty one box and start on the next.

When they're finished, they step back to admire their handiwork.

"How about a beer?" Tyler asks. "I think we've earned it."

He follows her up to the kitchen and settles onto a stool at the island. Hayley opens the fridge and pulls out two IPAs. She rummages in the drawer for a bottle opener, then opens both and passes one across the island. He takes a long swig.

"Thanks again for your help," Hayley says. "It's great to finally have those shelves up. Brandon promised they'd be finished weeks ago, but . . ." Her voice trails off.

Tyler takes another sip of beer. "Seems like he's always off somewhere. In the woods, right?"

"Yeah. Filling thc smokehouse."

"I've seen him come back with a turkey or two," Tyler says. "But entire days out there? Not my idea of fun, but every man to himself, I guess." He shakes his head. "I kind of thought we'd be working together on the property. But mostly I'm alone." His eyes meet Hayley's. "Seems like you're alone a lot too."

Taking a deep breath, she opts for honesty. "I am. Other than when I'm with Megan. I guess I've gotten used to it."

She's surprised by the perceptiveness of his observation, and even more by her own willingness to engage with it.

Tyler leans forward slightly, his voice softening. "I'm probably overstepping, but . . . is everything okay between you and Brandon?"

A charged silence stretches between them. Hayley finds herself acutely aware of Tyler's presence—his attentiveness, his raw appeal. She pushes the thought away. "Everything's fine," she says.

For a few moments, the quiet hum of the refrigerator is the only sound in the room. Tyler gestures to a large basket of eggplant and zucchini on the counter. "What are you doing with all those veggies? Freezing them?"

"You're welcome to take some, if you like. I was thinking I might make ratatouille." Hayley takes a sip of her beer. "Actually, what are you and Megan doing tonight? Would you want to join?"

"We don't have any plans," Tyler replies.

"Then come over." A small voice in her head warns her that she should have consulted Brandon first. But no—maybe it's time for a little spontaneity. This impromptu dinner might be just what she needs. Whether Brandon decides to show up for it or not.

An hour later, Megan breezes into the kitchen with her laptop tucked under her arm. "Thought you could use some company while you're prepping dinner." She pulls up the same stool Tyler sat in earlier, across the island from where Hayley is chopping vegetables. "Thanks for having us over tonight. I'm psyched for our party!"

Hayley scoops a pile of diced eggplant into a bowl and sprinkles olive oil over parchment in a sheet pan. "Me too."

Megan is focused on connecting to the finicky Wi-Fi. "Don't mind me, I'm just finishing a piece. It's hard to concentrate in the cottage. It's so small; I can hear it every time Tyler blows his nose."

Hayley feels a pang of irritation. It's getting a little old hearing Megan complaining about the cottage again. "Are you unhappy over there?"

"No, no, of course not! I hate to sound like I'm complaining—"

"No, tell me." Hayley cuts a green pepper in half and begins to chop it into squares.

"I mean, it's so much nicer than our crappy apartment in town, but at least I could walk to Bones & Leaves with my laptop for a change of scenery now and then. I just . . . I don't know, I miss that a little."

"Yeah, I get that," Hayley says, though she doesn't, not really. Megan can drive to town anytime she chooses. But Hayley wants to be amenable. "You know, the guest bedroom here is just sitting empty. Now that winter's coming, I can't imagine anyone's going to visit for months. You could work there."

Megan tilts her head. "Brandon would be okay with that?"

"Well . . ." Hayley thinks for a moment. She's honestly not sure. She slides the sheet pan in the oven, then washes her hands. "Use the room. We can take coffee breaks together."

"Yoga breaks." Megan smiles.

"Even better."

"I don't want to come between you guys. Are you sure it's not an imposition?"

"Absolutely."

Well, "absolutely" might be an exaggeration. But it's her place too.

Alone in the kitchen after dinner is prepped, Hayley looks around, feeling a mix of pride and nervousness. Candlelight flickers; a mellow playlist hums on the Sonos. Ratatouille simmers on the stove, its aromatic spices filling the air.

"What's all this?" Brandon asks as he comes through the door.

"Megan and Tyler are joining us for dinner. I know it's last minute, but Tyler built those shelves in the storeroom. I thought it would be nice to show some appreciation." She stirs the ratatouille, avoiding his gaze. Brandon's silence hangs in the air for a moment before he responds. "Sure." He reaches over her to dip a slice of baguette into the bubbling Dutch oven.

"So . . . you're okay with them staying, even if it goes a little late?" Hayley asks.

"It's fine," Brandon says, his tone clipped. "Probably good to do now and then."

Hayley nods. As she turns, she notices dried blood splattered across the front of his jacket. "God, Brandon. It looks like you murdered someone."

He doesn't respond.

As he disappears upstairs, Hayley exhales heavily. The ease between them that seemed so natural feels like a distant memory.

Hearing a knock at the door half an hour later, Hayley pulls it open to find Megan and Tyler giggling together on the stoop, their cheeks flushed in the chilly evening air.

"What's so funny?" Hayley asks.

"We're just marveling at the fact that all winter long, we'll only have to walk a few yards in the snow to have a dinner party." Megan holds up a bottle of cava. "We brought bubbles!" She gives Hayley a light hug. Tyler follows her inside, carrying a big bowl of salad.

Megan unwinds a scarf from around her neck and shimmies out of her coat. She has clearly dressed up for the night: a soft peasant blouse with a low neckline and layers of necklaces, a suede miniskirt. Handing the bottle to Brandon, she says, "It's nothing fancy. You must have some good vintages in your cellar. I've seen the deliveries."

Brandon nods. "The one thing I got from the big city was a taste for fine wine and spirits."

"You got me too," Hayley says lightly.

"Like I said, a taste for the finer things."

Hayley smiles. Brandon's words may only be a performance for their guests, but she appreciates the gesture.

"Speaking of which, I'll go down and grab a few bottles," Brandon says.

"I'll come with you," says Tyler.

As the guys tromp down the basement stairs, Hayley feels a surge of relief. Brandon's on good behavior. She's gotten so used to his grumpiness—maybe, at least for tonight, she'll be free from that humming concern.

Megan peels the foil off the cava and twists the wire. "The ratatouille smells fabulous."

"Aw, thanks. And you *look* fabulous," Hayley says, taking four wineglasses from the open shelf above the counter and setting them on the island.

"I wanted to dress up, for once." Megan pops the cork and pours two glasses. "Tonight is special. We're always running around in leggings and flannel."

Hayley looks down at her leggings and flannel. "It didn't even occur to me to change."

"Let's go upstairs and fix that."

"But I have to stir the—"

Megan takes Hayley's glass and sets it on the island. The two of them head up to Hayley's bedroom.

In the walk-in closet, Megan rifles through hangers and drawers, pulling out a floral dress, a black sheath, and finally a green velvet jumpsuit with spaghetti straps that Hayley bought on a whim but has never worn.

"That's it," Megan says appreciatively as Hayley twirls. "But you need to lose the bra."

"Really?"

"Trust me."

Hayley lowers the stretchy top, unhooks her bra, and wriggles back into the outfit. Megan turns her around by the shoulders so she can look at herself in the full-length mirror. Standing behind Hayley, Megan slides the ponytail holder out of her hair and fluffs it, letting it cascade over her shoulders. "See?"

Brandon and Tyler are back in the living room when the women descend. Hayley can tell by the look in both men's eyes that Megan was right. She feels loose and sexy, swept up in her friend's stylish vibe.

"Wow," Brandon says. "I've never seen you in that outfit before."

"Doesn't she look gorgeous?" Megan says.

"Uh—yeah." His smile deepens.

"You really do," Tyler says.

The night suddenly feels rife with possibility.

Tyler raises his wineglass, and they all clink.

By the time they move to the table, they're pleasantly buzzed. Hayley brings over her ratatouille and a salad, and Brandon opens two bottles of pinot noir. Settling into her chair, Hayley takes in the candlelit faces around her—Brandon relaxed and charming for a change, Megan rolling her eyes at his hunting tales, Tyler laughing, his arm draped casually across the back of Megan's chair.

After dinner, Brandon suggests a nightcap by the fire. He brings a small unlabeled oak barrel up from the basement, and they all settle in the great room.

"Springbrook Hollow bourbon, made near here. Their reserve batch," he says, pouring amber liquid into cut-crystal glasses.

Hayley takes a sip. A soft burn in the back of her throat spreads downward, leaving a lingering warmth in her chest.

Tyler throws his drink back like a shot of tequila. "Damn. That'll warm your bones."

Megan grabs Hayley's phone off the coffee table. "Let's change the music. What's the password?" She looks at her expectantly.

Only Brandon and Emily know Hayley's password. Hayley hesitates for a moment—is she ready to share it with Megan? Oh, what the hell. She gives it to her.

Megan switches the station to a sultry mix that Hayley recognizes from their yoga practice.

"What do you all say we take this evening to the next level?" Megan pulls a candy bar with a familiar-looking hand-lettered label out of her bag and breaks off three squares of chocolate before passing the bar to Brandon.

He looks at Hayley. "Okay. I'm in." He breaks off three squares for himself.

Hayley raises her eyebrows at Megan. Her usually reserved husband appears to have shed his inhibitions for the evening.

TWENTY-THREE

A lightening of the mood, a softening of the edges: The first effects are subtle. Hayley feels herself starting to trip more quickly than she did before. It must be all the wine and bourbon. The house pulses around her.

The four of them draw closer to each other, sprawling across cushions scattered on the floor.

"Okay," Megan says, "let's have some fun. Truth or Dare?"

Brandon groans. "Oh god. No. Someone always ends up saying too much."

"That's what makes it fun," she insists.

Hayley looks at her husband. "What are you afraid of?"

"I just don't see the point."

Megan leans forward. "The point is to let loose, get to know each other a little better."

"We already know each other," Brandon counters.

Hayley tilts her head. "Maybe you'll learn something new about me," she says.

Brandon sighs. "All right, all right, you win." He raises his hands in surrender.

"Listen," Megan adds, "you can always choose 'dare' if you're worried about revealing too much." With a smile, she pivots to Hayley. "I elect you to go first."

Hayley shrugs. "Ugh. Fine. I choose truth."

Tapping a finger against her lip, Megan studies her with a suddenly sober affect. "Hmm. Okay, so . . . exactly how rich are you?"

Hayley's neck prickles at the audacious question. There's a moment of awkward silence. "Uh—well—"

"Rich enough not to have to answer that," Brandon says, wagging his eyebrows. His silly expression breaks the tension and gets them all laughing again, and the topic is dropped. Hayley feels a surge of gratitude.

The first round continues with a dare for Tyler to execute a backward handspring, which he attempts, and fails, in good humor.

His audience claps.

"Your turn, Brandon," he says. "Truth or dare?"

"After that lame performance, I'm going with truth."

More laughter.

"Bold move," Megan says.

"Okay. What's something you've never told anyone?" Tyler asks.

"Oh. Jeesh." He shakes his head.

Hayley holds her breath. Brandon hates personal questions.

Shadows from the fire play across his face. "Well . . . I guess . . . it's that I'm angry at myself for holding on to a grudge against my dad." He swirls the bourbon in his glass. "I resented him leaving for so long, you know? If I'd been able to forgive him sooner, maybe we could've had more time together. Maybe we could've found a way to reconcile."

All of them, surprised by his sincerity, pause.

Hayley puts her hand on his knee. "I didn't know you felt that way."

"I did ask for something he'd never told anyone," Tyler says.

"And I obliged." Brandon covers her hand with his.

—

Colors seem brighter to Hayley now, more vivid. She sits back against the plush pillows, the warmth from the fire on her face, watching the flames dance and flicker. There's a feeling of camaraderie in the room, a soft glow that expands with each revelation.

Turning to Megan, she says, "Your turn. Truth or dare?"

"Dare."

Hayley hoped she'd say "truth." After Brandon's unexpected candor, she wants to ask Megan a question she hasn't had the courage to raise. "I dare you . . . to tell me the last time you felt jealous."

"Wait, isn't that a truth?" Megan protests.

"I say we allow it," Tyler says. "I want to hear the answer."

With a playful spark in her eye, Megan says, "It's not going to be about you, if that's what you're thinking."

"Damn, woman, you're cold."

She laughs.

"You're stalling, Megan," Hayley says in a singsong.

Megan sighs. "The last time I felt jealous? I mean—look around! I feel jealous right now, of you guys in this crazy beautiful house. But that's no surprise." She taps her lip again and turns to Hayley. "I must admit, seeing you and Emily together made me a little envious too. You have so much history. I felt like I was outside your little circle, looking in."

"Oh," Hayley says. "I'm sorry if I made you feel that way."

Megan shakes her head. "Nah. It's on me, not you."

Maybe it's only the candy bar, but Hayley feels as if the barriers that have divided them are dissolving.

"Okay, Hayley. Your turn," Tyler says.

"Truth."

"Again," Megan chides.

Hayley gives her a wry smile. "Sorry, I'm a scaredy-cat. I don't 'dare.'"

Tyler snaps his fingers. "That's my question, right there. What have you done that scares you most?"

"Um, having this conversation right now?"

"No, I'm serious," he says.

She takes a breath. "I guess . . . it was when I had to identify my sister's body in the morgue."

"Oh man, Hayley," Tyler says.

Brandon gives her a look. "Hayl, that's a lot of—"

"No, it's okay," Megan interrupts. "This is a safe space." She turns to Hayley and takes her hand. "I'm glad you feel comfortable enough to share that with us."

Hayley exhales. She feels exposed, a nerve laid bare. But strangely, she doesn't mind the sensation. "We're back to you, Tyler," she says.

Rubbing his back with a mock grimace, he says, "No circus act this time. Truth."

"Okay." Hayley thinks for a moment. She doesn't know anything about his background. "You asked me a tough question. Here's one for you. What was the hardest thing about your childhood?"

"Ah. Shit." He shakes his head. "I guess . . . I grew up in foster care. It felt like I didn't belong anywhere. Like I could never make real connections because they'd just be ripped away."

"Gosh, Tyler," Hayley says.

His eyes meet hers for a long moment.

"All right, let's shake up this pity party," Brandon says, clapping his hands together. "Megan, truth or dare?"

"It's your turn, not mine."

"I told you," he says, "I'm shaking it up."

"All right. Dare it is."

Brandon grins. "I dare you to start some trouble."

"Brandon!" Hayley says. "What are you doing?"

"She's the one who wanted to play this game," he says.

"All right, then," Megan says, "how's this for trouble? Tyler—I dare you to kiss Brandon."

"Nice," Tyler says. Leaning forward slowly, he locks eyes with Brandon—then turns to Hayley. He gives her a gentle kiss, a brush of the lips, more curious than passionate. She feels the scratch of his evening stubble against her cheek and, with surprise, something more: the pull of attraction. He leans in again and kisses her deeply. She feels herself respond.

"What the fuck?" Brandon scrambles to his feet.

Disoriented, Hayley pulls away.

Tyler raises his hands. "Whoa, buddy."

"Are you trying to fuck with me?"

"Brandon—" Hayley starts.

"Hey, man—I thought you wanted to shake things up," Tyler says. "My bad. I went too far."

"It's just a game, you guys," Megan says.

Brandon stares down at Tyler for a moment, as if he wants to say more. Then he pivots toward the kitchen.

Hayley's shock congeals into embarrassment. She pulls a throw from the couch and wraps it protectively around her shoulders. The slinky green jumpsuit suddenly feels all wrong.

"Shit. I'm sorry." Tyler looks at Hayley. "Brandon just . . ." He shakes his head.

"We're all pretty messed up right now," Hayley says.

Megan perches on the arm of the couch. "I guess Brandon's the possessive type."

Hayley follows Megan's gaze to the kitchen, where Brandon is aggressively scrubbing a pan over the sink. She sighs, feeling tired and a little defensive on his behalf. "He's just . . . Things got out of hand."

Megan gives Hayley a pointed look. "Tyler's right, though. Brandon was being provocative."

Hayley cringes. He was. From her spot on the floor, she can see Brandon's stony face as he stands at the sink. She attempts to rise, feels woozy, and sinks back against the cushions.

"Hey there," Tyler says, catching her and guiding her to sit.

"I have to talk to Brandon." She hears her own voice as if from the other end of a long tunnel. Gripping the coffee table with both hands, she pulls herself up. As she makes her way to the kitchen, she knocks into a side table, and the tall vase of cattails teeters and crashes. Glass shatters across the floor.

"Oh my god." Megan makes her way over to Hayley, sidestepping the mess.

Hayley grasps her friend's shoulder, attempting to steady herself, and sees, in Megan's hand, five words on the glowing screen of her cell phone: The kiss that changed everything.

Hayley squints at Megan, feeling her pulse thud. "What's that?"

Megan lets out a shaky laugh. "Just a text."

"To who?"

"Nobody. Myself." Megan smooths back her hair. Her cheeks are flushed in the dim light.

"'The kiss that changed everything'?" Hayley hears herself echo flatly.

Megan's expression turns momentarily distant. "The whole energy tonight was so . . . interesting. I want to remember every detail."

"Wait a minute." An alarm bell rings through the cotton wool stuffing in Hayley's head. "You're planning to write about tonight?"

Megan rubs the back of her neck. "I don't know. I just had an idea I might want to explore about . . . about how people try to create intimacy and openness. You know, firelight, music. But then everything gets screwed up when you bring in new dynamics midjourney."

New dynamics? Midjourney? What the hell is she talking about? And what does that have to do with "Woods and Wellness"?

"Don't worry," Megan says, pressing gentle fingertips on Hayley's wrist, "no names or anything." With a nod toward Brandon, she adds, "We should get out of your hair so you two can process privately."

Hayley starts to speak, but the movement of Tyler standing up distracts her focus. Ugh. How could she have responded to his kiss like that, with Brandon sitting right there? The whole thing makes her queasy.

Megan bustles around, picking up scattered cattails and stacking them on the table. She makes no move toward the kitchen, where Brandon glowers darkly. "I'll help you finish up tomorrow," she tells Hayley, hustling Tyler toward the door. He gives Hayley a long look over his shoulder as they go.

Hayley watches their outlines blur through the glass as they head across the yard to the cottage. Glancing around, she notes a second bottle of bourbon on the table, nearly empty. She doesn't even remember it being opened. A weariness descends over her, settling in her limbs. She's not going to make sense of any of this tonight. More than anything, she craves the oblivion of sleep.

Leaving Brandon to brood amid soapsuds and broken glass, she stumbles up the stairs.

TWENTY-FOUR

"Wake up, Hayley."

She stirs, emerging from foggy dreams. Brandon is shaking her with a hushed urgency.

The room is dark, with only a faint grayish light coming through the window. Bare branches outside, like bony fingers, reach toward the sky.

As she sits up, the room spins. She sinks back into the bedsheets. "What time is it?" she murmurs. "I can't."

"You need to see this." Brandon is barely visible in the semidarkness. "It's Megan."

With a start, Hayley recalls the giddy good cheer, the drinking, the shrooms, the game. The kiss that changed everything.

"She left her laptop here. She's writing a whole fucking book about you."

Brandon's face glows in the light of the open laptop between his hands. "Insinuating shit about why you're here in Crystal River. Questioning our marriage . . ." His eyes are unreadable shadows. "She's been digging into your past like an investigative reporter."

Hayley stares at him for a moment as the meaning of his words penetrates her groggy mind. Her eyes fall on the headline on the screen:

Heir of Mystery: What Drove Hayley Stone to Vanish into the Wilderness?

As she scans the first paragraph, her chest constricts:

After inheriting millions overnight in the wake of unspeakable tragedy, Hayley Stone fled quickly into marriage with a near stranger and moved to his remote mountain hideaway. Why did she delete her social media and sever all connections to her former life? And her new husband, Brandon—what's his story, and what is he hiding?

Does Hayley truly believe it's possible to leave everything behind? What are the ghosts she's trying to outrun, and what future is she so desperately seeking?

Bitter hurt wells up, soon overtaken by a flare of anger. Megan knows her darkest struggles—the depression that threatened to pull her under after her parents' deaths, the crushing pain of betrayal when her private life was made unbearably public. Yet here she is, weaponizing the moments when Hayley felt most understood by her. Just like Melinda. Just like . . . Olivia Blackwood.

Were Megan's confidences a ruse to dupe Hayley into telling all her secrets? Did Hayley mistake a con job for heartfelt connection?

Some part of her wants to believe there's an explanation that makes sense.

But no. Fuck that. Megan is just like the internet trolls who picked over Jenna's death with morbid fascination. Hayley shared her most intimate feelings, and Megan coldly appropriated them for her own gain.

Trembling and teary, Hayley slams the laptop closed. "She's worse than Olivia Blackwood. Worse than any of them."

Brandon sits quietly with Hayley until her breathing settles. For once, she appreciates his stoicism. She doesn't have to hash out the disaster of last night or the cataclysmic horror of Megan's betrayal. Anyway, no words could reassure her now.

The bleak sky outside the window, with its dull, eerie glow, reflects the emptiness she feels. She falls back into a fitful, restless sleep.

—

A jackhammer pounds behind Hayley's eyes when she awakens several hours later. Rain patters against the windows. Brandon is sleeping soundly beside her. She slides out of bed and dresses quickly in jeans, a sweater, and her slippers. She sweeps up Megan's laptop and softly pads out of the room and down the stairs.

In the kitchen, she makes coffee and unloads the dishwasher. Seeing the cattails piled on the table brings back the chaos of the night before. She sinks onto a stool and pours milk into her steaming mug.

The more she thinks about it, the more furious she is at the violation of her privacy. The more heartbroken at the betrayal by her supposed friend.

She needs an explanation. And she needs it now.

Clutching the laptop to her chest, Hayley crunches across the remnants of broken glass to the front door in her rubber-soled slippers and runs through the cold rain to the cottage. In the distance, tree branches cast spidery shadows across the pond's surface.

She knocks on the door.

Megan opens it. She breaks into a wide smile. "God, I'm so hungover! I just made a pot of Earl Grey. Join me?"

Hayley holds up the laptop.

"Oh yeah, I left that in my 'new office' last night," Megan says in a mockingly self-important voice. "I'm planning to start working there later today."

"Your 'new office'?" Hayley parodies Megan's tone. "You mean the room you conned me into letting you use so you can spy on me?"

Hayley registers Megan's stunned expression. In the silence, Hayley can hear the drip of rainwater from the eaves of the porch.

"What?" Megan says at last.

Hayley thrusts the laptop at her.

Megan stares at it. "I don't—"

"'Heir of Mystery'?"

Megan blanches. "How . . . how did you find that? I haven't opened that file in weeks. What—"

"Brandon showed it to me."

"He went through my computer?"

"I don't know how he found it, but—"

"He couldn't have seen this without digging through my history. He must've been looking for something to get back at me for last night."

"Jesus. That's not what matters here. Has this been your plan from the moment we met?"

"It's not what you think, Hayley."

"You don't know what I think."

"Please let me explain."

Hayley stares at her stonily.

Megan squints into the rain. "Will you come inside, at least? It's gross out there."

"Where's Tyler?"

"Upstairs. Still passed out. He won't hear anything."

Warily, Hayley follows her into the cottage.

Megan sits on the sofa, places her laptop on the coffee table, and gestures toward the rocker near the fireplace.

Hayley perches on a cushioned stool, feeling the distance between them grow. The weight of betrayal is heavy in her chest.

Megan inhales deeply. "Okay. So . . . when I saw you in Anderson's . . . yes, I knew who you were," she says.

Hayley crosses her arms.

"I wanted to meet you, Hayley. I couldn't believe what you'd been through. And that nobody was telling your side of the story."

"You pretended not to know who I was. To get access to me." Hayley's voice is flat, despite the turmoil she feels. A part of her wants to scream, to lash out, but another part is too numb with shock to do more than state the obvious.

"I knew you'd never talk to me any other way."

"You're right, I came here to get away from people like you," Hayley says, bitterness seeping into her tone. The irony isn't lost on her—she'd fled here for sanctuary, only to find herself ensnared once again.

They sit in tense silence, the air between them thick with things unsaid. Hayley feels the heat of her anger rising. How much of their entire friendship has been a lie?

"Was Tyler in on it?" Hayley asks, half dreading the answer.

"I'm the writer." Megan shakes her head. "But Hayley, I swear, I'm not like those assholes on the internet. I think it's criminal that your story is out there being manipulated, and you have no voice."

Hayley digs her thumbs into the upholstery of the stool. "Those people—those trolls—they stole what I had left of my . . . of Jenna." Hayley's voice cracks as she says her sister's name out loud. Her thoughts jump to the endless torrent of hateful online comments.

"I know, it's terrible. People who try to take advantage of grief like that . . . There's this line from *The Choice Conundrum—*"

Something clicks in Hayley's mind. The self-help books they have in common. The "guidebooks."

"Hold on," she says. "You had the same books I did before we even met."

"Oh." Megan winces. She clasps her hands in her lap and gives Hayley an earnest look. "Those books are amazing. They've changed my life. But . . . well, yes, when I was trying to learn more about you, I stumbled on a photo of your work cubicle on the *Sinister Sands* website, with those books lined up on a shelf above your computer. I knew they'd help me understand how you came through that trauma with such courage."

"Olivia fucking Blackwood." Hayley shakes her head, trying to take in the magnitude of Megan's admission. "Unbelievable." Even after all this time, those photos are still haunting her.

Another thought occurs. "And what about that Substack of yours. Is it even real?"

"Of course it's real. I mean, I have a lot of irons in the fire, you know? It's just—I'm not . . . it's not quite there yet."

"Is this some kind of game to you, Megan?" Hayley blurts out. "Because this is my life we're talking about. And I've been screwed over too many times—"

"I know, Hayley. And I know how this looks." Megan searches her eyes. "But I swear, taking advantage of you was never my intention." She leans forward. "I started this project because I genuinely believed I could tell your story with the insight and sensitivity it deserves. The friendship we've developed . . . it's real to me."

Hayley arches an eyebrow.

"I don't know how to convince you I'm being sincere," Megan says. "I know you've been taken advantage of before, and someone in your position . . . well, you're vulnerable. But if I may speak as a journalist for a moment . . ." She pauses, seeming to weigh her words.

Journalist. The word makes Hayley recoil. She drums her fingers against her arm, bracing herself for whatever Megan is about to say.

"I know this might sound rich coming from me," Megan continues slowly, "but I think you might want to take a hard look at your relationship with Brandon." Her tone gains urgency. "He persuaded you to move to a place that's way out of your comfort zone. You're making the best of it, but it isn't easy. And your money is funding this very expensive property." Megan hesitates before continuing. "I just think it might serve you to examine Brandon's motivations. Have you been paying close attention to your finances? Do you feel like you have a handle on where the money is going?"

The rejected credit card, those high bills. A cold, gnawing doubt wells in her chest. Megan has struck a nerve.

But no. Hayley forces herself to refocus. Megan is distracting her from the real issue.

"We're not here to dissect my relationship with Brandon," she says, her voice steady despite the turmoil she feels. "We're here to talk about the book you're writing. How can I believe anything you say when you've been hiding this from me all along?"

"I know I'll have to earn your trust back." Megan reaches for Hayley's hand.

Hayley pulls it away.

"Are you going to kick us out?" Megan asks, her voice low.

Hayley sighs. "Maybe. I don't know." The words sound cold, foreign to her ears, as if spoken by someone else.

"What can I do to make this right, Hayley? I'll do anything. Anything at all."

"You have no idea what my life was like," Hayley says. "I changed my number three times." She locks eyes with Megan. "I gave you my phone password last night. Now I have to change that."

"It was just for the playlist. I'm not—"

Hayley breaks in. "I ignored shit like that in the past because I was too trusting. I told you about Melinda—she went to CrimeHive with my wedding photos. Olivia Blackwood got half a million followers because of my family's tragedy. She tracked me everywhere. She even found us up here and tried to get to me through Brandon."

"I know. It's disgusting. The trolls who hounded you twisted the facts for their own agendas. But Hayley . . . that's not what I'm doing."

"Oh, sure."

"Please—change your passwords. Do anything you need to feel safe. But I'm not a threat, I promise."

"I'm supposed to believe that you're not going to use what you know about me?"

"I won't. I don't want to use you, Hayley. Please, hear me out." Megan leans forward. "The more I've learned about you, the more I think you're a fucking goddess. I mean, look at what you've survived. If you take control, you neutralize them. I think you should answer those shitty, invasive questions with your absolute truth."

Hayley is silent for a long moment, mulling over what Megan is saying.

"Tell your own story, Hayley. Let me help you. I know we haven't known each other that long, but think about how much we've shared in a short period of time. You've become my closest friend." Hayley studies Megan's face, searching for any flicker of deception.

Megan continues. "I've never known what it's like to have a sister, Hayley. If it's not too presumptuous to say this, now I feel like I do. And it means everything to me."

Sister.

Hayley stops short. Everything she longs for seems contained in that one word.

She feels herself waver. She remembers how isolated she felt before she arrived on the property.

Megan, seeming to sense her roiling doubt, reaches for her hand again. This time, Hayley allows her to take it. "Please, Hayley. You've become closer to me than my own family. Haven't we all made mistakes that require grace?"

Hayley would give anything to ask Jenna for grace now. How she wishes she could sit down with her and apologize for being so self-centered when she left for college that she thought only about her own future. How she wishes she could tell her that she regrets leaving her behind.

But Megan isn't Jenna. And Hayley isn't ready to forgive her.

She disentangles her fingers from Megan's. "I can't."

TWENTY-FIVE

When Hayley gets back to the house, Brandon is at the kitchen island, drinking coffee and scrolling through his phone. He glances up. "Where were you?"

"Megan's."

"Did you confront her? How'd she respond?"

Hayley pours herself a fresh cup. "I went through the whole thing with her. She apologized."

Brandon scoffs. "And you believe her?"

"I need to think it through."

"What's left to think about? She's a user and a liar."

Hayley shakes her head. She doesn't want to get into this with him right now.

After Brandon leaves the house, she sits alone at the kitchen island, letting the silence settle around her. She takes a sip of coffee. The confrontation with Megan replays itself in her mind, every word and gesture. Even if Megan is genuine in wanting to convey Hayley's absolute truth, her deception is hard to swallow. What's the riskier move here: To trust that Megan is being sincere, or to assume that she isn't?

She should tell Megan to leave, to never set foot on the property again. It seems like the logical next step. But a quieter, more cautious voice in her head whispers that she doesn't have all the information she needs.

She may or may not ever trust Megan again. Yet, despite her anger and sense of betrayal, Hayley can't dismiss everything she said. Megan's hard questions about Brandon have gotten under her skin.

Hayley finds herself connecting dots she hadn't seen before—a half lie here, an omission there. She feels a growing urgency to peel back the layers of her husband's carefully constructed story and learn what lies beneath.

It's later that afternoon. Hayley makes her way across the yard to the shed, where Brandon stores their firewood. She wants to bring some logs onto the porch, under the overhang, to keep them near. Blowing foggy breath into the gloom, she works quickly, back and forth, stacking logs under the eaves and returning to the pile for more. By the time she finishes moving all the wood she can manage alone, the sky is dark.

With her arms laden awkwardly with split oak and kindling, she elbows the front door open and kicks off her boots, then goes straight to the hearth, where she dumps the logs on the slate surround. She puts on her slippers and kneels at the hearth to build a fire. As recently as a month ago, the thought of doing this would have paralyzed her. Now she works quickly. After cleaning the old ashes from the previous fire with a small brush and shovel, she selects two of the driest oak logs and places them on the bottom. Over this base she constructs a lattice of kindling, laying smaller sticks perpendicular across the logs and adding another layer crosswise. She tucks dried leaves from a bucket between the lattice as tinder. With everything in place, she lights the tinder in several places to ensure an even spread.

The flames in the hearth settle into a warm glow as the room fills with the scent of burning oak. She inhales, her chest rising freely, unburdened by the old familiar knot of panic. Dusting off her hands, Hayley stands, observing the fire with satisfaction. She's proud of herself—not just for mastering the skill but for facing what once terrified her.

The flames are licking upward, beginning to char the logs, when she hears a knock at the front door. Now what?

She pads over and cracks open the door.

It's Tyler. Ugh. He's the last person she wants to see right now.

He shifts from side to side in the doorway. "Got a minute?"

Her instinct is to say no, to plead exhaustion, to tell him to go away. But the look on his face gives her pause. She pulls the door wider.

He steps inside, boots scuffing the floor.

"What's going on?" she asks.

"Megan left."

"What?"

"Yeah. I was out doing errands, and when I came back, she was gone."

"Are you sure—"

"She packed Ursula with all her stuff. Didn't even leave a note."

"Oh my god."

"It's my fault." Tyler begins to pace the floor, raking his hands through his unruly hair. "After you left the cottage this morning, I told her that writing a book about you behind your back is a shitty way to treat a friend."

"You heard us?"

"The cottage isn't that big." He stops pacing and looks at her. "I had to say something. It wasn't right. Even so, I didn't think . . ." He shakes his head. "In all honesty, she was also mad about last night. About the kiss. She said it seemed too real. That I seemed way into it. Into . . . you."

"Oh, Tyler. I think we were all just—"

"I told her she was imagining things, but she wouldn't listen. Remember when she was talking about how jealous she is of you? I think she just couldn't handle it."

An excruciating beat of silence passes. Everything in her life feels tenuous. Her marriage is unstable. Her new friendship has fractured. And now this.

She touches Tyler's arm. "I'm sorry. This really sucks."

Tyler steps closer and puts his hand over hers.

"No fucking way." Brandon stands in the doorway, shock etched across his features as he takes in the scene.

Oh god. This looks bad. Hayley moves quickly away, her mind searching for an explanation that won't sound like a lie.

Tyler clears his throat. "I should go," he mumbles, edging toward the door.

Brandon's eyes follow him. "Yeah, you should."

As Tyler slips out, Brandon turns to Hayley. "Wanna explain what I just walked in on?"

"Megan left," Hayley says. Brandon narrows his eyes.

She tries to keep her voice calm. "I understand why you might be upset, but you're jumping to conclusions. It's not what you think. I was just comforting him."

"Like how he 'comforted' you with that kiss last night?"

"Nothing is going on between me and Tyler," Hayley says. "That was a game."

Brandon's eyes remain wary.

"Please don't make this into something it's not. We have enough real problems to deal with." She takes a breath, trying to still the emotions churning inside her. "I mean, I can't believe Megan left without a word. We had that hard conversation this morning, but nothing she said made me think she was going to pick up and go." Hayley hesitates. She needs to steer them back to the heart of the matter that's been gnawing at her. She presses on. "Listen, Brandon. She said something . . . about you. About us, really."

Brandon tenses. "Oh?"

"She said I shouldn't trust you. That you're using me. For my money."

"She said *what*?"

"I know it sounds crazy—"

"It doesn't sound crazy, it is crazy," Brandon interrupts, his voice rising. "And you believed her, didn't you?"

Hayley feels her own frustration growing. "I didn't say I believed her. I'm telling you because I thought you should know."

Brandon lets out a sarcastic laugh. "Know what? That your so-called friend is a shit-stirrer? That she's trying to come between us?"

"I'm just trying to have an honest conversation with you."

Brandon's voice is thick with disdain. "An honest conversation? Based on what? The words of a woman who's been lying to you for months?"

Irritation twangs in Hayley's throat. But she swallows it down. "You know," she says, low and steady, "maybe Megan was right to question things. Because the way you're reacting right now? It's making me question everything too."

Brandon gives her a cold smile. "Come on, Hayley. You can't be this gullible. The woman is writing a book about you. Wake the fuck up."

—

Later that night, lying in bed, Hayley shifts uneasily under the comforter. Beside her, Brandon sleeps with his back turned, keeping his distance. His last words to her earlier were "Good riddance to Megan. I'm glad she's gone," before he made a plate of leftovers and took it to the den.

Now, still sleeping, he rolls onto his back. As she studies his profile, etched silver in the moonlight, questions swirl in her mind, each more disturbing than the last. She's caught between two untrustworthy narratives, unsure where the truth lies. Brandon's defensive anger over Megan's accusation does nothing to ease Hayley's doubts—if anything, it only intensifies them. What is he so defensive about? What is he hiding?

He isn't wrong, though, about Megan's manipulative streak: Her secret book project is a glaring betrayal. And her sudden, silent departure raises all kinds of red flags. If their conversation this morning was genuine, why hasn't Megan sent a single text to explain her abrupt exit? Why would she vanish without a word?

Hayley throws off the comforter. Her friendship with Megan might survive, or it might not. But this is her marriage. And its foundation feels increasingly unstable.

She rises and treads barefoot across the floor to the window. Gazing out at the field and woods that surround the house, she thinks back to Emily confronting her about living Brandon's dream, not her own. If that's true—if she reacted to the loss of her parents and sister by subsuming herself in her husband's fantasy—then maybe it's possible he's been doing the same with her. Playing house with Hayley in an attempt to banish his own ghosts.

Who knows. Maybe both of them have been hiding from their true selves.

She and Brandon need a reset. When she invited Megan and Tyler to live in the guest cottage, she'd envisioned their presence as something that would deepen her connection to this place Brandon loved so much. Instead, they became a distraction.

It's too destabilizing, now, to have Tyler, without Megan, living in the cottage next door.

Tyler has to go.

TWENTY-SIX

A ping from Hayley's phone wakes her in the early-morning gloom.

Megan?

She rolls over to squint at the too-bright screen:

NEWS ALERT: Crystal River Herald

Winter Storm Warning in Effect

Sudden weather shift expected, temperatures set to plummet. Freezing temperatures by late afternoon, with heavy snow forecast by nightfall. Take precautions.

She drops her phone onto the sheets. Despite her resolve to start making changes today, she knows that living in nature means living on nature's schedule. She can't exactly kick Tyler out right before a winter storm. What does she expect him to do, freeze to death in his truck? But she can make it clear that he'll need to ride out the storm alone at the cottage.

From the other side of the bed, Brandon stirs. "It's early," he mumbles without rolling over. "Go back to sleep."

"There's a big storm heading this way."

He turns toward her. "*Farmers' Almanac* says we have another week. The radar confirmed it."

"Well, the radar changed." She shows him the alert on her phone. "Do we have enough supplies? What if we lose power?"

Brandon sighs. "I'm up," he says, throwing off the covers.

After a quick shower, Hayley heads to the kitchen. Brandon isn't far behind. As he comes down the stairs, he's already talking about checking the smokehouse, cutting more firewood, securing tarps over the composting beds.

She starts cutting up vegetables for a pot of chicken soup and puts on some water to boil. She'll make beef lasagna later. Brandon's plan is to switch to the wild game he's been curing in the smokehouse once winter isolates them from the rest of the world. She might as well cook with conventional proteins from a civilized market while she can.

Over the pot of simmering soup, she watches clouds out the window chase each other across the mottled sky. She's surprised to see Tyler with Brandon at the woodpile, both of them chopping and stacking firewood. Given everything that's happened over the last twenty-four hours, she assumed they'd keep their distance. Maybe the impending storm is a useful excuse to put their conflict on hold. Watching them work without apparent animosity, she feels a twinge in her chest. Despite everything, she wishes Megan were here with her now, chatting and laughing as they prep for the storm together.

Hayley glances at her watch. It's 10 a.m. The farmers' market will be open for another couple of hours. She can stock up on fresh bread and more vegetables before the storm hits. It occurs to her that while she's there, it might be useful to have another conversation with Cheryl Snyder. As querulous and eccentric as she is, Cheryl knows the history here. And she isn't afraid to speak her mind.

As she steps out of the Jeep, Hayley winds a gray wool scarf around her neck. Despite the gathering clouds, the Crystal River Farmers' Market glows with pre-Thanksgiving cheer. String lights sparkle around stands piled high with pumpkins and gourds; vendors call out prestorm specials to passing shoppers. A flock of geese appears overhead, flying in ragged formation.

The wind is picking up. Shivering, Hayley burrows into her scarf and wraps her coat tighter around her as she makes her way past couples holding hands and parents pushing strollers.

After procuring her supplies, Hayley walks over to Cheryl's booth, where she is presiding over her pies, ever-present flask in hand. As Hayley approaches, Cheryl takes a long swig and rearranges the pies on her table, filling gaps.

"Morning," Hayley says, mustering a friendly expression. "Do you have a moment to chat?"

Cheryl screws the cap back on her flask and tucks it into her coat pocket. She flips the sign on her stand from Open to Closed. "Sure, you can buy me a doughnut."

They begin a slow circuit through garlands of corn and fading mums. Cheryl directs Hayley to a stand selling homemade pastries and selects a bag of maple sugar doughnuts. "Yum, still warm," she says, patting the bag in her arms while Hayley pays the vendor.

As they continue their stroll, Cheryl opens the bag and holds up a doughnut. "Want one?"

"I'm good." Hayley clears her throat. She isn't sure how to start.

Cheryl takes a big bite and gives her a sideways glance. "So what's up, buttercup?"

"I'm trying to understand more about Brandon's family history."

"Oh yeah?"

"Yeah." Hayley hunches deeper in her coat. "I read the police report about your husband's death."

Cheryl stops. She pulls the flask back out of her pocket and takes a long drink.

Rubbing her cold arms, Hayley asks, "Can you tell me a little more about what happened?"

Cheryl leads them toward a grove of picnic tables and motions for Hayley to sit on a bench across from her. "What do you know?"

"Only that your husband died after saving my husband's life."

Cheryl nods. "Tragic story, isn't it?"

"It is."

"But it's not the whole story," she says abruptly. "Rick was carrying on with Brandon's mother. Had been for years, right under his father's nose."

Wait—Brandon's mother was sleeping with Cheryl's husband?

Hayley feels her understanding of the situation slowly recalibrate, adjusting to this new information. Brandon has always spoken as if his father abandoned the family for no reason. "So . . ."

Cheryl steams ahead. "It was December. There'd been a bad storm the night before. Rick stayed over in the cottage when the weather made it too dangerous to drive—that was his excuse, at least. Convenient, eh? I was a dupe back then. So anyway, Brandon caught them in the act over there and lost it. He sat in his mother's car with a fifth of Jim Beam from his dad's stash. Drank himself stupid sitting in the driveway, then got the bright idea he was gonna peel out of there and never come back.

"Idiot kid couldn't handle the black ice, though. The car hydroplaned down the driveway, and Rick came out to save the day. Next thing you know, my husband is trapped underneath. There was no saving him. He lasted a week in the ICU before his body finally quit." Her voice hardens. "Brandon's dad got a slick city lawyer. Came up with some argument about the car being on their own property, and the DUI just disappeared. No charges filed."

Shock steals Hayley's breath. She presses a hand to her mouth.

"No damages, no accountability." Cheryl spits the words out like a curse. "Your husband killed Rick, and I got nothing."

"It was a terrible accident," Hayley says.

"'Accident,'" Cheryl snorts. "I don't think so."

"What do you mean?"

"Brandon didn't even try to stop that car," Cheryl says, leaning closer.

Hayley fights the urge to pull back from her boozy breath. "Before he died, Rick told me he could see the rage in that boy's eyes, even as the car spun out of control. Your husband wanted my Rick dead."

Hayley pictures Brandon, drunk and furious at his mother's betrayal, impulsively gunning the engine.

It's not impossible to imagine.

On the other hand . . . maybe it was an accident. Cheryl isn't the most reliable of narrators.

"They left town right away?"

Cheryl studies her with calculation. "How could they live together after that? All three were ghosts of their former selves, I reckon. Brandon's dad stuck the 'for lease' sign up as soon as the ground thawed. By summer, he'd filed for divorce. Brandon and his mother disappeared to Florida. The whole mess buried, neat and tidy. 'A terrible accident.' And I'm left to pick up the pieces."

Cheryl's voice wobbles before she steadies it again with liquor. "Old ghosts linger if you don't face them. Brandon's got a lot to answer for, even now." Rising abruptly, she says, "Well, thanks for the doughnuts. I best be getting to my booth." She pauses, then turns back with a sardonic smile. "I hope you'll still enjoy your little slice of paradise up there, now that you know what really happened."

As she heads to her car in the deepening cold, Hayley feels the wind nipping her neck and realizes she must've dropped her scarf. Shit. She gets in behind the wheel, too drained to return to hunt for it. After snapping on her seat belt and cranking the heat, she pulls out her phone. She's got to tell Emily what she's learned—after all, she's the one who discovered the police report. Even though Cheryl's story will confirm Emily's worst suspicions about Brandon.

Lots going on here, Hayley texts. Is this a good time?

Almost immediately, three bobbing dots appear. Then: Hi! Almost out of range. Sorry I can't talk! Luv ya!

Luv ya? Hayley sits back in her seat. The goofy slang is so unlike Emily.

Or is it? What does she really know about anyone anymore?

Hayley resorts to their fallback: multiple heart emojis.

Emily doesn't respond.

TWENTY-SEVEN

Hayley pulls up to the house. Clouds hang low over the mountains, casting slanting shadows across the driveway. She parks the Jeep in the garage, gathers her groceries, and heads inside. As she steps into the kitchen, she glances out the window. Brandon and Tyler are still at it, stacks of split wood now piled high.

She turns the burner back on beneath the pot of soup, her mind replaying Cheryl's story in fragmented pieces. Whether or not Cheryl's version is entirely truthful, Hayley can't ignore how disturbing the revelations are. There's a deeper layer of pain and violence in Brandon's past than he's ever shared.

Hayley unties her apron and heads back out into the bracing wind. Brandon nods as she approaches, meeting her eye.

"Can I talk to you?" She glances at Tyler. "Privately?"

Brandon swipes an arm across his sweat-damp brow. "I'll be in soon."

Just at that moment, they all turn at the scrape of tires on gravel as Cheryl's battered truck pulls up.

"What the hell is she doing here?" Brandon says.

Cheryl cuts the engine and emerges, swaying slightly as she slides out. Even from a distance, Hayley can see her bloodshot eyes.

Ambling toward them, Cheryl clutches what Hayley recognizes is her own gray wool scarf.

"Missing something?" Cheryl holds it up. "Reckon you'll be needing this." With a careless flick she sends the scarf sailing sideways to land at Hayley's feet. Turning to Brandon, she says, "Your wife and I had quite a chat. As I'm sure you've heard."

Shit. The last thing Hayley needs is Cheryl confronting her husband before she's talked to him herself.

Brandon shoots Hayley a questioning look.

She shakes her head. Bending to retrieve the scarf, she wraps it around her neck and says, "Thanks, Cheryl, but you really shouldn't be out with the storm coming! I'll walk you back to—"

Cheryl waves a dismissive hand. Her focus swings to Tyler. "Who's this?"

"Uh . . ." Tyler, holding an armful of logs, looks alarmed to have been roped in. "Just helping out."

"Well, you be careful. Funny things happen to the help around here."

Brandon's brow furrows.

"I'm interested in why you never told your bride what happened." Cheryl glares at him.

His face darkens. "Hayley's right. You should get home before the storm hits."

Cheryl barks a laugh. "I appreciate your concern for my safety. It's rich, coming from the punk who wrecked my life." She sways, leaning against a stack of firewood to steady herself. Turning to Hayley, she says, "Why don't you ask him what he did to my husband? I'd love to hear his answer."

Hayley holds up her hands. "Please, let's all just take a beat. I think—"

Cheryl shrugs her off. "Don't you try to shut me up." Pointing an accusing finger at Brandon, she says, "And don't you tell me for a second you didn't want my Rick dead."

Brandon shoves his hands into his pockets. Hayley can hear his keys rattle. "You're drunk," he says. "I want you off my property."

Tyler chooses this moment to heave the logs in his arms onto the stack with a clatter.

Cheryl wheels around at the noise. She narrows her eyes, staring straight at him. "And what the hell is up with you? You better hope history doesn't repeat itself. Or has it already?" She turns on Hayley. "He's a looker! Did Brandon marry a woman just like his mommy? Faking it in the fancy house so hubby won't guess she's banging the help in the cottage?"

Hayley's legs are about to give out from under her.

Tyler is frozen in place.

Turning back to Brandon, Cheryl says, "I may not know everything, but I know trouble when I see it. And that boy?" She points to Tyler. "He's got his eyes set on something. Or someone." Her words are slurred from alcohol, but her eyes are sharp with malice.

Brandon pulls his hands from his pockets and grabs Cheryl's arm. "That's enough. I'm taking you to your truck."

Cheryl tries to twist from his grip. "Get off me!" Her voice rises to a shout. Holding her firmly, Brandon steers her toward her pickup as she attempts to claw at his face.

"What else are you hiding from her?" Cheryl shrieks. "Does she know what happened in Florida?"

Reaching the truck, Brandon hauls open the door.

"The Coyote Kid," Cheryl spits. "How'd ya feel when you found one of your old friends in the yard? Did my little gift make you nervous?"

Hayley feels a sudden tightness grip her chest.

Cheryl was the one who left the coyote.

"Jesus Christ, Cheryl," Brandon says. "You're a fucking lunatic."

She jabs a finger at him. "I suffered for twenty years, Brandon. Alone. Then you show up out of nowhere, acting like you're the star of the show. Ripping open old wounds. I needed you to see what you did to me. To feel the pain you left behind."

With a final shove, Brandon maneuvers Cheryl behind the wheel. "We're done here," he snaps before slamming the door.

The pickup engine revs to life. Pebbles fly as Cheryl throws the truck into gear before rumbling backward down the driveway.

"It's not safe for her to drive like that," Hayley insists. "We should—"

Brandon, fists clenched, doesn't budge. "She's a cockroach. She'll be fine." Shaking his head, he adds, "Unfortunately."

—

Back in the kitchen, Hayley braces her hands on the island. She draws slow breaths as she lets her body warm up, absorbing the impact of what just happened.

What kind of person would kill and gut a coyote and leave it on your property? It isn't just the act itself that's so unsettling; it's the message behind it. The dark, twisted echo of Brandon's nickname.

Cheryl is a damaged soul. And she's clearly unhinged. But she got under Brandon's skin. Though she had no idea what was going on between Brandon and Tyler, she instinctively grasped the tension between them. She zeroed in on the fact that Brandon feels threatened. Her goal was simple—to rattle Brandon, to make him doubt his standing with Hayley—and she succeeded.

And what was she insinuating about Brandon's life in Florida?

Hayley can't stop thinking about Cheryl's slurred indictment:

What else are you hiding from her? What else, what else, what else . . .

A blast of cold air startles Hayley from her reverie. She turns to see Brandon in the doorway, brushing a few snowflakes off his coat. Hayley takes in his pale face and haunted eyes, the slight shake of his head that means he doesn't want to talk. In the fraught silence, she goes over to the range and stirs the soup. It occurs to her that the storm might present an opportunity.

Once they're prepped for the weather and hunkered down, she and Brandon can take all the time they need to talk while the world grows white and quiet outside their door. Cry if they have to. Yell if they must.

She ladles hearty helpings into two wide bowls and places them on the island. Neither of them speaks, aside from murmured requests to pass the water pitcher, the bowl of salt, the pepper grinder. Outside, wind rattles the eaves, filling the charged space between them.

—

When they push back their empty bowls, Hayley meets Brandon's gaze.

"I know there's still a lot to do before the storm hits," she begins shakily. "But when the work is done, you and I are going to talk. And I mean really talk. I want to know everything that happened here the day Rick Snyder died."

"Hayley, I—"

She puts up her hand. "Wait. I'm not done." Has she ever cut him off midsentence before? "And I need to know what Cheryl meant about Florida."

A rap at the door jolts them both. Once again, it's Tyler, peering through the glass.

"Done with the wood," he announces as he enters, shaking off snowflakes. "What's next?" His eyes flicker between them as he absorbs the tension in the room. "That was some weird shit, right?"

Brandon shakes his head and stands up. "C'mon," he says brusquely to Tyler. "We can get a supply run in before the roads become impassable. Let's take separate cars—divide and conquer."

He leaves without looking Hayley in the eye.

Through the window, Hayley watches the two men walk to the driveway. Behind the tall pines, the sun has begun its rapid descent. Wind launches brittle leaves across the frozen grass like spiky ghosts.

Brandon and Tyler drive off, disappearing into the gloom.

TWENTY-EIGHT

As Hayley loads the dishwasher, her thoughts drift to Emily, out there on the trail with the storm closing in. Hayley tells herself not to worry—Em assured her that Trailblazers has storm protocols in place. Still—a little confirmation wouldn't hurt.

She texts her friend: Assume you made it to a shelter. Get in touch when you can.

Setting the phone aside, Hayley pulls out the ingredients for lasagna, trying to focus on the rhythm of chopping and assembling.

Half an hour later, as she's sliding the pan into the oven, Hayley hears a muted ping and reaches into the back pocket of her jeans for her phone. Em? She glances at the screen. No. Another news alert. She focuses:

NEWS ALERT: Crystal River Herald

Local Resident Fatally Injured in Orchard Accident

Cheryl Snyder, 66, Dies Following a Fall from a Ladder

"What the fuck . . . ?" Hayley whispers aloud in the empty room. The news is surreal. Impossible. She clicks through to the story, pulse racing. The local police were conducting safety checks on the community's older residents in advance of the storm when they discovered Cheryl's body in her orchard.

Cheryl—here just hours ago, unloading fury and recriminations—now dead from a fall?

With shaking fingers, Hayley pulls up her message thread with Brandon.

You won't believe this, she types. Cheryl is dead.

Brandon's reply is immediate. Car accident?

Fell off a ladder. Wtf.

She stares at the screen, trying to absorb the information. After several long moments, she sees Brandon's dancing dots.

Yeah wtf. Then On my way. Home in half an hour.

Hayley sets down the phone. Emotions whir through her—disbelief and sorrow at Cheryl's sad end mingled with what she has to admit is a twinge of relief. Cheryl is out of their lives. Not that Hayley wished anything bad would actually happen to the woman . . .

Though Brandon did.

He said so out loud.

She shakes herself. Stop it, Hayley. Wishing something can't make it so.

Did Brandon only wish it? Or did he . . . ?

The dead coyote. Cheryl threatened him. He felt cornered.

No, she chastises herself. This is madness.

God, she wishes she could talk to Emily. She longs for her insight. Emily met Cheryl; she'd understand the enormity of this news. She might not be a fan of Brandon's, but surely she wouldn't believe he's capable of . . .

Does this qualify as an emergency? Hayley picks up her phone.

It rings in her hand, startling her.

Caller Unknown.

Ordinarily, she'd never pick up. But maybe Emily is calling from a shelter with a landline, or from someone else's phone.

"Em?"

"Hello. Am I speaking to Hayley Stone?"

The voice is unfamiliar. She tenses. "Who is this?"

"Hayley, it's Olivia Blackwood."

Hayley's world narrows to a pinpoint.

Olivia Blackwood—the name is a physical blow. Then she remembers: the deadline for a written response to the cease-and-desist letter she sent is tomorrow.

"Legal forwarded your letter." The woman's tone is measured. "I thought I should just pick up the phone."

"Why? I think it was pretty clear."

Olivia sighs. "Despite what you think, I'm not your enemy, Hayley."

Hayley feels herself flush with anger. "Yes, you are."

"If you cooperate with me instead of treating me like a criminal, we'll get a lot further."

"That's bullshit," Hayley spits out. "You're a muckraker with the morals of a snail. I'm the victim here."

For a moment, Olivia is silent. Then she says, gently, "You're right. You are the victim here."

"I am. And you exploited me."

"It's my job, Hayley. Not a personal vendetta. True crime podcasts aren't going away, no matter how much you wish they would. But woman to woman, I want to say . . . I have a lot of empathy for you."

Hayley gives a short laugh. "If you care about me so much, why did you call my husband after all this time?"

"What?" Olivia says, sounding genuinely confused. "I never called your husband."

"There were five messages on his phone from a Florida number. He said they came from you."

There's a pause on the other end of the line. When Olivia speaks, her voice is serious. "Hayley, he's lying."

She feels her chest tighten. "I don't believe you."

"I'm calling you, Hayley. I'm trying to make amends. To explain. Why would I make this up?"

Hayley pauses, gathering her thoughts. She's played this moment in her head for two years: the opportunity to tell Olivia Blackwood what she really thinks.

"I get it, Olivia," she begins. "You have a popular podcast. You need to feed the beast. But I need to say this. It's one thing to take this whole story and blow it up, with all of its sordid details. But you did something worse—you told the world that my sister was an addict and connected her drug use with the fire that caused my parents' death. I hate you for that."

There's a long pause. When Olivia speaks, her voice is gentle but firm. "I'm not responsible for your sister's actions. I'm really sorry, but it's not my fault."

Hayley feels drained, her anger giving way to a deep, aching sadness.

"The truth is important," Olivia says. "Even when it hurts."

Tears well in Hayley's eyes. The podcast, the public scrutiny, the relentless speculation about her family's tragedies—it all comes rushing back. Part of her wants to scream, to hurl the phone across the room. But another part, a quieter, more insistent voice, whispers that this might be her chance for answers. "Then tell me the truth. Which of my sister's asshole friends told you that she was an addict? I really want to know."

"Why, Hayley? How will it make anything any different?"

"Because I'm sick of all the secrets and lies."

A heavy silence fills the void between them. Finally, Olivia sighs. "Okay. Well . . . I got a hotline tip from an anonymous source. We only interacted through email, and I didn't ask their real name."

"And you just ran with that? Without verifying?"

"We did our due diligence. The information checked out with other sources."

"What was the email address?"

"I can't disclose that." Olivia pauses again, then adds, "But I'll never forget the name they used. It was . . . distinctive."

Hayley holds her breath, waiting.

"They called themselves the Coyote Kid."

TWENTY-NINE

The Coyote Kid.

Brandon.

Hayley is reeling, unable to process her husband's betrayal.

A cold, hollow feeling spreads through her chest as the implications sink in. The man she married, the one she'd run to for comfort and a fresh start, was the architect of her pain all along.

Everything she thought she knew about him, about their relationship, crumbles in an instant.

How could he? Why would he?

A tangle of emotions—rage, disbelief, heartbreak—threatens to overwhelm her. She's dizzy, as if the ground beneath her feet has suddenly given way.

The knowledge she was so desperate to uncover now feels like poison in her veins.

A shard of truth lodges itself in Hayley's mind: Megan warned her about Brandon. Now, amid the barrage of revelations, it's Megan's insight she craves. Megan would truly grasp the magnitude of his deception.

With trembling fingers, Hayley types out a message: You were right about Brandon. He's been lying since day one. He was Olivia Blackwood's source. I'm shattered.

She hits Send.

Hayley hasn't heard from Megan since she left. Will she even respond? She stares at the screen, willing it to light up.

Nothing.

Hayley can't wait any longer. She needs to talk to someone, to share this burden before it crushes her. The ghosts Cheryl talked about seem to have seeped into the very floorboards below her feet.

Emily. That's who she needs right now.

Hayley taps in the override code Emily gave her to use in case of an emergency and puts the phone on speaker. The line rings once.

Twice. Three times.

Four times, five . . .

Ice, ice, baby . . . duh nuh nuh nuh-nuh-nuh-nuh . . .

Hayley hears faint music trickling into the living room from seemingly nowhere. She strains to hear the tinny melody. It only just pierces the sound of the crackling flames in the hearth, coming in a beat behind the ringing on her phone.

Ice, ice, baby . . . duh nuh nuh nuh-nuh-nuh-nuh . . .

Strange. Hayley hits End Call just as Emily's voicemail picks up. Even then, the faint singsong continues, wafting eerily through the air as if on a delayed echo.

Why does Emily's ringtone sound like it's reverberating from somewhere?

Hayley stares at her phone for a moment. Then she turns the speaker off and hits Redial.

She picks up the phone. It rings in her ear.

The distant opening tune chimes once more. *Ice, ice, baby . . . duh nuh nuh nuh-nuh-nuh-nuh . . .*

Emily's ringtone is coming from inside the house.

THIRTY

With mounting panic, Hayley calls Emily's number again, straining to pinpoint the location of the tune.

Ice, ice, baby . . .

It's upstairs.

Instinct kicks in now. She jumps up and goes to the kitchen. She grabs the knife Brandon gave her as a birthday present from its storage block on the counter. Clenching the cool metal handle, she races up the stairs, past snow swirling outside the floor-to-ceiling windows.

She pauses on the upstairs landing and presses Call again.

Ice, ice, baby . . . duh nuh nuh nuh-nuh-nuh-nuh . . .

It's coming from their bedroom.

She rushes into the room, following the ringtone to Brandon's bedside table, and opens the drawer.

There it is. Emily's phone in its familiar case: the *Trailblazer* logo with blue hands cradling an orange flame.

Hayley picks up the phone. It turns on with a touch. Strange—the battery has full power.

She taps in Emily's password and opens her messages.

Hi! Almost out of range! Sorry I can't talk! Luv ya!

Luv ya!

She knew it. After a decade of texting, Emily's voice is as familiar to her as her own.

This isn't it.

Emily didn't write that text. She didn't have her phone.

Hayley's knees buckle, and she sinks to the floor beside the bed.

How many times can reality crash into her before she runs out of ways to deny it? She has tried so hard to dismiss her qualms, lean on her mantras, talk herself out of her reservations and suspicions, ignore the red flags. *It's my trauma,* she told herself. *I'm reading signs where there are none.*

The truth settles in her bones. Cheryl's dead. Emily's gone. And here's her phone, hidden in Brandon's drawer.

The real danger was never fire or coyotes. It was her husband, lying beside her in bed every night.

Hayley had believed that she and Brandon just needed a reset, time to relearn each other in this new life. But now? Emily was right. Hayley refused to listen. And now all she can think—hope against hope—is that Emily is out there somewhere. That she's okay. "Please," she whispers in a desperate prayer to the universe, or nature, or a spirit guide, "let her be alive."

Oh god, Brandon. What have you done?

Suddenly Hayley is seized with fear. She has to get off this remote property before her husband comes home. She runs to her closet and tosses clothes into a duffel bag, burying Emily's phone in the folds of her sweaters. Her hands tremble as she zips up the bag.

Back in the bedroom, peering out the large windows at the thickening curtain of snow, she realizes that the parking space is empty.

Fuck, she forgot. Brandon has the Jeep.

She pulls her own phone from her back pocket and holds it up to her face. The phone vibrates, rejecting her. She tries again, willing her features to compose themselves. Damn it. Her own device doesn't recognize her. The face staring back from the mirrored surface is a stranger's—eyes wide, skin pale, features distorted by fear and disbelief.

Twice, with fumbling fingers, she tries to enter her password before successfully unlocking it.

She opens the Uber app and types in the address of a Holiday Inn Express on the outskirts of town. An alert pops up: Winter storm warning in effect. Service temporarily suspended.

She shoves the useless device back into her jeans. Tears stream down her cheeks. She has always hated this godforsaken house. She was right to. Did Brandon know all along that one day she would be trapped here? Was it part of his plan somehow?

Outside, a flash of light, barely visible in the storm, catches the corner of her eye. Hayley can make out two faint pinpricks floating up the driveway through the trees, blinking intermittently through the curtain of snow before they disappear.

Headlights. A vehicle.

Either Tyler or Brandon has made it back up the mountain.

If it's Tyler, she can jump in his truck and beg him to drive her off the property.

If it's Brandon . . .

She squints, desperately trying to discern whether it's the truck or the Jeep. Snow obscures her view. As the vehicle pulls into the parking area, she can just make out the headlights.

She hears the slam of a car door, muffled by the howling wind, and then a shadowy figure approaches the house.

Gripping the knife in her shaking hand, Hayley runs to the bathroom and slides the door shut. Fuck—the pocket door has no lock. This house will literally be the death of her!

She pulls up her phone again. As she tries to call 911, *No Signal* glows, mocking her, across the top of her screen.

Ear to the hollow door, she strains to hear.

Please be Tyler.

The door bangs open downstairs. Terror floods through her veins. She forces herself to breathe quietly, despite her dread.

A familiar but unexpected voice calls her name: "Hayley?"

It's Megan.

THIRTY-ONE

From the landing outside the bedroom, Megan calls, again, "Hayley? Are you there?"

A spark of relief cuts through Hayley's panic, and she exhales just a bit. She slides open the bathroom door and steps out.

Megan is wearing a fisherman's sweater and jeans and, despite the storm, canvas sneakers. Her hair is damp, her footprints wet on the wide-planked oak floor. "I got your text about Olivia Blackwood. You sounded so upset that I just jumped in my car. I was worried I wouldn't get to you before the roads closed."

"Thank god you're here," Hayley says. "I'm freaking out. I just found Emily's phone in Brandon's drawer."

"What?" Megan pauses, taking this in. "He stole her phone?"

"I think . . . it's worse than that." She shakes her head. "And he's on his way home now. We have to get out of here."

"I knew he was bad news. I just didn't know how bad."

"She's a liar, Hayley!" It's Brandon, at the foot of the stairs. He must've entered quietly through the back door. Before they know it, he's pounding up the staircase.

Time seems to slow. Who should she trust? What's happening?

Megan turns to Hayley. "Give me the knife!"

Hayley hesitates, her fingers tightening instinctively around the handle. Megan wrests it away from her, then turns as Brandon reaches the top of the stairs.

With a forceful blow, he smacks the knife from Megan's hand, and it clatters to the floor. He grabs her arm.

"No!" she shouts, struggling in his grip. She writhes sideways and lands a sharp kick on his shin.

Grunting, he hurls his weight against her, and she teeters, crying out as she loses her balance. Arms flailing, she crashes backward down the full flight of stairs. A series of sickening thuds punctuates her descent.

When she hits the bottom, there's silence.

Brandon straightens. His chest is heaving, and he's staring directly at Hayley. His dark beard is iced with snow.

Her breath comes in short, sharp gasps. This can't be real, a part of her mind insists, even as her body trembles with the undeniable truth of it.

Summoning every ounce of strength she possesses, she picks up the knife from the floor and moves toward the stairs. "Get out of my way!"

"Hayley, stop!" With startling speed, he grabs her wrist and pries the blade from her grip.

She drives her elbow, hard, into his sternum, and he doubles over. Seizing the moment, she shoves past him, leaping recklessly down the stairs and nearly tripping over Megan's inert form at the bottom.

Hayley shakes her shoulders, desperately trying to wake her, but Megan's bloodied head lolls, no movement at all.

Spying car keys on the floor, spilled from Megan's pocket, Hayley scrabbles for them as Brandon's footsteps thud down the stairs. Then she sprints for the front door, flinging it wide into the full wrath of the blizzard.

THIRTY-TWO

Outside, the storm is so heavy that the amber porch light barely penetrates the darkness. Hayley can hardly make out the shape of the pond, its edges blurred and indistinct in the swirling snow. She plunges off the steps into ankle-deep powder. Sliding in her slippers, she stumbles toward Megan's old sedan.

As she reaches the driver's side door, Hayley scrapes frantically at the handle before she gets a solid grip and pulls.

Just as the door opens a crack, she sees Brandon's hand, from behind her, slam it shut.

"Get the fuck away from me!" she yells into the howling storm.

"What are you doing?" Still holding the knife, he pins her against the car.

Hayley sobs, struggling to break free. "Let me go. You killed Megan!"

"It was an accident, I swear."

"What about Emily? I found her phone," she shouts.

"What?"

"Where is she?"

When Brandon pulls back to look at her, Hayley sees her chance. She pushes him away, and he loses his balance on the ice. His feet slip out from under him, and he crashes to the ground.

Hayley takes off in a sprint—not toward the house, where Megan lies in a heap, but toward the smokehouse, across the frozen yard. Halfway there, she slips, too, going down with a flash of pain. *Fuck.* She pulls herself up and hobbles forward, feeling the searing jab in her right ankle with each frantic step. At the smokehouse, skidding on the icy dirt, she wrenches open the heavy door with its iron ring and tumbles inside. She pulls the door closed behind her, panting.

Shit. No lock. Again.

Spying a ladder against the wall, she heaves it sideways across the door.

The dusky space is silent, the air heavy with the scent of smoke and cured meat. The dirt floor is hard beneath Hayley's feet, and cold air seeps through the cracks in the boards. Her breath is visible in the gloom. She leans against the door, ankle throbbing, listening for any sound of Brandon. She can't believe how resolutely she's ignored her husband's darkness, his secrets. All the signs were there. Ranging free on the mountain, howling in the forest. And now, cornered, his animal instinct has taken over.

Once her eyes have adjusted to the dim interior, the shelves stocked with tools lining the walls come into view. Hanging from hooks spaced along the ceiling are the carcasses of turkeys and rabbits, their forms suspended in various stages of curing. The wings of the turkeys are splayed slightly, their skin taut and shriveled. Their legs hang heavily, their clawed feet a stark reminder of their once-living state. The rabbits are smaller and more delicate, their slender bodies stretched out, their fur long removed. Their smooth, pale flesh has darkened from the smoke. The ribs faintly visible beneath the surface give them a fragile, skeletal appearance. The ears have been trimmed away, leaving only the heads with closed eyes, their expressions eerily solemn.

Time slows. Hayley scans the room, searching for something, anything, that might serve as a weapon. Her eyes alight on the tools lining the shadowy walls: rakes, coils of rope, a rusty saw . . . there, a metal spade for clearing ash from the pit. She limps over and grabs it. The worn wooden handle feels reassuringly substantial as she grips it in both hands like a baseball bat.

All at once, Brandon's yell, raw and primal, carries through the planks. "Hayley! Let me in!"

As he pounds on the door, the ladder shudders violently. The sound of its metal rungs scraping against wood fills the air.

Then—the shaking stops.

For a moment Hayley hears nothing but her ragged breath and the pounding of her heart in her ears.

A sudden, thunderous crack shatters the silence: the sound of splintering wood. Hayley stands frozen, watching with horror as wooden boards in the door begin to give way. Through the widening gaps, she sees the glinting tip of the kitchen knife's blade slide in and out of the doorway, methodically destroying the barrier between them.

With one final heave, the door splinters open. Hayley's breath catches in her throat as Brandon's figure, silhouetted in the dim light, fills the doorway. A rush of cold air hits her in the face.

"Stay away!" Hayley shouts, her voice trembling. She swings the spade in a wide arc.

Brandon ducks, the metal edge narrowly missing him.

She swings again, desperation fueling her movements.

He keeps pressing forward. "Hayley!" His voice is guttural, almost unrecognizable. "You have to listen—"

"No!" She holds the spade up in front of her like a shield as she backs away.

Her shoulder hits the wall with a painful thud. Rough wood scrapes her skin through her shirt.

She's trapped.

This is it, Hayley realizes with a sinking sense of doom. The end. Her mind grasps at fragments of memory—her father's deep-throated laugh. The lilac scent of her mother's perfume. Baby Jenna's warm body nestled in her eight-year-old arms. The Florida sun on her eyelids as she lies by the pool at the Platinum Shores clubhouse. An entire lifetime condensed into one fleeting moment.

She wants to scream, to fight, but her body refuses to obey. Is this how it felt for Jenna in those final seconds? Hayley closes her eyes, bracing for the inevitable—

A whooshing sound splits the air, so unexpected that for a moment Hayley thinks she's imagining it.

Then a hollow thwack.

Hayley opens her eyes.

Brandon goes still, arm aloft, frozen midlunge. He pitches forward onto the dirt floor, the knife skittering from his grip and sliding across the uneven ground.

An arrow protrudes grotesquely from his back, its shaft quivering with the force of impact. Her own scream echoes in her ears, alien and primal.

THIRTY-THREE

In a swirl of snow and ice, Tyler appears, grim purpose carved into his features as he lowers Brandon's crossbow.

Hayley's breath comes in jagged gasps. Blinking hard, she creeps forward. Tyler throws out a hand to halt her advance. He crouches to check Brandon's collapsed form.

After a long moment, he says, "He's gone."

The smell of sweat mingles with the coppery scent of blood.

Hayley's legs give out. The spade falls to the floor with a thud. The enormity of what just happened crashes over her with such force she can barely take it in.

Her husband . . . murdered Megan . . . and tried to kill her. And now he's dead.

Her vision blurs with tears.

Tyler has saved her life.

"Brandon killed Megan," she cries in anguish.

Tyler's eyes widen. "What?"

She points a shaking finger toward the main house through the shattered door. "He threw her down the stairs. She was trying to warn me, I think. Emily . . ." Her voice trails off. Is there any possibility Emily could still be alive, after what Hayley has been through today?

"My god." Tyler shakes his head.

Hayley is shivering violently now. Tyler bends to her side. Removing his jacket, he wraps it gently around her shoulders. The heavy coat, with its warm lining, immediately calms her.

Taking her cold hands in his, Tyler says, "Let's get you cleaned up. We can figure out our"—his voice catches, and he clears his throat—"our next steps, once the storm lets up."

With a steady grip, he guides her through the wrecked doorway of the smokehouse and across the frozen yard toward the cottage.

—

Though the living room is snug and warm, Hayley can't stop shivering. She burrows into the quilted flannel lining of Tyler's jacket. "Okay if I keep your coat on till I warm up?"

"Of course." Tyler leads her to the sofa. "I'll light a fire," he says. "Then I want to take a look at that ankle."

She nods.

Crouching at the hearth, Tyler arranges logs and kindling and strikes a match. The flames flicker. He retrieves a pile of blankets from the closet and tucks a mohair throw around her legs, elevating her injured leg and placing it carefully on a pillow. He lights a wide green candle on the coffee table. It glows with the scent of artificial pine.

Only the wind's muffled roar and the spitting flames in the hearth break the quiet. Hayley pulls Tyler's coat tight around her, its collar snug against her neck.

"I'll make some tea. Herbal?" he asks.

"Okay."

He goes around the corner into the kitchen.

Outside, snow is piled high on the window frames. Hayley leans back and closes her eyes. As her breathing slows, she begins to try to make sense of what she's just been through. Brandon, her husband, is dead. And is—was—a murderer.

Megan.

And possibly, probably, Emily.

And—oh god—Cheryl.

But . . . why?

She hugs her knees to her chest. Only days ago, she was arranging furniture and planning dinners with their new friends. She'd thought the presence of Megan and Tyler was all she and Brandon needed to get through their little marital rough patch.

If only.

Brandon and Emily were the two people she counted on most, the ones she believed would be with her forever.

She thought her new life with Brandon would be her salvation.

Emily never liked Brandon. She thought it was fishy that he proposed so quickly. Megan thought he was a gold digger from the start. Hayley wants to shake her old self, tell her to open her eyes. Look at the signs. Stop seeking portents that don't exist and face the ones that are right in front of her. The man who claimed to love her, slept next to her, fooled her into a false sense of safety, was the real danger all along.

As she gazes at the fire, a wave of despair washes over her. Her life has shattered.

She is so grateful to Tyler for saving her.

And she is very, very tired.

Hayley shivers again, unable to get warm despite the fire. She pulls Tyler's coat closer around her shoulders. As she adjusts the collar, her hand brushes against something hard.

Curious, she slips her fingers into the inside breast pocket. They close around a small circular object. She pulls it out.

She stares at the ring resting in her palm.

A black-and-gold band, glinting in the firelight.

THIRTY-FOUR

The realization hits her like a punch to the gut.

This isn't just any ring. It's the one she saw countless times on her father's finger throughout her childhood. The one in Jenna's torn photograph.

But it can't be.

Her mind stutters, caught between what she knows and what she sees in front of her. That ring was lost forever. Yet here it is, tangible and undeniable, in Tyler's possession.

How? Why? Jenna gave it to . . . Hayley balks at the implication.

She stares at the band, willing it to make sense, to transform into something else, anything else. But it remains stubbornly, impossibly familiar.

A sickening suspicion begins to emerge from the shadows of her mind.

She has never seen Sean Wilder's face, not once—not in photos, not in person.

No. It's ridiculous. And yet, the thought is there, growing, taking shape.

Could Tyler be . . . Sean?

The thought is outlandish. Absurd.

And yet . . .

Once the idea takes hold, Hayley can't shake it.

Memories flash through her mind, each one taking on a new significance.

Tyler's appearance with Megan in Crystal River. The way he insinuated himself into her life once they moved into the cottage. His uncanny knack for being nearby whenever she was alone—gardening by her porch, working on the sprinklers, materializing in the basement.

The pattern is undeniable, but the truth of it is horrifying.

Tyler.

Sean.

He's been right here in Crystal River all along.

The ring in her hand feels heavier now, a tangible link between Tyler and his true identity. Between Tyler and Jenna.

It all makes sense.

The man making her tea in the next room is her dead sister's fiancé.

A chilling clarity descends.

The meeting at Anderson's between Brandon and Tyler was no coincidence.

Brandon had met Jenna's fiancé. Both of them were working on the house in Platinum Shores.

Brandon and Tyler—Sean—knew each other in Florida.

Hold on. Sean was part of the electrician's team working at her parents' house. The fire that killed them was blamed on faulty wiring, ruled accidental by the inspector. Hayley had never thought to question it, too numb with grief to probe further. And when Olivia Blackwood insinuated that Jenna had started the fire, Hayley's fury had blinded her to other possibilities. She'd been so fixated on proving her sister's innocence that Sean's possible involvement hadn't even crossed her mind.

Cold sweat prickles the back of Hayley's neck. *Sinister Sands* floated the idea that Jenna messed with the wiring. But Jenna wouldn't have known how to do anything like that. An electrician's assistant, on the other hand, could easily rig something during a party when everyone was distracted.

Hayley clutches her father's ring, the metal warm against her skin.

Were Sean and Brandon plotting together? Or was it only Sean?

Moments from the past few months bubble up in Hayley's mind: Brandon's irritability whenever Tyler showed up. His willingness to let them move into the guest cottage despite his visceral dislike of the man. Brandon's lies. The argument by the mud pit.

Oh god. Her heart pounds against her rib cage.

She has to get out of here.

Frantically, she looks around the room, searching for options. The windows rattle with the fury of the storm outside, sheets of snow obscuring the view. Even if she could reach one of the cars (and with her twisted ankle, that's in doubt), there's no way she'd make it off the property in this weather.

She fumbles for her phone in her back pocket and taps 911.

No signal. Of course there's no signal. Damn it, Cheryl was right about landlines! If only she'd listened.

She shoves the phone back into her pocket, her breath coming in short, panicked gasps. There has to be something in this room, something she can use to defend herself. As her gaze sweeps the living room, her attention falls on a pile of self-help books stacked on the bench next to the stone fireplace—the books she now knows Megan read to get closer to her.

Above the stack, a quote transcribed in Megan's looping handwriting is taped to the wall: *Open your eyes, and the choice will be crystal clear.*

It's from *The Choice Conundrum*. Megan must have left it for her to find.

Hayley's senses sharpen.

Open your eyes.

Her gaze falls on the iron fireplace poker leaning against the bench.

The teakettle whistles.

"Be there in a sec!" Tyler calls.

Sean. Sean calls.

Hayley rises, the mohair blanket falling to the floor at her feet. Shrugging off Sean's coat, she drapes it on the rocker. She stuffs the ring into the front pocket of her jeans.

There's no one she can rely on now but herself.

From the kitchen, she hears a cabinet door open and shut.

Her lawyer's words echo in her mind: *Documentation is crucial, Hayley. Every article, every report, every word.*

She pulls her phone from her back pocket. She might make it out of here. She might not. Either way, she needs to record what happens next.

She silences the ringer and opens the voice memo app, then taps the red Record circle. Heart pounding, she slips the device back into her pocket.

She limps over to the fireplace.

Slow, casual movements, she tells herself. She can't betray what she knows.

Hayley remembers how Megan helped her conquer her panicked response to smoke. *This fear does not control me.*

She looks down at her trembling hands and takes a breath. Steadying herself, she grips the poker.

THIRTY-FIVE

Hayley is stoking the flames when Sean returns with two steaming mugs of tea.

"Come over here," he says. "Sit with me."

"Just a sec." She pokes at the logs. Her hands still shake, just a bit.

He gazes at her.

In the lengthening quiet, Hayley forces herself to meet his eyes. Can he tell that the atmosphere in the room has shifted?

"I'll take care of the fire," he says.

"I'm just—"

"Be careful." His voice is blandly polite. "A single spark can start a blaze, you know."

Spark. Blaze. Is he toying with her? Stay cool, she tells herself. If you react to every little thing he says, you'll never make it out of here.

She has no choice but to put the poker down. She sets it inside the hearth and perches stiffly on the rocking chair.

When Sean sets the mugs on the coffee table, she glimpses the edge of his praying mantis tattoo from beneath his rolled-up shirtsleeve. As she observes the easy grace of his movements, his disarming smile and attentive gaze, a small part of her can't help but understand how he's fooled them all for so long. His magnetism is undeniable, even now.

He sits on the sofa. "This must be hard," he says. "Come here." He holds out his arm, beckoning her, and though it's the last thing she wants to do, she rises from the rocker and limps over to join him. He draws her into a hug.

She feels a wave of nausea as she thinks: This psychopath is touching me the way he touched Jenna. But she can't let him know she's onto him. "It's all just so much," she says.

He sighs. "I understand it's difficult to believe that Brandon was trying to kill you. But there's a lot about him you don't know."

"Like what?"

"He was in major trouble when he met you. He was running out of options. You were his golden ticket." Sean shakes his head, seemingly in contemplation of how corrupt Brandon was. "You can't be blind to the fact that you came with certain . . . assets."

"I suppose I did."

"I went on supply runs with the guy that ended in detours to the bank in Crystal River. He inherited a mountain of debt with this place. He was paying off some serious liens on the property, decades old."

Hayley feels a jolt of recognition. She knew those credit card bills were too enormous to be explained away by high-end farm equipment and furniture purchases. Sean's words echo her own doubts about Brandon—doubts Megan planted before she left. But why didn't Brandon tell her about the debt? It wouldn't have mattered to her; she would've paid. And it's hardly evidence that he was so desperate he'd kill.

There's more to the story, she's sure of it. Sean is laying the groundwork for something. She needs to play along without revealing how much she's piecing together. "I had no idea."

Sean gives her a knowing smile, clearly relishing this moment. "He begged me to keep it from you. But you must've noticed a change in him."

Brandon *had* become increasingly erratic—that irritability that flared up suddenly, sending him stomping out of rooms. His moodiness.

She takes a sip of tea from her mug. Lemon Zinger. Too hot; it burns her tongue. She puts it back on the coffee table.

Sean moves his hand lightly up the side of Hayley's neck. There's a tension in his touch that sends a chill down her spine. She fights the urge to recoil and meets Sean's eyes, forcing warmth into her own that she doesn't feel.

His smile is tight and controlled. "Let's talk about what really matters here."

"What's that?"

"You and me."

She stops breathing but forces herself to remain composed. "Um . . . what?"

"That day in the basement . . . Truth or Dare . . ."

She's repulsed by the thought that she ever allowed him to kiss her. But she can't let him know that. "You're not wrong. I admit we had a . . . some kind of connection."

He moves closer. "And the way it felt when you and I—"

"Oh . . . Tyler . . . I was drunk and—"

He shakes his head, gesturing back and forth between them. "No, Hayley. This—us—is real."

He lifts several strands of her hair, rubbing them between his thumb and forefinger.

She winces. Before she can stop herself, the words slip out: "Sean, no—"

His posture shifts. He blinks once, twice.

Oh god.

What has she done?

THIRTY-SIX

A long moment passes between them. In the sharpening silence, Hayley is aware, once again, of the storm raging outside. The whine of the wind as it rattles the windows. The light from the moon filtering through dense snowfall.

Sean's expression is carefully masked. She can almost hear the gears turning in his head: he needs a new plan.

So does she.

The warmth in her pocket reminds her that her phone is silently capturing every word. The only thing she can do now is get him to tell her as much as possible.

Matching her expression to his, Hayley forces the air from her lungs.

"You knew Brandon in Florida." Moving to the other side of the sofa, she pulls the ring from her pocket and holds it out in her palm. "When you were engaged to my sister."

Sean's eyebrows lift, just a fraction.

Hayley feels her throat constrict, but she's determined to continue. "My parents threatened to disown Jenna if she married you. How convenient that they died the night of your engagement party. But then Jenna dumped you. I guess you didn't count on her being so torn up, did you?"

Hayley would do anything to dial back time. She longs to run into her parents' house, where Jenna is about to throw the engagement party that will soon turn deadly, and do whatever it takes to wrest her sister away from this terrible man.

Focus, she commands silently. She has to see this through, to be the bait that lures out the truth.

For Brandon. For Jenna. For herself.

She places the ring on the coffee table. "It's strange, isn't it?" she says. "How everyone was so quick to blame Jenna after the fire. They said she tampered with the wiring in the house." She swallows hard, trying to steady her voice. "But Jenna couldn't even change a light bulb, let alone mess with the wiring." Hayley pauses, watching for his reaction. Sean stiffens, barely.

"It makes you wonder," she adds, forcing herself to stay composed. "Maybe the trolls were onto something, but they weren't looking in the right direction."

Sean's eyes meet hers, and for a split second, she sees something flicker—something dark, something hidden. It's gone as quickly as it appeared. "What are you accusing me of, Hayley?"

The room feels suddenly colder. Silence stretches between them. She takes a deep breath, steeling herself.

"I don't know," she says, her voice sharper now. "You tell me."

Sean laughs a little. "You know, Hayley, sometimes the things we're looking for are right in front of us, but we're too close to see them clearly. Have you ever thought about why Brandon was willing to let a couple of random strangers move onto his property?"

His eyes are fixed on her, tracking her every reaction. "Brandon was Jenna's dealer, Hayley. He got her hooked on fentanyl."

The news slams into her. "What?"

"Yep. And after your folks died, he sold her out for a reward to some podcaster."

Though Hayley doesn't want to believe this, it does connect with what Olivia told her about her source, the Coyote Kid.

"He'd cleaned up his shit by the time he met you," Sean continues, "but I knew he'd do anything to keep you from finding out. It would ruin his whole life, right?"

"So . . . you were blackmailing him," she says.

A look of smug satisfaction crosses his face. "It didn't take a lot of convincing; he knew what was at stake. Pretty soon he was all in, calling me 'Tyler' and tolerating your girl crush on Megan."

Hayley flashes back to her first encounter with Brandon, at the clubhouse after Jenna's funeral. His contrition when he spilled his beer on her, his later admission that while the beer-spilling was an accident, the meeting wasn't. He'd been watching her all day, he told her, hoping for a chance to talk to the beautiful woman with the sad eyes. Hoping for a chance to comfort her.

If Hayley had ever found out that Brandon was Jenna's dealer, let alone that he'd sold her out to Olivia Blackwood, she would've walked. She knows it. Brandon knew it too.

A sudden draft of air snakes down the chimney, sending the low flame in the stone fireplace into a burst of sparks. Flames flicker sapphire and gold. The smell of ash lingers, then fades.

Despite the devastating blow Sean has dealt, Hayley can't afford to lose her concentration. She needs to keep Sean talking. "So did Megan know who you really were?"

He scoffs. "She knew me as Tyler Madden. She had no clue I was ever with Jenna. I met her on the CrimeHive site. I was always in and out of those chat rooms, following your story. Megan posted all these questions about the 'Banking Heiress'—'I'm a writer, blah blah blah, based in Crystal River. Does anyone know Hayley Stone?' And that's when I got this great fucking idea. She wanted to meet you, and I wanted to get what belonged to me. She was a means to an end."

"What do you mean, what 'belonged' to you?"

He tilts his head slightly, considering. When he speaks, his voice is unnervingly composed. "Brandon copied my playbook: marry the rich heiress. I want what he stole from me."

Marry Sean? Is he out of his mind? Revulsion sweeps over her, but she keeps her voice neutral. "What did you tell her?"

"I DMed her and said I did some work for your husband in Florida, back in the day. I told her Brandon was a shady guy, that he sold fenty to your sister and you didn't know anything about it. That got her attention. We FaceTimed for a few weeks. She was hot, there was a vibe. When she asked to meet in person, I knew it was on."

"So you came to Crystal River," Hayley prompts.

He nods. "Yeah, I drove up here, and we met at that coffee place—Bones and whatever. I'd already scoped out your property a few times by then. Knew this guesthouse was sitting here empty."

A tremor runs through her. He'd been here without them knowing. Casing the place. Watching them through their soaring windows.

All those times she felt as if something, or someone, was watching her . . .

Sean continues. "By the end of the hour, we'd come up with the idea to 'run into you' in town. It was too easy. Megan called it karma, but it was all my plan. You never would've let me live on the property without her. And you'd never willingly talk to a journalist. It worked for both of us."

Hayley's memories slowly recalibrate as she takes in this new information. The hikes with Megan, the yoga—god, tripping together. "So Megan was here just to get my story?"

"I don't know what her motivations were. And I really don't care. When she started feeling guilty about all of it, she became a real pain in the ass. She said she hadn't expected to become actual friends with you and that it changed everything for her. When you found out about that book, she was genuinely upset." Sighing, he says, "Truth is, Megan and I never had much in common."

"Were you faking the relationship with her the whole time?" she asks.

He shrugs. "We were having fun. It was good until it wasn't, you know?"

Her chest tightens. Megan was caught up in Sean's lies. And those lies got her killed.

Sean laughs a little. "We stood in the aisle at the hardware store with that damn toilet plunger for a good half hour before you noticed us."

Hayley thinks back to what she assumed was Brandon's jealous reaction to Tyler the first time they met. "So seeing you—Sean—that day was a total surprise?"

"It sure was. Though Brandon knew what I'd come for the moment he saw me. I called him the next day and laid it all out."

"From a Florida number," Hayley says. The pieces click into place: those calls Brandon claimed were from Olivia Blackwood were actually from Sean.

Sean has been here the whole time, manipulating events from the shadows.

The image of Brandon in the smokehouse, collapsing at Hayley's feet to reveal Sean holding his crossbow, appears before her.

You have to listen . . . Brandon's last words, desperate and urgent.

With a shiver it hits her: Brandon wasn't attacking her. He was warning her.

"You weren't protecting me from Brandon," Hayley says. "He was trying to tell me the truth about you, and you silenced him."

A muscle feathers in Sean's jaw. "I thought it wouldn't be necessary. But in the end, he left me no choice."

Bingo. Hayley's phone, with the proof she needs, burns in her pocket.

But Sean keeps going. "Once I was on the property, I knew if I needed to get rid of him, it wouldn't be hard. That crossbow he was so proud of. The woods. There are a lot of ways to stage an accident up here."

Except for the crackle of logs in the fireplace, the room is silent.

Sean's eyes flicker with a calculated intensity, his veneer of concern slipping away.

Ah, she thinks. Here he is. This man is capable of murder.

A ripple of fear runs through her. Sean killed Brandon on purpose. And now Hayley is alone with him. The storm shows no signs of relenting, and even if it does, she'll still have no way out. Since escape is impossible, she might as well uncover what she can.

Does he know what happened to Emily?

Hayley thinks back to the night in her study when Emily scrutinized the torn photo of Jenna. She'd zeroed right in on the ring her sister's fiancé was wearing. Could Emily have found it in Sean's possessions?

Emily didn't go to the trailhead in the Jeep. She went in Sean's truck. Hayley imagines herself in Emily's position, settling into the passenger's seat, enacting the ritual the two of them jokingly disparaged but faithfully preserved: opening the glove compartment to see if it held gloves.

And finding the distinctive black-and-gold ring.

Hayley gestures to it, lying on the coffee table. "Did Emily see that in your truck?"

Sean's expression shifts, almost imperceptibly.

Hayley's breath hitches. "Did you kill her?"

"I'm not a monster, Hayley," he says, his voice strangely calm. "I don't want anyone to die. I just have to protect myself."

She gives him a long look. "Was Brandon there when Emily found the ring?"

He shakes his head. "I'd already dropped him in town. You know, it's too bad—it never would've happened if she didn't go snooping around when I stopped for gas." His voice takes on an almost wistful tone. "We'd been having such a nice conversation about hiking gear. But when I got back in the car, the glove compartment was open and she was holding up the ring, saying, 'I know who you are.'" He doesn't rush, doesn't raise his voice. "I tried to reason with her. I wanted her to just get on that trail and be gone. But she worked herself into a frenzy. 'I'm calling the cops, I'm calling Hayley, I'm calling the FBI,' whatever. Threatening me. What else could I do?" He shrugs, as though the answer is obvious.

"So what *did* you do?"

"I did what I had to."

The words land like a blow. Emily is dead.

Hayley, desperate for more information, presses on. "Did you plant her phone in Brandon's nightstand drawer?"

"Wait a minute." Sean's expression hardens. "Speaking of phones, where's yours?"

Shit. She's gone too far. Hayley is sick with dread. "I left it back at the house."

"You're lying. Stand up."

Slowly, she stands.

"Hand it over."

She pulls out the phone and gives it to him.

"Oh, Hayley." Sean shakes his head, balancing the phone on his palm. "So many bad decisions."

THIRTY-SEVEN

Sean pushes the red button on Hayley's phone, stopping the recording. "Did you really think you were going to get out of here with this?"

As she watches him delete their conversation, her heart sinks.

"Look what you've done," he says. "Now we're both out of options."

"Wait." She can hear the desperation in her own voice. All she can do is keep asking questions. Her life depends on it. "How will you get my money if I'm dead too?"

"Well, it's not ideal," he says. "But those trips to the bank with your dumbass husband always had something in it for me. I'm leaving with a lot more than I came with." Shaking his head, he places her phone on the coffee table next to the ring. "You know what sucks? You and me, we could have left this shit place. Gone to a beach somewhere. I guess it's too late for that now."

"The fact that you think I'd go anywhere with you is insane," she says.

"Now, that's unkind."

"This is all going to catch up with you. Your fingerprints are everywhere. You faked your identity and stole money. Too many people are dead already. As soon as the police start putting two and two together—"

"Who's going to come looking for you up here on this mountain in the winter?" he asks. She fixates on his eyes. They're disturbingly placid. "I'll be long gone before anyone starts poking around."

Hayley's mind races, searching frantically for a lifeline. There must be someone nearby who could help. A friend? A neighbor? Cheryl's name floats to the surface of her thoughts.

But Cheryl is dead.

A realization settles in her gut, heavy and undeniable. Sean killed her too.

"So why did you get rid of Cheryl?" Hayley's voice quavers. "She was harmless."

"I didn't want to do it. But the way that woman was insinuating things—"

"Her beef was with Brandon, not with you."

"It's true—she hated him. That coyote she sliced up? Hardcore." He nods admiringly. "Sadly for her, I knew that anyone who could do something so twisted was a loose end. She was bound to keep meddling. I had to do damage control." He appears untouched by conscience or remorse. "She made it easy for me, being drunk and all. One wrong foot on a ladder . . ."

"So that's how it works. Somebody gets in your way, and they end up dead," Hayley says. "But you can't kill everyone."

"Not everyone," he says. "Just a necessary few."

Sean speaks as if he has all the time in the world.

Hayley knows she doesn't. She feels the conversation slipping away from her, like water through her fingers.

He rises slowly and steps closer to her, his gestures sharp and deliberate. "I'm sure you can see the logic in all of this," he says.

The room begins to close in on her, the walls seeming to bow under the weight of her own fear, as if darkness itself is tightening its grip.

She looks around. The poker is out of reach. Pillows, blankets, books—useless.

The mug on the coffee table catches her eye.

In one quick motion, she grabs it and flings the hot tea toward him. It splashes across his face and neck.

"Fuck!" He claws at his eyes, momentarily blinded.

Just as he lunges toward her, the door bursts open.

THIRTY-EIGHT

It's Megan. Her face is bruised, her hair matted with blood.

"Tyler!" she screams.

He turns.

Hayley's gaze darts to the fireplace. The poker lies there, its end glowing a dull red from the coals. She limps toward it, trying not to draw his attention back to her.

Her fingers close around the metal handle. She takes a deep breath and swings the poker through the air, striking Sean hard on the shoulder from behind.

With a cry of surprise, he staggers forward. Hayley swings again, and again, aiming for his arms and his head this time. Her survival instinct has kicked in.

"Stop!" Sean twists, trying to evade the blows. He reaches toward her, grasping for the poker, and his hand closes around its glowing end. There's a sickening sizzle. The acrid scent of burning flesh fills the air.

Writhing, he recoils, stumbling backward until he hits the sofa and collapses. His face contorts, a mix of pain and fury. "I'm gonna kill you bitches!" he shouts, his speech slurred.

Megan springs into action. She grabs a thick blanket from the pile and unfurls it, tossing it over his form.

Sean kicks wildly beneath the blanket. His hands grip the edges, but the heavy fabric smothers his movements.

Hayley hobbles forward. Together, she and Megan work to tighten the blanket around Sean, wrapping layer upon layer, pinning his arms to his sides.

He continues to thrash, his movements becoming more restricted with each turn. Soon, he's cocooned, immobilized like a mummy in its shroud.

Hayley sits on his chest, her weight an anchor.

The room grows quiet, save for their labored breathing and the occasional curse from Sean.

Megan retrieves Sean's tool kit from the pantry. She pulls out a roll of silver duct tape and unrolls a strip, pressing it against the blankets covering his legs. His skin is streaked with angry welts, a purple mark rising on his temple where Hayley struck him with the hot poker. She passes the roll to Hayley, who finishes wrapping Sean's torso and arms. Sean groans faintly, his face tight with pain. Hayley tears off the strip and hands the roll back to Megan, who winds the tape around Sean's ankles. They work in determined silence until he is fully subdued, leaving just his head and neck visible over the tightly bound casing. Only then does Hayley exhale.

She looks at Megan. "My god," she breathes, her voice shaky. "You're alive."

"Yeah. Head wound." Megan touches her hair. "Looks worse than it is."

Hayley takes in the blood smeared on her forehead and across her shirt. "Nothing broken?"

"Nah. I have a killer headache. But when I came to, and realized I was alone, I knew I had to find you."

"I liked you better dead," Sean says thickly.

They both look down at him.

"Charming as ever," Megan says. "Now shut the fuck up or I'll tape your mouth closed." She turns back to Hayley. "Let's call the police."

"I tried. No signal," Hayley says, limping toward the armchair. "We're stuck with him." She lowers herself into the chair.

"Your foot—what happened?" Megan asks.

Hayley sighs. "I slipped on the path when Brandon was—when I thought Brandon was chasing me."

"Oh. God. Yeah." Megan's voice drops. "I saw him in the smokehouse when I was trying to find you."

An ache spreads through Hayley's chest. Brandon's death—it's too raw, too fresh. She can't even begin to make sense of it.

Megan turns to Sean. "You killed Brandon."

"I had no choice."

"He's lying," Hayley says, her voice steadier than she feels. "It was cold-blooded murder."

Megan gapes at Sean.

"I got his confession," Hayley continues. "Recorded on my phone. But he deleted it."

"Don't worry, it doesn't matter," Megan says. "Forensic experts can retrieve the data from your phone. You're a hero, Hayley."

She doesn't feel heroic; she feels exhausted, scared, and somehow both numb and hyperaware at the same time.

"Fuck you both," Sean spits. "I—"

"That's enough." Megan seals his mouth, wrapping the duct tape around his head.

"How much did you know about all of this?" Hayley asks her.

"I knew this asshole was a grifter," Megan says. "But I had no idea he was capable of murder."

Hayley gives her a grim nod. "And not just Brandon. He killed Emily. And our neighbor too."

"Holy shit." Megan shakes her head. "I thought Brandon was a criminal. But it was Tyler all along."

"It was." Hayley glances over at him. "And his name isn't actually Tyler. He's Sean."

Megan looks back and forth between them. "*Jenna's* Sean?"

Hayley nods.

Sean glares at them, his eyes narrow slits above the strip of silver duct tape covering his mouth.

"Wow." Megan regards him with disgust. "Hayley, I had no idea."

"I know," Hayley says.

Megan sighs deeply. She tilts her head to one side. "Maybe we should wrap another layer around his arms and legs."

As they work, Hayley says, "Did he know you were planning to leave?"

"No. I didn't tell him I was going."

"So . . . why did you?"

Megan cuts a strip of tape. "When you showed up with my laptop, it was a wake-up call. I couldn't turn a blind eye to Tyler's—uh, Sean's—bullshit any longer. And I'd been taking advantage of you. It was wrong. I was sitting here, trying to decide what to do next, and I noticed that book, *The Choice Conundrum*, on the bench. I started leafing through it and came across a line: 'Open your eyes, and—'"

"'—the choice will be crystal clear.'" Hayley looks toward the wall, where the quote still hangs.

"I wanted you to find it," Megan says. "Those words gave me the courage to take myself away so I could think straight. I needed to figure out how I was going to tell you the truth. To make everything right between us."

Sean, trussed like a turkey, starts panting heavily and whining through his nose.

"Shh," Megan says.

"So where did you go?" Hayley asks her.

"Back to that shithole apartment in Crystal River. It wasn't rented yet, surprise, surprise. I just needed to think about everything."

Hayley sets the roll of tape on the coffee table and gives Sean an appraising look. "That should hold him for a while, don't you think?"

The two of them stand back and assess their work.

"I'd say so," Megan says. "I guess we should try 911 again, huh?"

"We can try. It might take a while. We'll probably have to ride out the storm with him."

They both eye Sean. He starts whining again.

"If you keep doing that, we're gonna have to cover your nose," Megan says.

THIRTY-NINE

The storm outside is beginning to abate, its roar fading to a whisper. Inside, the fire casts restless shadows on the walls.

Megan sits in the rocking chair, her face illuminated by the flickering light. Her hair is disheveled, and a bruise purples her cheekbone. A small cut has left a smudge of partially dried blood across her brow. Gingerly touching her forehead, she flinches.

Hayley, in the chair opposite, rubs her throbbing ankle. As adrenalin ebbs from her system, the reality of her ordeal sinks in, leaving her drained and heavy. She's relieved that Megan's alive, and grateful for her help, but a kernel of suspicion remains.

Megan breaks the silence. As if reading her mind, she says, "I owe you an explanation, Hayley. I have to tell you the truth."

Hayley listens, wary but attentive.

"When I agreed to this whole scheme, I truly thought Brandon was bad news." Megan leans forward. "I believed that Tyler was justified in going after him. That *Sean* was justified, I mean." She pauses, swallowing hard. "But everything changed when you confronted me about the laptop. I realized I'd been lying to myself."

She continues. "I was devastated by how deeply I'd hurt you. I wanted to come clean—about Sean's deception, about the fact that he and Brandon already knew each other. About my role in all of it."

"Why didn't you come to me sooner?" Hayley asks.

"Fear. Shame. I didn't know how to begin to make it right." Megan's voice catches. "I was sitting in that miserable apartment, trying to figure out how to make amends. When I got your text about Olivia Blackwood, I didn't even think; I just jumped in my car. I knew if I waited, the storm would make it impossible. I had to find you."

Part of Hayley wants to cling to her anger. But, as she studies Megan's face, another part of her recognizes that human nature is complex, filled with murky contradictions. In Megan's story, in her own choices, in the very air between them, Hayley senses the vast expanse of gray that lies between right and wrong. "And you saved my life," she says.

A log shifts in the fireplace, sending up a flurry of sparks.

Both women glance at Sean's inert form on the sofa before turning back to each other.

Megan shakes her head. "I cannot believe how much pain and anguish that man caused. He's responsible for every terrible thing that happened to your family."

"Not everything," Hayley says. "My family was already dysfunctional. Jenna was broken. Our problems were the tinder. Sean just lit the match."

As she and Megan sit quietly, Hayley's breathing slows and deepens. She is fully present, here, now. Suspended between all that has happened and what will come next.

Grieving her parents and Jenna changed her fundamentally. Mourning Brandon and Emily will change her even further. Hayley looks at Megan, at Sean's bound figure, at her own trembling hands, and a truth settles over her. Moving forward isn't about leaving the past behind. It's about threading the pain and strength, the doubt and wisdom, into the fabric of who she is becoming.

She will never be the same. Maybe that's not such a bad thing.

TWO YEARS LATER

FORTY

The soothing rhythm of waves breaking on the shore. Feathery palm trees and white sand, framed by the striped curtains in the cabana. The coconut scent of sunscreen . . .

Hayley takes it all in as she stretches languorously after a dip in the Pacific waters. The breeze is just cool enough to be refreshing, not so cool that she needs to cover up. Beads of water on her tanned stomach will evaporate quickly in the midafternoon sun.

She crosses her legs, adjusting the cushions on her lounge chair for a better view of the azure sea. The scar on her right ankle is paler against her newly acquired tan after three days at the Cabo Serenity Resort and Spa. She marvels that this tiny incision—the orthopedic surgeon's handiwork—is the only physical reminder of her ordeal in Crystal River.

Well, there is one other thing. The hardcover book, with its image of snowy pines, lying next to her beach bag and Grecian sandals, with "#1 *New York Times* bestseller" splashed across the cover:

First Frost: A Season of Darkness, A Life Reclaimed
by Hayley Stone, as told to Megan Sinclair

Settling back on her recliner, Hayley takes a sip of cucumber-infused water. The cabana, with its thatched roof and billowing pink-and-white curtains, is a perfect sanctuary. A small table beside her chair holds a plate of fresh-sliced mango, papaya, and pineapple. In the distance she can see the main resort building, its architecture blending seamlessly into the landscape. The expansive windows mirror the undulating waves of the ocean. The infinity pool appears to merge with the horizon, creating an illusion of endless blue.

A breeze picks up from the east, sending a delicate chime into song. A silver bell on a driftwood signpost, nestled in a cluster of purple bougainvillea near Hayley's cabana, announces the daily weather report, which ranges from sunny to rainy to breezy.

No snow. No frost. No ice. Just how Hayley likes it.

She opens her tote, searching for her sunglasses case. Inside, a folder embossed with the image of blue hands cradling an orange flame holds notes for the speech she'll deliver tonight at the Sol y Luna Retreat Center. Nearly a thousand registrants from around the world have gathered for Trailblazers' first international women's conference, many of them supported by the scholarship Hayley established in Emily's name last year. Trailblazers is now her central mission, dedicated to ensuring that Emily's legacy of bravery and personal transformation endures.

Hayley pulls out her notes, marked with the topic of her talk—"The Rejuvenating Power of Sisterhood"—and sets it next to her on the chaise.

Ah, here's the sunglasses case. She opens it, dons her shades, and picks up the necklace she stashes in the case when she swims. She fastens the delicate chain around her neck and adjusts the ring that hangs from it—her father's black-and-gold band—against her clavicle.

In the quiet of the moment, with nothing to distract her but the sound of the waves and the distant laughter of resort guests, she'll review her speech one last time.

Opening the folder, she begins to leaf through the stack of news alerts from her final months in Crystal River. Though her remarks tonight will be upbeat—she's here to inspire women to forge a path ahead, after all, not remain stuck in the painful past—she likes to skim the headlines before each talk, to keep the order fresh in her mind. She knows all too well how facts can get scrambled by emotion, even in one's own memory.

Crystal River Herald (November 13, 2023)

Deleted Confession Nails Florida Man in Landlord's Death

For the first few days after the storm ended, the *Crystal River Herald* was the only news outlet interested in Sean Wilder's arrest. (Murder and identity fraud appear on the police ticker in the Adirondacks with surprising frequency.) The shift in weather patterns that took the region by surprise was a bigger headline.

When Cheryl Snyder's death was reopened for investigation, the Utica and Albany papers began to take notice. But the news didn't go viral until the *New York Post*, under Megan's byline—and with Hayley's cooperation—revealed that the widow who recorded the murder confession on her phone was none other than the infamous Florida banking heiress.

New York Post (November 16, 2023)

Heiress Scammed: Accused Crystal River Murderer Found to Have Siphoned Savings from Florida Widow

With Megan's reporting setting the tone, the media deemed Hayley both hero and victim. Gone were the gossipy insinuations of collusion, conspiracy, ulterior motives, and greed that had plagued her in the past. Thanks to Megan, Hayley was in control. From the lobby of the Holiday Inn Express on I-87 near Crystal River, she held a press conference with Emily's tearful mother by her side. Hayley demanded a thorough investigation into Emily's disappearance, including an immediate search through the treacherous terrain of the region.

Even now, two years later, on a sunny beach thousands of miles away, the headline of the next article gives Hayley shivers:

USA Today (November 19, 2023)

Body of NYC Woman Discovered in Adirondack Ravine

Emily was found sixty feet below the hairpin turn on Route 8, the back road between the town and Brandon's property. Dense brush obscured the site, and snowfall during the storm had buried her body completely. It took the New York State Police three days to find her. Without Hayley's advocacy, and the subsequent national pressure, Emily's remains would not have been located until spring—if ever.

Hayley runs a finger around the ring that hangs from her necklace. This ring has meant different things to her at different times. First it represented the comfort she craved from her father. Then it was about Jenna's trusting nature and her simple desire to find love. Now Hayley wears it for Emily—for having the courage to voice her honest opinions, no matter how much Hayley resisted hearing them. For fearlessly confronting Sean, whose lies she uncovered when she found the ring in his truck.

After Sean was arrested, one question still nagged at Hayley. Why did he keep the ring, knowing it was the only physical object that tied him to Jenna? The answer she and Megan uncovered when they delved into research for the book was unsettling: narcissistic psychopaths often keep mementos of their victims.

After the trial was over, Hayley received a package in the mail from the Albany courthouse. It contained both the ring, released from evidence, and a letter from Sean Wilder, bearing the return address of the Clinton Correctional Facility in Dannemora, New York. The note, penned on lined paper in a semiliterate scrawl, said, "Their making me send this back to you, Halee. I hope your greatful."

She sighs. At least Jenna didn't marry him.

Hayley will always grieve her sister's death, but now she's channeling her pain into helping others. She founded Jenna's Place, a group home for recovering opioid addicts in South Florida, with a second location planned on the Crystal River property. The logo features a green-and-magenta hummingbird in Jenna's honor.

During the trial, a seemingly minor detail shook Hayley to her core. Sean's praying mantis tattoo, he revealed, had no connection to composting or regeneration. It represented predation—the mantid's patience, its ability to blend in, to wait.

Its largest prey, he said, is the hummingbird.

Daily Mail (US edition, May 3, 2024)

Ice Storm Killer's Murder Trial Kicks Off in Crystal River, New York, as Mountain Town Reels from Chilling Crime

In court, Hayley discovered the extent of Brandon's involvement with Sean. A raft of witnesses testified about all the times they had crossed paths in Florida, long before she knew either of them. One witness was the director of the wilderness program where Brandon and Sean had met as teenagers. Brandon's mother sent him there after the car crash that killed Rick Snyder left her son with several shattered bones and an addiction to painkillers—Vicodin, Percocet, OxyContin. During that same period, Sean, a foster kid with a propensity for starting fires that had gotten him kicked out of home after home, was placed there by the state.

Another witness was the manager of Platinum Shores Estates. While Brandon was renovating the Pierces' house, Sean was brought on short term to work with the electrical team. The manager testified that no one on-site knew that the two men were previously acquainted.

A handful of Jenna's old friends were also called to the stand: some former club kids, some acquaintances from her stints in rehab. They confirmed that Brandon sold fentanyl from his car at the Walmart parking lot but noted he had cleaned up his act months before Jenna's fatal overdose. By the time Hayley met him, he was in recovery, seeking a new path.

Hayley has found comfort in this detail.

There's no way to know whether Brandon wanted to kill Rick Snyder or whether his death was an accident. But in some ways, it doesn't matter whether it was intentional or not. Brandon was responsible for Rick Snyder's death. If he hadn't gotten behind the wheel, drunk and raging, on an icy, treacherous night, it never would have happened.

Over the past two years, Hayley has mourned the chance they never had to overcome the traumas that haunted them both. Despite everything she's learned about how damaged Brandon was, Hayley still feels his absence like a physical ache. Her grief is a complex thing, tangled with anger and disappointment. Many nights she's played a scenario in her head: What if they were alone together in the house, snug and cozy, while that terrible storm raged outside—and had the conversation she'd wished for? Would it have been the reset they needed, or would it have been the beginning of the end?

She'll never know.

Hayley truly believes that the man she met, and grew to love, was trying to make a fresh start—that he sought happiness with her in Crystal River, that he wanted to build their future there, together, and let go of his past.

But the past refused to let go of him.

Crystal River was slow to forget. And Florida followed him to the mountain.

New York Times (June 5, 2024)

Ice Storm Killer Found Guilty on Three Counts of First-Degree Murder, Receives Consecutive Life Sentences without Parole

When Hayley's lawyer called her with the news of Sean's conviction, she'd just moved to San Diego. "Congratulations. This is a major victory," he told her. "Justice has been served. Now you can put it all behind you and move forward with your life."

"I know," she said. "I will."

But Hayley found that in order to move forward, she first needed to go back: To delve into exactly what happened, and why. To try to make sense of it all. She ignored the barrage of queries she received: Emails, texts, and DMs from news producers; social media comments, messages, and mentions; and requests through her lawyer. This time, the story would belong to her. On her schedule.

And she knew just how to start.

Ever since that final night in the cottage, with Sean trussed on the sofa and the storm raging outside, Megan has talked with Hayley about writing this story together.

"But only when you're ready," Megan said. "It has to feel right."

Megan was living in a studio in Brooklyn. Her bylines in the *Post* had gotten her enough work to leave Crystal River; after she broke the story of the "Ice Storm Killer," her Substack exploded with subscribers. In the year following Sean's arrest, she'd carved out a niche for herself in true crime, focusing on the victims'—usually female—perspectives.

Hayley was hesitant at first. But Megan never pushed, giving her space when she needed it and offering a listening ear when she was ready to talk. They started small, with brief phone calls where they'd discuss anything but that night in the cottage, gradually progressing to longer conversations where they began to delve into what had happened on the property. Megan's honesty and her genuine desire to understand Hayley's point of view helped to bridge the gap between them. As time passed, Hayley found herself looking forward more and more to their calls and video chats.

As she read through Megan's articles and essays, Hayley began to understand her own objectives. Yes, she yearned to gain clarity on everything that had happened. But even more, she wanted her story to give other women the strength to believe in themselves and trust their instincts. With Megan's help, she would find her voice.

I'm ready, Hayley texted after Sean's conviction. Come to San Diego. Let's do this.

Megan's reply was immediate: I'm there.

—

Variety (August 18, 2024)

Murder Heiress Set to Release Highly Anticipated Tell-All; Stone and Coauthor Sinclair Score Major Advance, Sparking Streaming Rights Bidding War

Hayley smiles to herself. Tomorrow, at a press conference, she'll announce that the eight-part limited TV series will drop next fall: *First Frost*, with the tagline "When Hell Froze Over."

Tonight, though, is all about Trailblazers.

"Thought you might be thirsty." Megan, wearing a macramé bikini and floppy sun hat, stands at the foot of Hayley's recliner. She's holding two supersized frozen drinks with requisite mini umbrellas and bright-pink straws. "Whatcha doing?"

"Just prepping for tonight."

Megan places the drinks next to the fruit plate on the small table and stretches out on the lounge chair parallel to Hayley's. "I'm sure whatever you say will be perfect. Just speak from the heart."

"You know what? You're right." Hayley closes the folder and slides it into her beach bag.

"So guess who reached out to my agent, trying to get in touch with me?" Megan takes a sip of her drink. "Olivia fucking Blackwood."

"No way. What did you say?"

"I said when hell freezes over. Oops, I forgot—"

The two women finish in unison: "It already did."

Hayley shrugs, laughing. "You know, I don't care about that bottom-feeder. Feel free to—"

"Nah. We don't need her. My Substack just passed a million subscribers."

"And I'm booked with speaking engagements for the next twelve months."

"Exactly," says Megan. "Olivia Blackwood can buy a ticket to one of your appearances, like everyone else."

The table between them vibrates—Hayley's and Megan's phones are both buzzing with a news alert. They pick them up at the same time.

CrimeHive Exclusive: Ice Storm Killer's True Story Sells for Seven Figures!

"Holy shit," Megan says.

Hayley shakes her head in disbelief.

They both start scrolling.

Journalist Olivia Blackwood has inked a jaw-dropping deal for *The Ice Storm Killer Tells All*, which has been kept under wraps for the past year and is set to be released tomorrow.

In a twist that could only happen in real life, Sean Wilder, a.k.a. the "Ice Storm Killer," gave exclusive access to the reporter whose true crime podcast, "Sinister Sands," meticulously examined every detail of the lurid Florida scandal that sparked it all. Blackwood, known for her no-holds-barred reporting, sat down at the Clinton Correctional Facility with the killer in a series of interviews that are sure to make this book an instant bestseller.

"Sean Wilder is the most magnetic, charismatic man I've ever known," says Blackwood. "He seduced two sisters and a journalist whose new book about him, *First Frost*, is irrevocably compromised by the fact that she was desperately in love with him. It will be a gift to the world to hear the unvarnished true story."

The killer's recounting of his spine-tingling crimes, combined with Blackwood's propulsive style, will undoubtedly captivate—and horrify—readers worldwide. Love it or hate it, *The Ice Storm Killer Tells All* will be the most talked-about book of the year. And CrimeHive will be there every step of the way to bring you the latest. Stay tuned!

Hayley looks at Megan.

Megan looks at Hayley. She removes the straw from her drink and takes a long swig straight from the glass. "We should've taped that idiot's nose shut when we had the chance."

"Um . . . excuse me . . ."

Hayley and Megan look up to see two twentysomething women with Trailblazers tote bags hovering on the path in front of the cabana. "Are you Hayley Stone?"

Hayley sits up straighter, reflexively cautious. Then she relaxes. They're at a spa in Cabo, for god's sake. "Yes?"

"Oh, wow!" says one of the women. "We came all the way from Vancouver to see you tonight!"

"And for the workshops," the second one adds, "but mostly for you."

"Would you mind signing my book?" the first one blurts out.

"Michele, not now," the second one stage-whispers; "she's in a bikini."

"It's fine. I'd be happy to," Hayley says.

Michele, blushing, pulls a copy of *First Frost* from her tote.

Hayley takes the book, her fingers tracing the raised words on the cover. The pages inside are a part of her now, a record of her darkest hours and hard-earned insights.

"Today's your lucky day," Hayley says as she writes her signature. She nods at Megan, who is slurping on her straw. "This is Megan Sinclair. She can sign it too."

The second woman gapes at Megan. Now she's as starstruck as Michele. "Oh my god! I want to be a writer too. Wait—this bit is my favorite." She pulls out her own copy of the book, stuffed with Post-its, and thumbs through it. "Ah, here: 'Sean's rules have been in play the whole time. His game isn't Truth or Dare. It's Kiss, Marry, Kill. He got his kiss. Failed at marriage. Now all that's left is . . .'" She looks up. "That line gives me chills." All of a sudden, she pivots to Hayley. "I'm so sorry. You actually survived it!"

Hayley smiles from behind her sunglasses.

Megan thrusts out her hand. "Who do I make this out to?"

The girl gives her the book. "Can you make it to Ashley? 'With love'?"

"Um—sure."

After Michele and Ashley back out of the cabana, gushing thanks, Hayley and Megan settle back on their lounge chairs. Hayley takes a long sip of her cocktail. "Ooh, this is good. What is it?"

"I asked the bartender to make us something special. White rum, coconut water, fresh lime, and simple syrup. I'm calling it an Icebreaker."

Hayley laughs. "Perfect." She lifts her frosty glass. "To Icebreakers."

Megan tips hers toward Hayley. "And Trailblazers."

Hayley gives her a wry smile. "And Olivia fucking Blackwood. She and Sean deserve each other."

They clink glasses.

As Hayley sips her drink, she reflects on Ashley's observation. Yes, she survived. But publishing a book doesn't put it all in the past tense. She feels as if she is simultaneously shedding a skin and growing a new one. Each word has been an act of reclamation, a way of owning her past rather than being consumed by it.

Once, Hayley believed her trauma defined her. She moved to Crystal River to try to overcome it. But although the world still holds shadows for her, she's found an unexpected source of peace. The book has connected her with others who share the knowledge that everything can shift in a heartbeat—and that overcoming your fears is just the beginning.

She isn't just surviving anymore. She's truly living.

ACKNOWLEDGMENTS

Our friendship began twenty-five years ago, when, both newly settled in Montclair, New Jersey, we met in a bookstore. We've shared our lives from those early parenting days to empty-nesting and beyond, trading manuscripts and ideas, debating plot twists and story arcs, and engaging in a conversation about books and writing that has never ended.

When we coedited a book of essays, *About Face: Women Write about What They See When They Look in the Mirror*, we discovered the joy of true collaboration. Years later, working on a television pitch together revealed to us how intuitively our creative minds merged. Writing *Please Don't Lie* felt like a natural evolution—challenging, invigorating, and above all, fun.

We found our rhythm sitting across from each other with our laptops in our New York City apartments and at an Airbnb in the Adirondacks, where we escaped to write several key scenes and absorb the atmosphere. The work was intense and rewarding, full of surprises and discoveries.

This book emerged from a rich community of writers and readers. Our weekly novelists' group—Marina Budhos, Alice Elliott Dark, Alexandra Enders, Bonnie Friedman, and Pamela Redmond—has been a source of encouragement and wisdom. Susan Davis, Amy Ferris, Gina Frangello, Susan Golomb, Lisa Gornick, Jane Green, Katherine Howe, Gina Hyams, Paula McLain, Mary Morris, DK Nnuro, Priya Parmar, Haley Sharp, Ayelet Waldman, S. Kirk Walsh, Brooke Warner, Meg Wolitzer, and Laura Zigman have all offered support and insight at various points along the way. Our Montclair writers' group and long-running book club have provided both inspiration and steadfast friendship over the decades.

Venturing into suspense and thriller territory, we leaned on the counsel of friends who've mastered the genre—Danielle Girard, Greer Hendricks, Angie Kim, Jean Hanff Korelitz, Jean Kwok, Jenny Milchman, John Searles, Danielle Trussoni, and Amanda Eyre Ward, among others. We appreciate the valuable feedback of our early readers, Cindy Handler and Nancy Star.

We are grateful to our publishing team: Selena James, whose vision for this book matched our own; Charlotte Herscher, whose sharp and perceptive notes elevated our manuscript at every turn; and the entire editorial, marketing, and public relations staff at Thomas & Mercer. Special thanks to our agent, Eric Simonoff at WME, who embraced our collaborative venture with enthusiasm and skill.

This book also carries within it the memory of two fierce advocates: author Louise DeSalvo and literary agent Beth Vesel, each a champion of our work together from its beginnings.

Christina thanks her husband, David Kline, whose support and enthusiasm for each new adventure are unwavering; her sons Hayden, Will, and Eli, always eager to hear "just one more" plot twist; her three sisters—Cynthia Baker, Clara Baker, and Catherine Baker-Pitts—who make her life richer in every way; and her mother-in-law, Carole Kline, who sets a beautiful example of how to live a creative life.

Anne thanks her children, Tessa and Delayna; her partner, Joshua Cohen; her mother, Linda Burt; her sister, Jess Burt; and Ann

Birmingham, Mari Brown, Tommy Christaldi, Dana Cohen, Julia Cohen, Ross Cohen, Sue Cohen, Anna Morgan, Mark Rose, and Ted Rose for their support, encouragement, humor, love, and patience throughout the process.

Lastly, we thank our readers. We hope this story keeps you up late turning pages, just as it kept us up late writing them.

ABOUT THE AUTHORS

Photo © 2025 Cowbird Creative

Christina Baker Kline is the #1 *New York Times* bestselling author of eight novels, including *The Exiles*, *Orphan Train*, and *A Piece of the World*. She is the recipient of the New England Society prize for fiction, the Maine Literary Award, and a Barnes & Noble Discover Prize. Kline has also written and edited five nonfiction books. *Please Don't Lie* is her first thriller.

Anne Burt's debut novel, *The Dig*, was an American Booksellers Association Indie Next pick, the Strand Book Store's mystery selection for spring 2023, and the IndieBound.org Indie Next list's lead "Thrills & Chills" reading group title for summer 2024. She is also a nonfiction writer and editor and a past winner of the *Meridian* literary magazine's Editors' Prize in fiction.

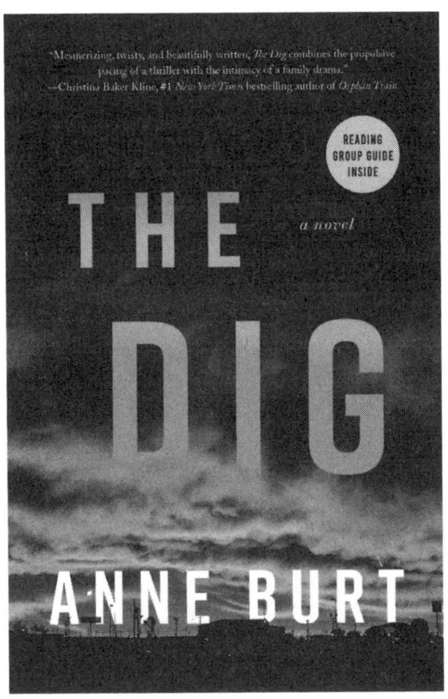

When Sarajevo-born siblings Antonia and Paul join a wealthy Midwestern family in the 1990s, a series of events with deadly consequences is set in motion. Now, with her career on the line and her brother missing, Antonia must race against the clock to confront long-buried family secrets.

Informed by timely issues of immigration, capitalism, and justice, yet timeless in its themes of love, identity, and competing loyalties, *The Dig*, inspired by the Greek tragedy Antigone, portrays a woman at odds with her history, forced to choose between her own ambitions and her loyalty to her beloved, idealistic brother.

Read it now! Available wherever books are sold.